Wrong Side Girl

by

Julia Goda

Copyright

ISBN: 978-0-9940944-5-2.

Dedication

This book is dedicated to all the girls and boys who have to fight every day, who feel unworthy and unloved, who want to give up, who want to run away, to escape,
to leave it all behind.

You are strong.

You can make it.

I know you can.

And, as always,

To Andre.

My very own Hero.

Chapter 1

Lizzy

Fifteen years ago.
Lizzy is nine. Cole is twelve.

I am hiding in my cave.

It's not really a cave, more like a hole just big enough for me to sit in. It's probably dangerous since it's nothing but a hole I dug into the side of one of those ridges in the woods a few years ago when I needed to get away. It's just big enough to hold my now almost ten-year-old body. I like that it's close to the creek in the woods behind my house. I can hear the water running over the rocks.

It's peaceful in my cave.

Nobody can find me.

The sand beneath my bare feet feels cool and I dig my toes in deeper. It relaxes me and lets me think of nothing but the sand on my skin. I've had lots of practice in how to not think about anything. To shut everything out and just sit here.

This is the only place where I can do that. It's my favorite place in the whole wide world.

It's my escape.

The place where I come to find peace and quiet.

I come here whenever things at home or school get too much. It's like a cocoon that surrounds me and keeps everything else out.

I take my shoes and socks off and bury my hands and feet in the soft cool sand and let it run through my fingers and over my toes again and again.

Then I stare.

At the sand.

Or the creek.

Or the sky.

And I listen to the sounds of the woods, to the wind in the trees above me, the trickling of water in the creek to my right, the birds chirping, the leaves rustling.

To anything that will drown out their words in my head.

And I think of nothing.

Not of the screaming and shouting and name-calling.

Not of the smell of alcohol on my mother's breath.

Not of the sound that man's hand makes when it slaps my mother across the face.

Not of the struggle that follows.

And definitely not of the sounds that follow after.

My mind is completely blank.

And I am all alone.

Two weeks later.

It's my birthday.

My special day.

I turned ten today.

I've been waiting for this day all month.

It's July and it's hot outside, so I picked my favorite skirt to wear this morning. It used to be a sleeveless dress that I wore when I was five or six. It has a stretchy top with little spaghetti straps. Now, the stretchy top sits on my hips and I tuck in the straps at the side. The fabric is worn and soft and I love the colors. Kinda like a soft rainbow from light pink through purple and blue to soft green. It's the prettiest piece of clothing I own and I only wear it for special occasions.

And since today is special, I chose my favorite skirt to wear.

I was excited for my cake and present. I was sure that this year would be different; that this year surely I would get a cake and a present.

Turning ten is a big deal.

I was so very excited.

But when I bounced down the stairs and called out for my mom, I didn't get an answer. I checked the kitchen, but it was empty. And quiet. I went into the living room and there they were lying on the couch.

It looked like they were both sleeping.

The room was a mess: beer cans and cigarette butts everywhere. The smell was overwhelming and it made me scrunch my nose in disgust. My mom was only half-dressed. Her skirt had ridden up and sat around her hips and she was not wearing any panties. A man's body was half on top of hers. He wasn't wearing a shirt and his pants were undone. His arm was slung around my mom and his hand was holding one of her boobs. Not a pleasant sight, but nothing I hadn't seen before. I walked over to the couch and shook my mother's arm.

Nothing.

I tried again and called out, "Mom, wake up!"

Still nothing.

They were totally out of it.

I looked around then went back into the kitchen. I didn't

see a cake anywhere. I even checked the fridge and the freezer but found nothing but beer, a jug of milk, and pop tarts.

No cake.

No candles.

No present.

Not even a card.

She forgot.

I couldn't help but start crying. Silent tears of disappointment were running down my face. I swiped them away, but they kept coming. I couldn't keep up.

I felt alone.

So terribly alone.

With nowhere else to go, I ran outside to escape to the woods, to sit in my cave and forget.

To spend my special day in my special place by myself.

That's where I am right now. I am still crying and it annoys me that I can't stop. I should have known that she would forget.

That today wasn't a special day at all.

That I am not special.

I hear it often enough. Every day to be exact. If not from my mother, then from someone in town.

I should have known better.

Lost in my sorrow, I jump when a boy appears beside me at the opening to my cave and looks down at me. He has curly, blond hair and big, blue eyes that search my face. I have no idea who he is, have never seen him before. Not in town, not in school, not anywhere. He looks like he is a year or two older than me, but still, I should know him because our town is really small.

"Are you crying?" he asks me in a weird voice.

Embarrassed at being caught, I turn my head away and shrug my shoulders. I'm hoping he will just go away. This is my place. Nobody ever comes here. I want to be alone. But instead of leaving, he sits down next to me, facing me.

"What's your name?" he wants to know. I keep my face averted and shrug my shoulders again. "I'm Cole," he says. I stay silent and watch as I let the sand run through my fingers over and over again. He still doesn't leave. Instead, he tells me about himself. He just moved to town a few days ago. Into one of those big, old houses I love so much on Old Hollow Street at the other end of the woods. He is twelve and going into grade six after the summer. He was exploring the woods behind his house when he saw me sitting here. He wishes he had a dog. He would name him Cash and he would be an Australian Shepherd. I'm not sure what that is, but I do love dogs. I keep listening to him, quietly watching the sand running through my fingers as he tells me about all the adventures he and Cash would have. It sounds like they would be best friends and have a lot of fun together.

I wish I had a dog to be my friend. That had been my birthday wish.

Thinking about that makes me cry again. I try to wipe my tears away without him noticing, but of course he notices and asks me in a sad voice, "Hey, did I say something wrong?" I shake my head and stay quiet. He stays quiet with me for a while until I stop crying, and it actually feels nice to have him sit with me.

When my tears dry, he repeats his earlier question, "What's your name?"

This time I answer him. "Lizzy," I whisper.

He smiles at me and holds out his hand to me. "Hi, Lizzy, I'm Cole. Pleasure to meet you." That makes me giggle and I take his hand. He shakes it then lets it go and gets up. I realize he is going to leave and that makes me sad. Before he leaves, though, he looks down at me, still smiling, and asks, "Wanna meet here again same time tomorrow?" I think about it for a minute while I look up into his blue eyes and then nod. His smile grows wider. "See you then, Lizzy," he says, then turns around and leaves me with a smile on my face.

From that day on we were inseparable.

Chapter 2

Lizzy

I was running late.

Chloe and Jesse had appeared in the common room at the shelter just as I was about to leave and I had sat down to talk to them for a little bit. Chloe was one of my favorites. I know, technically I wasn't supposed to have favorites, but I couldn't help it. She reminded me of myself when I was her age. I was worried about both of them. They stuck together like glue and didn't let anyone else get close. Chloe was reserved and always talked real quiet, trying not to draw attention to herself. Jesse was her protector. I was guessing they were around the same age, maybe a year apart. Where Chloe was quiet and shy, Jesse was serious and didn't mind sharing his opinion. He was always looking out for her, always making sure nobody messed with her, and made it clear that if they did, they would have to deal with him. A lot of the other kids that came in on a regular basis either respected him or were intimidated by him, so they didn't go there. But there were a few boys that concerned me, who would go through Jesse to get to Chloe. They would see it as a challenge. I had been worried that one of them had been successful and that had been why they had disappeared for a few days. I was so relieved when I saw them in one piece today. When I had again offered them a room at the shelter for the night, they had turned me down, just like they had the other twenty times I had offered. Our rules stated that boys and girls weren't allowed to sleep in the same room. So they never stayed. I needed to come up with a solution. I was very tempted to ask them to come and stay at my place, but that was against the rules. First thing tomorrow, I was going to talk to my supervisor to see what we could do to help them.

I hadn't gotten through to them yet, so I didn't know exactly why they were so scared and closed off, but I had an idea. It always followed the same pattern. The same pattern that I most definitely would have succumbed to if Cole hadn't saved me from it: living on the streets, having no one to trust and no place to go. I would be forever grateful to Cole for keeping me strong enough to fight that constant urge of running away. To this day, he was the most important person to me. Even if he couldn't fill the place in my life I had hoped he eventually would, he would always be a priority in my life. No matter what, I would always be there for him. I had promised him that when we were kids and I would keep that promise if it killed me. There was no way I could disappoint the only person that had ever loved me and cared for me.

And protected me.

Sometimes that protection had made things worse for me, especially when he wasn't around and the other kids in town would taunt and bully me without fear of retaliation from Cole, but I had never told him that. I was stubborn, always had been. I had heard and seen a lot of things before Cole came into my life, and those things had made me seem tough to the outside world.

And I liked it like that.

I never let my emotions show to anybody but Cole.

Our jobs kept both of us busy these days, but we made a point of getting together as often as we could. And we talked on the phone daily. It was important to both of us to stay connected, to be a part of each other's lives. When he didn't have a flavor of the week—or day— we went out clubbing or bar hopping together, and it was always a blast. When he did have a girl, he would often ask me to come out with them, but I always found excuses why I couldn't make it.

That was something I didn't need to see.

Another girl hanging all over him, his hands touching her in places that I wanted him to touch me.

I had accepted the fact that that would never happen, but that didn't mean I wanted it shoved in my face that he wasn't interested in me that way. Currently, he was single and I was supposed to meet him fifteen minutes ago at a bar down the street from my apartment. It had been a few weeks since we'd had a chance to actually meet up for more than a quick coffee because I had been so busy at work. At my last evaluation meeting with my supervisor, Taryn, I had presented her with the idea of setting up regular tutoring sessions and career info meetings for our street kids. She had loved the idea and told me to go ahead with it. That meant I had to set up interviews with tutors and career counselors, get flyers printed, go out on the streets and talk to the kids about it, head staff meetings to fill everyone in on what was going on, and get a team together to support me. I had been so busy that I'd had to cancel on Cole a few times.

On that thought, my phone started ringing. I checked the display and saw that, yes, it was Cole. Speaking—or thinking—of the devil.

"Hey," I answered after the third ring.

"Where are you?" He sounded really angry. Rude much?

Taking a deep breath I told him, "I'm on my way to the car. Something came up at work and I had to stay a little longer. I'll be there in ten minutes."

"Held up at work again, huh? You think you could have called?" Very angry now. His attitude was starting to piss me off. What the hell was his problem?

"Are you serious right now? You know I don't work a nine to five job, Cole! I'm sorry I've been so busy lately and you're upset, but I'm not sorry I stayed to try and get through to the kids that worry me. My job is important to me. You know that!"

"Yeah, believe me. I know that." It sounded like he had a hard time keeping his annoyance under control. That incensed me even further. What? He was mad at me for being passionate about my profession? He could not be serious.

"What the fuck is your problem, Cole?" I practically shouted at him. I was ready to just head home. It had been a long week and I didn't need this shit.

I heard him sigh at the other end of the line. Then he said in a calm voice, "Nothing, baby. I just miss you, is all."

Just like that my anger evaporated and my heart melted. I loved it when he called me 'baby'. I'm the only person I've ever heard him call that. For his babes he usually reserved 'gorgeous' or 'sweetheart'. But I was his only 'baby'. Call me stupid and naïve, but I liked it. I liked the fact even more that he was possessive of that endearment.

We'd gone out with our significant others together once, which had been huge for me because I never brought the guys I dated to meet Cole. I don't know. It just felt wrong. When Peter had called me 'baby', Cole had totally lost it on him. He was furious and threatened to beat the shit out of him if he ever heard him call me that again. His date— for the life of me I cannot remember her name now—had given me weird looks and had turned into an even bigger bitch after that. For the rest of the night, Peter had been kind of distant with me. He had ended it the next day, mumbling something about encroaching on somebody else's territory. I had tried to explain to him that it wasn't like that, but he hadn't listened to me.

That had been the first and last time I had introduced any of my boyfriends to Cole.

It kinda pissed me off that Cole got away with almost anything as long as he called me 'baby', but I couldn't help it. It showed me that I did have a special place in his heart and that on some level he considered me his. Call me crazy, but I needed him to own that part of me.

I closed my eyes and said quietly, "I miss you too, Cole. I'll be there in ten minutes." We both knew that everything was forgiven when he said, "All right, I'll see you in ten. Drive safe," and hung up. I closed my phone and threw it on the passenger seat, then started my car and went to meet Cole.

Cole

I was going to beat the shit out of that guy if he didn't stop ogling her ass. "Yo!" I called and stared him down when he lifted his eyes to mine. He got the message loud and clear and trained his eyes on the tits sitting on the stool next to him at the bar. I took a deep breath in the hopes of keeping my shit together. It wasn't easy. I felt like every guy in the bar was staring at either Lizzy's tits or her ass and it was driving me fucking insane with jealousy and possessiveness. I knew I had no right to those feelings since she wasn't mine in that way, but that didn't change a goddamn thing. The problem was that I wanted her to be mine in *every* way possible, but I knew I had no right to make that so.

She was totally out of my league.

She could come across as rough and arrogant, especially when she didn't like someone, but really, she was sweet and funny and loyal to a fault.

That was my Lizzy.

I had taken her under my wing when she was ten and I was twelve. Even as young as I was back then, I had known that she needed someone to care for her and I had wanted that to be me. One look at the sad little, red-haired girl with bright, green eyes sitting in a hole in the woods behind my house, tears running down her face, but trying so hard to be tough, and I had been a goner. I had fallen in love with her right then and there. And my feelings for her haven't changed since. On the contrary, they have only grown stronger over the years. I knew she had had a crush on me when she was still in high school and I had started college, but I'd chalked it up to her missing me because I only came home every other weekend or during breaks. It hadn't lasted long and shortly after, she had started dating. It made me a damn pussy, but that had been hard to watch and I had been grateful to be away at college so there wouldn't be a chance to run into her and her boyfriends.

I never let on how much in love with her I really was.

Yes, she knew she held a special place in my heart, knew we had a bond that nobody would ever be able to break, that I considered her my best friend. But she had no clue that I was head over heels in love with her.

And I would never tell her.

I was too scared of losing her.

My track record with women wasn't the best. None of the

women I had hooked up with could keep my interest for long. The longest period of time I had ever been with the same woman was four weeks.

Pathetic, I know.

In college, I had pretty much fucked everything that had a vagina. Most of the time, I hadn't even known their names or remembered their faces the next morning. I had slowed down a little after I graduated and started my job as an architect at one of Boston's most successful companies, but I was still a bastard and treated women like shit. I wasn't capable of giving them more than a good time in bed and I didn't want to do that to Lizzy.

I couldn't lose her.

Not ever.

And if my mother ever found out that I acted on my feelings, she would destroy Lizzy and I couldn't let that happen, either. I didn't want that bitch anywhere near my girl. So I stayed away from her and told myself to be grateful for being able to call her my best friend.

That it was enough.

But tonight, I had a hard time convincing myself of that fact. I didn't know what it was. I hadn't lied to her earlier when I told her that I missed her. I did. Terribly. Yes, we called each other almost daily, but I had missed looking at her, smelling her, hugging her, being close to her. I was two years ahead of her in school, and when I had gone off to college, it had been like this for a while until I buried that feeling with my cock in any girl who would have me.

But now it was worse.

Lizzy was like a drug to me and I had been forced to go cold turkey for the last few weeks. Taking a different woman to bed every other night had only made it worse. None of them were her.

Not even close.

It had gotten so bad that I'd had to close my eyes and imagine I was fucking her to be able to come. I was pathetic, and the fact that I had no solution to this dilemma pissed me off and freaked me out at the same time. That's why I had lost it on her when she was running late.

I had really missed her.

I turned my eyes back to the pool table and watched Lizzy take her shot. Her ass pointing in my direction when she leaned over the table made my dick twitch.

Jesus, Cole, get a handle on it. You're not a fucking teenager.

She pocketed two of her striped balls and threw me a smirk over her shoulder. God, she was sexy. And the fact that she didn't even know it made her irresistible.

Never had I seen her play those games women play to get a guy's attention. She didn't strut—well, she did, but not in the fake way that ninety-five percent of the female population did. To her it came naturally. She didn't flick her hair, she didn't make big sexy eyes at anyone, she didn't show off her goods. She was classy and hot in a way that every guy knew she was the total package. To be honest, I was surprised that nobody had snatched her up yet, but I didn't complain. I knew it would be impossible and incredibly painful for me to watch her fall in love with some guy that wasn't me. My heart wasn't ready for that yet. Only a dick would be so selfish, but hey, I never said I wasn't a dick.

This way, I could at least pretend that she was mine.

Her next shot went wide, which made her narrow her eyes at the ball and straighten up with an attitude.

Fucking adorable.

I chuckled. "Your glare is too cute to magically make that ball jump into the pocket in fear. You gotta at least try and mean it," I teased her.

She transferred her glare to me, and my dick twitched again. As hard as it was to appear unaffected, I succeeded by giving her a wide grin. I walked toward her and crowded her body so she had to move out of my way to let me set up my shot. She walked over to the table to take a sip of her beer.

I was focused on my shot when a body pressed into my side. The smell of an awfully sweet perfume almost made me gag. I turned my head and laid eyes on a busty brunette that looked kind of familiar.

Shit. Had I fucked this one?

Out of the corner of my eye I could see Lizzy watching us. It annoyed her when I got hit on during our time together. I couldn't blame her. I was just as possessive of her time as she was of mine. If it had been just me out alone or on the prowl with my buds tonight, I would have taken this one up on her offer. It was always easy to find someone to fuck. But tonight was about getting my fix of Lizzy.

"You mind?" I rumbled in the brunette's direction.

"Come on, baby, I know you like it when I touch you. You said so last month when I took you home and you fucked me all night," she said in a put-on seductive voice that had the opposite effect while she was running one of her long fingernails down my arm and biting her lip suggestively. The half hard-on Lizzy had given me shriveled into nothing.

So I *had* fucked her.

I searched her face, trying to spark a memory, but I couldn't come up with a name or even the faintest recognition. I must have been completely blitzed when I hooked up with her.

Lizzy caught my eyes when she was passing behind the skank's back. Her face seemed impassive, but her eyes were flashing, which told me she was anything but.

"I'm getting us some fresh ones," she told me in a bored voice while waving our empty beer bottles at me. She walked over to the bar where I witnessed two guys automatically making room for her to reach the front.

My teeth clenched.

Yeah, it was real hard tonight to keep my possessive streak under wraps. Those guys better not ogle or touch her.

A hand on my chest reminded me of the woman that was pressed into me, and I turned my head back to face her. I never dipped in the same pond twice. Once I was done with a chick, I was done and never went back. Seeing this one standing next to Lizzy made me wonder how I could have gotten it up for her a month ago. She didn't hold a candle to my Liz.

My lip curled in self-disgust.

"I'm not interested in fucking you again. You need to get lost." Yeah, I was a dick, but I needed her gone. Looking at her reminded me of what I would never have and it pissed me off. The skank narrowed her eyes at me then swung her head to look at Lizzy. She hadn't missed my focus on her and the bitch came to the forefront. Turned out she wasn't as stupid as she looked, though. Her smirk was downright evil when she hissed, "Forget it, asshole. A stuck-up bitch like her will never end up with a guy like you. All she'll ever see in you is a friend. Call me when you've figured that out for yourself," the distaste and incredulity was clear in her voice. As if she was disappointed in me for being stupid enough to think I could ever have a chance. Yeah, she was smarter than she looked, but she had also just insulted my girl.

Poking a riled lion was a mistake.

"Listen, bitch, if what you're saying is true, you must have been a damn lousy fuck, seeing as I don't remember a fucking thing about you. Not even your fucking face. Now leave." My voice was cold and threatening and she flinched. With one last nasty look in Lizzy's direction, she turned to leave and got lost in the crowd of the bar. My body was shaking. Fucking bitch had nailed it right on the head. I didn't need any more reminders that Lizzy was too good for me. What I needed right now was time to cool off before Liz came back with our drinks, so I decided to take a quick piss break to get myself under control.

Chapter 3

Lizzy

This was exactly what I didn't need. Time and time again I had watched girls and women throw themselves at Cole. It started during his first year of junior high. Being two years younger than him, I had still been in elementary school, but we lived in a relatively small town and I always knew when he had a girlfriend. He never told me about them or introduced them to me, but the fact that he wasn't around that much always clued me in pretty quickly. I also saw him around town with his babes. And girls talk.

It got worse when I started my freshman year and he was a junior in high school. Two years of pure torture. Of watching him make out with girls in the school hallways, during games, and at school dances. Of hearing all the girls talk about his skills in the sack. Judging by the amount of girls that had bragged about their experience, he had been a total pig. That had killed. Thinking badly about him was new for me and I had had a hard time reconciling the two Coles: my partner in crime, my best friend, my protector, and the love of my life, with the player who had no compassion for the feelings of the girls he screwed, who was an arrogant prick. During that time,

I felt like a pathetic little girl with an unrequited crush on her best friend. Still, I couldn't not be his friend. I was the only person he let get close, the only person who knew he had feelings and whom he would share his soft side with. He meant everything to me. Still did. And deep down inside I had always kept a spark of hope that as soon as I was old enough, he would make his move and claim me as his. A stupid little girl's dream that got crushed when I was a junior in high school and Cole had come back home from college for Thanksgiving.

But even after I realized that Cole would never feel what I felt for him and accepted that we would only ever be friends, watching him with other girls or hearing about his conquests never got any easier.

After our initial little tiff over the phone earlier tonight, we were having a great night. Until skanky bitch number five thousand four hundred and twenty-three made an appearance.

No, I didn't really believe that Cole had had that many women, but sometimes it felt like it. I really didn't need to know that he had fucked her all night. She was gorgeous of course, but I could smell bitches from a mile away. Why did he always hook up with those worthless pieces of ass? I knew he didn't even like them. He had told me. So why did he waste his time with them? And why couldn't he give me what he was giving out freely to most of the female population of Boston? Was I that unattractive to him? Was the thought of having sex with me that revolting?

Tonight showed me once more that I needed to get my head out of my ass and let someone else into my heart. Yes, I dated. But more often than not, nothing ever came of it. Most of the guys I went out with never made it past first base.

I had had sex with three guys.

Again. Pathetic.

I was twenty-five years old for Christ's sake!

Now that I had escaped that hellhole I had grown up in, had finished my degree, and had a job that I loved, it was time to work on my personal life and find someone to be happy with.

I looked over my shoulder to see if Cole was still busy with that bitch, but couldn't find him anywhere.

Figures.

Didn't take him long to drag that skank somewhere for a quick fuck. Still, he usually didn't do that when he was with me. If not subtle, he had always been respectful enough to not hook up right in front of my eyes.

Guess times had changed.

I heard the bartender put the beers on the counter in front of me and turned back around to give him a smile.

"Thanks, looks like I only need one of those now."

Not knowing the rules to this new arrangement of Cole hooking up while we were out, I decided to enjoy my beer at the bar instead of going back to the pool table to wait there for him like an idiot. The bartender was kinda cute and, following my own advice from a few seconds ago, I started chatting him up in an effort to be more open. His name was Mike and bartending was only his sometimes job. He was a cop and was helping out his buddy from college, who had inherited the bar from his dad two years ago. While we were talking, he was called away a couple of times to serve drinks, but we kept a pretty good conversation going. He was a funny guy and his intensive over-the-top flirting had me laughing out loud a few times.

During one of those times, I felt a light hand touch the

small of my back, then felt lips at my ear and heard whisper, "Looks like you're having a good time without me."

It was Cole.

I was, actually. And why shouldn't I? He had gone off to enjoy himself with the skanky bitch and left me hanging.

"I am, actually."

The clenching of his jaw told me he wasn't happy about that, but right now I honestly couldn't care less. He had thrown a fit when I was running late because of my job and then he went and got himself laid in the bathroom in the middle of a game of pool. In my eyes, he had no grounds to stand on.

"Your new conquest gone?" I asked, annoyed.

"She's not my new conquest," he said through clenched teeth.

"Your old conquest, then." What was his problem? Nobody forced him to fuck everything that moved, so why was he in a bad mood all of a sudden? You'd think he would be sated and mellow after having just gotten off.

He looked at me sharply, then caught sight of Mike and narrowed his eyes at him.

"Yeah, she's gone," he said darkly. "You make a new friend while I was in the bathroom?" Ah, so he had taken her to the bathroom. Very classy.

"I did. That's Mike. He seems like a real nice guy."

"You were laughing just now. He make you laugh?"

What the fuck? Why was he so angry? Did he know Mike?

"You know him or something?" I asked.

"Nope. Never seen him before."

"Then what's your problem?"

Cole caught Mike's eyes and tipped his chin up at him, indicating he wanted another beer. Mike tipped his chin up at

Cole in answer and reached under the bar.

"My problem, honey, is that I came back from the bathroom to find you flirting with the bartender instead of waiting for me over by the pool table like a good girl so we can finish our game."

He could not be serious. Was he trying to piss me way the fuck off? Well, mission *fucking* accomplished!

"Are you fucking shitting me right now, Cole?" My voice was getting loud. There was no way Mike hadn't heard what I said since he was only a few feet away with Cole's beer in his hand. He placed it on the bar in front of Cole before he looked at me and asked with concern in his voice, "You okay, Lizzy?"

I opened my mouth, but before I could assure him that I was fine apart from the fact that I thought my head was about to explode, Cole threw his arm over my shoulder, jerking me roughly into his body while he growled, "Yeah. She's fine. Move along."

Oh. My. God.

I didn't only think it. My head *was* exploding. Here he was, leaning against the bar, freshly fucked by one of his walking vaginas, and he was staking a claim on me because a guy had made me laugh?

My elbow shot out and connected with Cole's side while at the same time I got up from the stool I was sitting on so that it was now between us, dislodging the arm he had around me. My hands landed on my hips as I leaned over the stool into his space to hiss into his face.

"What the fuck is your problem, Cole? You're not my boyfriend! You have no right to tell me whom I can and can't talk to! Drop the overprotective big brother attitude! I'm twenty-five years old and perfectly capable of choosing the people I want to spend time with! Which, right now, is not you! So maybe *you* should move along!" By the end of my tirade I was breathing hard. I didn't think I had ever been this mad at him before.

Cole was watching me, anger flashing in his eyes. "Believe me, Lizzy, I am well aware of the fact that I am not your boyfriend! What pisses me off is that as soon as I turn my back for five minutes, you're making goo-goo eyes at the first asshole that catches your fancy! Really? You're gonna hook up with the bartender? I hadn't pegged you as trashy!"

My head jerked back as if he had slapped me across the face.

Pain sliced through me, obliterating everything in its path.

Tears were pooling in my eyes—too many—and they overflowed and silently ran down my cheeks.

Cole had never talked to me like that. He knew what it did to me, knew how it made me feel when people I cared about treated me like shit, knew how deeply words could cut me.

Since I was ten, he had been the one person in my life that I knew with absolute certainty wouldn't talk down to me.

But he had just literally called me trash.

He was right, of course, I had been born into that life, had grown up surrounded by trash, had lived on the wrong side of town my whole life before I could finally escape, but Cole had never let me feel it.

Until now.

"Shit, Liz, I didn't mean that. I—" I cut him off, moving my hand in front of his face, palm out, my eyes cold on him. I didn't want to hear any of his apologies. I dug some money out of my pocket and threw it onto the bar, ready to leave. I needed to get the hell out of here before I lost my hold on my emotions. But Cole stepped in front me and kept talking, his voice slightly panicked, "I don't know what's going on with me. You're right. I don't have any right to tell you who to hook up with, but you have no idea how frustrating that is for me. You know how possessive I am of my time with you. Maybe that's why I lost it on you just now. I missed you. Please, baby—"

"No," I interrupted him again, my voice filled with rage and pain at the same time, "Don't you dare call me that! You just lost every right to ever call me that again!" My bottom lip was quivering and I knew I wouldn't be able to hold it together for much longer. I tried to walk around Cole to get to the exit, but he grabbed my arm and pulled me back to him.

"Shit, Liz. I never meant to hurt you. I—" he was pleading with me, but I couldn't deal with that right now. I was too hurt to even look at him. With a hard twist, I wrenched my arm out of his hold, turned around, and bolted. I made it to my car before Cole could catch up to me. When I heard him come to a stop right behind me, I whirled on him and let fly. All the pain and hurt and disappointment he had inflicted in the last ten minutes curled up in my stomach and turned in to an anger so hot I could feel my eyes alight with it.

"Leave me alone, Cole! I don't want to hear it! You can take your remorse and shove it up your ass for all I care! You think you can treat me like you just did, talk to me like you just did, then give me a bullshit apology and expect me to forgive you? Not gonna happen! You were the one person in my life that knew everything about me, everything that happened, and has never judged me for it! I won't let anyone ever treat me like trash again! And that includes you! You know damn well how hard I've worked to leave that life behind, Cole! So go to hell!" Without giving him a chance to respond, I got into my car, cranked it up, and shot out of the parking lot and headed home.

By the time I got to my apartment, I had three missed calls and two messages, all from Cole. I turned my phone off and collapsed onto my bed, too emotionally drained to even get undressed before I climbed under my blanket. I didn't cry, but instead stared blindly at the wall in the dark, trying to push down my pain, to not feel anything.

But for the first time in my life, I was unsuccessful.

So I let the tears fall while big sobs shook my body. I don't know for how long I cried. What I did know was that, for the first time in fifteen years, I cried myself to sleep.

Cole

In the breezeway outside of Lizzy's apartment, I could hear her heart-wrenching sobs. On my way over here, I had thought of nothing but finding a way to make her hear me out, of letting me apologize. She must know that I hadn't meant what I said, that I could never consider her trash. I had just been so frustrated and angry that I could never make her mine when that's all I wanted. But of course, she wouldn't know what that felt like.

Hearing her crying was breaking my heart. I had seen her cry silently often throughout our childhood and during our teen years, but that sobbing... God! It was killing me! Lizzy was the strongest woman I knew. She didn't let anyone beat her down, although lots of people have tried. I had made it my job to take care of her, to console her when things at home were bad, to build her back up when she was down, to protect her from the assholes in our town. She had always let me, had expected me to be there for her.

But tonight was different. She had needed to get away from me, hadn't wanted to talk to me. For the first time in our lives, she had pushed me away. And that left a gaping hole inside me that was tearing me apart. I couldn't lose her. Not ever.

She was my everything.

And I would show her exactly that.

I didn't know for how long I sat leaning my back against her door, my head in my hands, the fear of losing her so strong I was shaking. I couldn't lose her. I just couldn't. And if nothing else, tonight proved that I wouldn't be able to watch her fall for another guy. Just seeing her talking and flirting with another guy, a guy who had made her laugh, drove me absolutely insane with jealousy. I couldn't stand it. What would I do when she eventually found someone she was actually going to date long-term, move in with, marry, have babies with? No. Absolutely not! That was not going to happen! Ever!

Yeah, I was a selfish bastard but that laugh was mine, those bright green eyes were mine.

She was mine.

The crying had stopped. She must have fallen asleep. I shouldn't wake her. I would give her the space she needed from me tonight.

But tomorrow, things would change.

Tomorrow, I would show her exactly how I felt about her.

Chapter 4

Lizzy

Fourteen Years ago.
Lizzy is eleven. Cole is thirteen.

Cole is taking me to get ice cream. I love ice cream. It's one of my most favorite things in the world. Getting ice cream with Cole makes it my most, most favorite thing in the world.

Cole is my best friend. We do pretty much everything together. Every day, as soon as I come home from school, I dump all my stuff in my room and go to our special place as fast as I can. Then I wait for him. Sometimes I don't have to wait long, sometimes I have to wait longer, and sometimes he doesn't come at all. But I'm never mad at him for not showing up. He explained to me that sometimes his mother won't let him go outside and keeps him with her inside all day. First I thought his mother must really love him if she wanted him around so much, but he told me that wasn't it. I didn't know what it was, he didn't share that with me. And I didn't ask. He will tell me if he wants me to know. And then I will be there for him like he is always there for me when my mom makes me cry or when I can't stand the fighting anymore and need to get out of the house.

I will always be there for him, because I love him.

Today, I don't have to wait for him at all. He is already lying down in front of my cave, looking up at the sky, when I get there, waiting for me, smiling up at me when he sees me standing above him. I love it when he smiles at me. It gives me butterflies. He takes my hand and leads me out of the woods to the ice cream shop in town and I love that, too. Him holding my hand. It feels nice and I smile the whole way there.

I know exactly what I want: an ice cream sundae with chocolate sauce and whipped cream and sprinkles on top. When I give the lady at the counter my order, Cole grins and says, "That's my sweet Lizzy."

That gives me butterflies, too.

I like it when he calls me his.

Cole orders his banana split and we sit down outside at one of the tables with the umbrellas and devour our treats in silence. I don't mind it when we don't talk. It isn't awkward or anything. We understand each other perfectly fine even when we don't say anything. We are both comfortable that way.

It's not long before some of the kids in Cole's class see us. I don't like them. They are mean to me when Cole isn't with me. When I see them coming towards us, I look down at the table and my body stiffens a little bit. "You okay?" Cole asks me and I nod without looking at him. He knows me too well, though. I can never lie to him without him knowing.

"Lizzy, what's wrong?" I'm about to tell him how those kids had called me names on my way home from school the other day when they reach our table. I can tell by the look on their faces that they are up to something, and the feeling of dread makes me lose my appetite.

"Hey, Cole! Why you keep hanging out with that little girl?" One of the boys asks snidely.

"Back off, dude. She's my friend." Cole isn't happy to see them either. I can tell.

"Your friend, huh? How can you be friends with that piece of white trash? Your mother would go apeshit if she knew." He is laughing now and it sounds ugly and mean.

"I told you to back off, Marc. And don't call her trash or I'll kick your ass!" Cole has gotten up from his seat and is nose-to-nose with that Marc guy. I don't think I have ever seen him this angry with anyone. They are having a staring contest and Marc loses. He gives me one last disgusted look before he turns away and goes inside the shop to get his ice cream. His friends follow.

Cole sits back down and looks at the table, but doesn't finish his ice cream.

I feel bad, so I try to apologize. "I'm sorry, Cole."

He whips his head around and looks at me. "Don't you dare be sorry, Lizzy. You have nothing to apologize for. Those guys are assholes. Don't listen to what they're saying."

I nod at him, but again he knows I don't mean it. "I'm serious, Lizzy. Don't listen to them. You are not trash and don't you ever let anyone tell you otherwise. You're my Lizzy and you're perfect the way you are."

Okay, that makes me feel better. I give him a genuine smile and he smiles back at me, then we finish off our ice cream before he has to take me home. His family is going to a dinner party tonight and he has to be home on time to get ready. He doesn't want to go. He hates those dinner parties. I know. He told me. I don't know exactly what a dinner party is—at my house we hardly even have dinner—but I hate them for him.

Chapter 5

Lizzy

I woke up the next morning feeling miserable. Must be all that crying and tossing and turning. Oh yeah, and the fact that the most important person in my life had ripped my heart out last night.

Opening my eyes was hard. They felt swollen and crusty. It was too bright in my room and the light streaming in through my window made me flinch in pain. My head was throbbing. I needed some painkillers.

I rolled out of bed and made my way to the bathroom. When I got a glimpse of myself in the mirror, I couldn't believe what I was seeing. My eyes were red and puffy and the black rings underneath them combined with my pale face made me look like one of those emo people. The left-over makeup from last night looked horrendous and my hair was a complete disaster. I needed a shower. Stat. *Get your shit together, Lizzy.* I couldn't go into work looking like this. In my job I needed to be strong for the kids, not walk around looking like a zombie all day. So shower first, then coffee.

After my shower, I still felt like shit, but at least I looked marginally better. I decided to blow out my hair today and put makeup on. Maybe looking good would boost my self-esteem and put me in a better mood. A girl could hope. I purposely avoided thinking about last night, thinking about Cole. I couldn't deal with that right now. Not yet. I wasn't sure when I could face my feelings of disappointment and hurt, but I knew that time wasn't now.

I was out of coffee, so a trip to the coffee shop was in order. On my way out the door, I grabbed my cell phone to throw it in my purse and saw that the alerts from last night were still active on my screen. I didn't want to listen to his messages or read his texts. There weren't any new ones, so I swiped my finger on the screen to at least clean up my home screen. While I was taking care of that, the phone chirped in my hand with a new text message. It was from Cole. I hit 'ignore' as soon as I saw his name, and threw my phone in my purse. *Don't go there. Just go and get some coffee, then go to work.*

That's what I did.

Standing in line at the coffee shop, I decided to get everyone else at the shelter a coffee as well. It would be another busy day today and I appreciated all their help and hard work, so I wanted to bring in a little thank you.

"Morning, Lizzy. Looking good today," Grant, the barista, smiled at me.

"Why, thank you, Grant," I said playfully and smiled back at him. Good confidence booster. After taking my order and writing my name on the cups, he made me giggle by giving me a wink before I moved to the end of the counter to wait for my coffees with a small smile on my face.

When I made it to the shelter, I saw Jesse and Chloe hanging out at the front of the building, waiting for someone to unlock the door. Looked like I was early today and was the first one here apart from the night supervisor. I called over to them and waved them towards me. When they got closer, I could tell that living on the streets was taking a toll on them. Their clothes were dirty, almost filthy, and the rings under their eyes looked worse than mine had that morning. They had also lost weight, judging by the way their clothes were hanging off of them. I needed to get through to them and soon before something worse happened to either of them.

"Have you guys eaten?" I asked when they reached me at my car. I knew they hadn't. The last food they had was probably the snack I gave them yesterday afternoon. Both of them shook their heads.

"Neither have I and I'm starving. Wanna join me for some pancakes and eggs at the diner down the street?" I was lying. I wasn't hungry, but I needed to get some decent food into these guys, and taking them out for breakfast might give me a chance to talk to them on neutral ground, away from the other kids. Yes, this could be considered bribery, but I didn't care. Bribing kids with food that they loved but couldn't afford usually went a long way.

Chloe's eyes got big at the mention of pancakes and she looked pleadingly at Jesse, who gave her a small nod in return. "Yeah, that would be great, Lizzy. Thanks." I could tell it was hard for him to accept help from someone, but Chloe needed food and that was his priority. I stored that very useful information away to think about and use later.

"All right! Just let me drop these coffees off at the office and we'll walk down there together." I unlocked the front door and told the night supervisor, Jimmy, I would be back in an hour after I handed him his Americano. He grunted his thanks at me and went back to reading his magazine. Gotta love Jimmy. Always such a ray of sunshine, but I had a soft spot for him, and I knew he liked me to.

At the diner, we found a corner booth and I told them to order whatever they wanted. For myself, I ordered some eggs and toast. The thought of actually eating made my stomach roll, but I knew I needed food to get me through the day without getting a major headache later. They both ordered, but not enough in my eyes, so I changed my order and added some waffles that I then wouldn't eat and offer to them.

While we waited, I contemplated how I could get to the point without scaring them away. Chloe seemed like a sweet girl, so talking to her was easier than trying my luck with Jesse. But I also knew that I needed to gain Jesse's trust if I wanted to get anywhere, and that was not going to be easy. He was hard and serious and didn't trust anyone other than Chloe. He was also her protector, which meant if I took advantage of her sweetness, he might read it as me playing her and never trust me. So I had to tread carefully.

"You okay, Lizzy?" Jesse, to my surprise, interrupted my thoughts. I was surprised because he sounded worried about me. Maybe I was already further in with him than I thought and he did trust me a little bit.

I smiled at him and said, "Yeah, Jesse, I'm fine. Why do you ask?"

"Your eyes look sadder today than usual." Damn, he was perceptive. And not afraid to call me out on it. Which told me that, yes, he was worried about me, which meant he cared about me. It also told me that he thought my eyes always looked sad, but today they were sadder. Not a lot of people could read me like that and it shocked me a little that Jesse could. I looked deeper into his eyes and there it was. He was a broken soul. Just like me. And he had read me way before I had realized it. Yeah, he was perceptive. Which meant he would know if I lied to him or stretched the truth a little. That wouldn't do me any good, so I decided to be honest with him. Only honesty would get me through to him. It would show him that I respected him.

"You're right. I am sad today. A very important person in my life hurt my feelings last night and I'm not over it."

"He apologize?" Smart guy.

"Yes, he did. But it still hurts."

"You gonna forgive him?"

I hesitated. Was I going to forgive him? I wasn't sure. "I don't know." Jesse nodded at me, eyes searching my face as I took a sip of my coffee.

"How are you guys getting on?" Now that I had shared, I wanted to see if he would reciprocate.

He was silent for a little while, still searching my face, then he sighed and relaxed into his seat. I saw that as a good sign and was rewarded when he answered me.

"It's hard, living on the streets. I'm worried about Chloe getting hurt, but we don't have another choice." A lot of children ran away from home because of some stupid fight with their parents, thinking anywhere would be better than home, but I could tell by the hardness in Jesse's eyes and face that for them, there really wasn't another choice. This was bad. I ran my eyes over Chloe, reading her posture, her face, the guilt and apprehensiveness in her eyes. She wouldn't make eye contact with me and kept her gaze on the table.

"Chloe," I called her name softly. Jesse squeezed her shoulder, telling her it was okay, so she lifted her eyes to mine. I don't know why I hadn't seen it before; she must have been hiding it too well. Maybe something happened that she couldn't hide it now or maybe it was getting too hard and she was breaking, but the stark pain she let me see now broke my heart.

"Honey," I whispered as I lifted my hand to her cheek and started stroking it with my thumb. That was new for me. I had never called any of my kids that, but there was something about her that made me want to snatch her up and take her home and just give her the love she so desperately needed. She was broken. Just like Jesse. Just like me. Tears pooled in her eyes and her lower lip started quivering. I closed my eyes and swallowed hard, trying to control my own emotions. When I opened them again, I could feel Jesse watching me intently. He made no move to interrupt Chloe's and my moment, though, which gave me hope.

"Please let me help you," I kept whispering. I saw Jesse's body stiffen, but powered through. "I'm not gonna make you go back home. I can tell there is a reason why you prefer to live on the streets. Believe me. I know how hard life can be. But I can help you. Please let me. I swear you can trust me." Chloe was crying silently now and Jesse pulled her into his side, comforting her. I looked at Jesse. His eyes were still searching, reading me, and I could see the exact moment when he made up his mind. Determination and resolve evident in his manner, he leaned toward me over the table and demanded, "Promise you won't send us back. I will kill him if he ever lays a hand on either one of us again."

"I promise," I answered in a firm voice without hesitation.

He believed me. Thank God.

He leaned back into his seat and relaxed again, which made Chloe relax as well. She was staring at me with hope in her eyes when our food arrived.

"Okay, guys. Get some food in your bellies and then we'll talk."

By the time we were leaving the diner, I knew their entire story. Jesse didn't sugarcoat anything. They were siblings.

Jesse was sixteen, Chloe fifteen. He told me straight up what their father had done to them and it made me want to commit murder. In the most agonizing and torturous way. My heart ached for them and I would do anything in my power to help them through this. Jesse had promised me that they would spend the night at the shelter. It was getting too dangerous on the streets for Chloe, and he didn't want her to get hurt any more than she already had been. He hadn't been sleeping at all the last few nights since someone had tried to rape her while he was asleep. I promised them that the shelter was safe at night, that nobody would harm his sister.

I was sitting in my office, contemplating my options of how to help them when I heard a knock on my door before Marie, one of our student volunteers, peeked her head in. She was a tall, trim woman in her early twenties who exuded passion and commitment. She had a big smile on her face, a smile that told me she knew something that I didn't. I raised my eyebrows at her in question and she opened the door further to reveal a big bouquet of red roses in a crystal vase. I narrowed my eyes at the roses, confused, then watched as she placed the vase on my desk.

"Look what a nice young man delivered a second ago," she said teasingly. She knew I hated surprises. "Looks like someone has his eye on you. Red roses!"

Hesitantly, I grabbed the card that was on one of those sticks in the middle of the bouquet and opened it. When I saw who was responsible for sending the flowers, the hurt from last night came crushing back into me.

Liz.
I didn't mean what I said last night.
I am so sorry.

Please forgive me.
I love you,
Cole

Just like last night, I couldn't hold back the tears. They were now running freely down my face as I kept staring at the card. I knew he didn't think I was trash, he had proven that over and over again all my life, but it still hurt that he could get so angry and lose control to talk to me like he had last night. I wanted to forgive him, but it was hard to let go of that disappointment and insecurity that was rooted deep down inside of me. When you hear people call you white trash, when your own mother, the one person who is supposed to love you unconditionally, treats you like shit and calls you worthless your whole life, then at some point, you start believing that there is some truth to their words. It was hard not to. And those words coming out of Cole's mouth last night for no apparent reason had made those insecurities come to the forefront. It made me angry that I couldn't get over that feeling of not being worth anything and it absolutely broke my heart that Cole was the one who made me feel that way.

"Lizzy," came a voice from the door.

It wasn't Marie's voice.

It was Cole's.

I couldn't look at him.

I had to close my eyes to try to control my tears, but it was no use. My hands flew up and covered my face when the sobbing started. Cole was behind my desk in a flash and wrapped his arms tightly around me, whispering in my ear how sorry he was, how much he loved me, how much it hurt him to see me like this, that he was the reason for my misery.

I stood in his arms and cried for a long time. I didn't know how to stop.

"Liz, baby, please stop crying. It breaks my heart to see you like this." He framed my face with his hands and made me look up at him, but I kept my eyes closed. "Look at me." The tremble in his voice was what made me open my eyes. From behind my tears, I could see the remorse and guilt that was written all over his face. As was the pain at seeing me hurting.

"It's not an excuse, but I need to tell you why I lost it last night." He took a deep breath as if he needed a second to gather his courage. Then he shocked the hell out of me.

"I have been in love with you since I found you in your cave fifteen years ago. I'm not good enough for you, Liz, but I don't give a shit anymore. I want you. All of you. You belong to me." All I could do was stare at him wide-eyed as he continued rocking my world. "I stayed away from you because you deserve better than me. I'm a bastard and treat women like shit. I've never had a girlfriend, never wanted one, don't know how to have one. But I always wanted you and not being able to act on what I want has been driving me crazy. It's gotten worse over the last few years and, baby, I'm done with that shit. Watching you with that guy last night, knowing that he made you laugh like that, pissed me off and I took it out on you. That was wrong and I am so sorry. Please, honey, you have to forgive me, because I don't know what I'll do if you don't." He was searching my face, looking for a reaction, but I was too shocked to give him one. My brain was trying to make sense of his actions last night and his words now, but wasn't very successful. If he loved me, was *in* love with me, then why did he screw that woman in the bathroom with me being right outside the door?

"Say something, Liz," Cole whispered pleadingly.

It took me another second to unscramble my thoughts.

"You're in love with me?" I asked him.

"Yeah," he was still whispering as he touched my nose with his.

"But I don't understand. If you love me, why did you take that bitch to the bathroom to fuck last night?"

Cole flinched then narrowed his eyes at me in confusion. "I didn't fuck anyone last night. Wait, you thought I fucked that skank in the bathroom while you were sitting at the bar?" I nodded. He cursed.

"Fuck, Liz, no wonder you were so mad at me." His hands at my face pulled me into him more until the fronts of our bodies were touching and I had to lean my head back to see his face. "I didn't fuck her. I wouldn't do that to you. It makes me look like an asshole, but honestly, I didn't even remember her. She said something about you and me yesterday that hit too close to home. I told her off and made her leave. I was mad because she was right and I needed time to cool off, so I went to the bathroom. When I came out, I saw you flirting with another guy and saw red and hurt you. I can't tell you how sorry I am about what I said. I swear I didn't mean it. I was just mad and frustrated that I could never have you the way I wanted. But that's done. I don't give a shit if you're too good for me. It's you and me, Liz. It's always been you and me."

"You thought you weren't good enough for me?" He nodded, his face serious, waiting.

"I always thought...I thought that..."

"What? You thought what, Liz?" he asked when I stopped.

I swallowed then whispered, "I thought...I don't really know what I thought. I just knew you didn't want me that way."

He looked deep into my eyes before he leaned in another

inch and kissed me. Slowly at first, carefully, his eyes open to gauge my reaction, but when I didn't push him away, he closed his eyes and *kissed* me like I've never been kissed before. It felt like a promise, a promise that he would always want me. And it was needy. He gave and asked me to give back in return. And I did. My arms went around him, my hands fisted in the back of his shirt, and I kissed him back with everything I had. He said he had always wanted me, had always been in love with me, and the pain I had felt turned into pure bliss. When his tongue touched mine, we both groaned and the kiss turned wild. We were devouring each other. I couldn't get enough and neither could he. His hands were in my hair, holding me in place while he went deeper and deeper, his body pressing into mine.

A knock on my door made us come back to reality, and we both moved back in surprise but didn't let go of each other. We were breathing hard. My door opened and I had to tear my eyes away from Cole's to see who it was. Jesse was standing there, his unhappy eyes on Cole.

"You okay?" he asked me in a dark voice. Judging by the look he was still giving Cole, he was about a second away from coming to my rescue. "I heard you crying." God, he was a good kid! I gave him a reassuring smile when his eyes came to me and told him, "Yeah, Jesse, I'm good. Can you give us a minute?" His eyes roamed my face then he nodded and closed the door behind him. I looked back at Cole.

"Competition I need to worry about?" he asked teasingly, his lips tipping up. I smiled.

"No. Just protective. He saw that I was sad and was worried about me. He's a good kid." Remorse entered Cole's eyes again and he touched his forehead to mine, then kissed me there and hugged me tight.

"I'm so sorry, Liz. Can you forgive me?"

"I'm not gonna lie and tell you what you said didn't break my heart, Cole," he hugged me tighter, "but I want to forgive you. I missed you. You're everything to me, too," my voice was shaking at the end. Cole kissed me again and this time it felt like relief.

"Does that mean you're gonna give us a chance? I'll do anything to make it up to you, baby. I love you." I believed him.

"I love you, too. I always have," I whispered. Then it was my turn to kiss him, and I was rewarded when he groaned into my mouth again. This kiss was shorter, sweeter, full of love. I had no idea a kiss could be like that and I hoped that he didn't either. I wanted this to be ours.

When he broke the kiss, he stared into my eyes with hope and relief. "I wanna take you out tonight to celebrate. There are things we need to talk about. I want it all out in the open so there are no misunderstandings. I'm gonna do this right and make sure you'll never want to leave me standing in a parking lot again. I'm never letting you go, Lizzy." Tears pooled in my eyes again, but this time they were happy tears, tears of hope.

"Those better not be sad tears, baby," he mumbled against my mouth. I shook my head and giggled.

"I'll pick you up at six. Wear something sexy. I want to show you off." I scrunched my nose at him. He knew damn well I didn't have any sexy clothes. He chuckled, then gave me one last quick peck before he let me go and walked out of my office.

I sunk back into my chair, completely blown away. Funny, how things could change so quickly. The last ten minutes would change the rest of my life forever. They already had.

No matter if in the end Cole and I didn't work out, I would always remember his words and his kisses as something to treasure.

Jesse's look was assessing when I entered the common room. When I gave him a bright smile, even I could feel my face light up. He grinned at me and gave me a smirk. A smirk! For weeks I had seen him do nothing but frown and glare and now he was smirking at me.

"So what they say in the movies is true. Roses and kisses really do work as legit apologies. I need to remember that." Oh, my God. And now he was teasing me! In my head, I jumped up and down in glee for having had a hand in this fun side of Jesse making an appearance. On the outside, I remained cool and collected when I returned his teasing, "Yeah, buddy. You should take note. Roses and kisses go a long way," then I lowered my voice and gave him a serious look, "Some honest and heartfelt words also don't hurt." I was being serious because I wanted him to know that yes, people screwed up, that was life. But an honest apology would go a long way. It was never too early or too late to learn life lessons.

I had set up a meeting with my supervisor first thing tomorrow morning to discuss Jesse's and Chloe's case, but for now, I had them settled in one of our rooms. Now that I knew they were brother and sister instead of a couple, they were allowed to sleep in the same room. Jesse had been relieved when I told him that. Even if the shelter was safe for them at night and he didn't have to worry about Chloe being attacked, he still didn't want to let her out of his sight.

The rest of the day went by without any more drama. Or maybe that was just me riding my high from this morning. Daily drama is unavoidable at a youth outreach shelter, but today I took it in stride. Because Jesse had opened up to me, and now I had a chance of getting them off the streets and finding a good home for them.

And because Cole had blown me away with his revelations. To be honest, it scared me a little, our relationship changing that dramatically. Yeah, I had always wanted him to be mine in every way, but dreaming about it and actually having it were two completely different things. I had no idea if we could make this work. Neither one of us had any experience with romantic relationships. The thought of Cole not realizing that he would have to commit to me and only me, scared me. After hooking up with and treating girls like shit since he was sixteen, it must be hard for him to break that habit. And he was right. I did deserve better than that and would not accept that kind of behavior from my boyfriend while in an exclusive and committed relationship.

But I wanted him.

I hoped to God that he wanted this badly enough to really give it a try, because the alternative was a nightmare. If after everything he had told me today, he turned out to be a massive jerk of a boyfriend, I don't think we would be able to recover from that. In any way. We would have to part ways, cut all ties. And that thought scared the ever-living hell out of me.

Chapter 6

Cole

It was five minutes to six when I was knocking on her front door. I had a key and she knew I was coming, but this was a date and I wanted to treat it as such. I was new to this, had never cared about how a boyfriend was supposed to behave, but this was my Liz and I had to try my absolute best. She deserved to have the best boyfriend, someone who made her feel special and loved and appreciated in every way. And I was going to do anything and everything to be that man for her. There was absolutely no going back from this. Yes, it did scare the shit out of me, but seeing the hurt I inflicted last night had broken something inside of me. Since I knew I wouldn't be able to watch her fall in love with someone else, the only alternative to that would be not being a part of her life, which wasn't an alternative I could live with. So I needed to claim her as mine and work my ass off to make it worth her while. She had surprised me today in her office when she gave in to my kiss without hesitation. I thought I would have to work harder to convince her to take a chance on me. There was a lot we needed to talk about tonight, and I wanted to get every little doubt she might have out of the way. I knew her well enough to know that how I had treated women in the past was something she hated. She had never had a problem telling me so. But it ran deeper. She had been disappointed in me for treating women like pieces of meat, free for the taking, and that had burned. I wanted her to be proud of me, to believe in me, and I *would* prove myself to her.

My game plan was to be honest and straight to the point. Lizzy wasn't a person who liked to sugarcoat things. She was always straight up and to the point. No bullshit. She never played any of those games most women like to play. I don't even think she knew how to play them. My sweet Liz. That was the reason why a lot of women didn't like her. She wasn't like them and didn't strive to be. But the fact that other women were either scared of her or thought she was an arrogant bitch didn't change her one bit. She would rather be honest and alone than dishonest and have fake friends. What you see is what you get. Always. So that was my game plan. Bare my soul to her, be honest in every way, and hope it wouldn't make her run in the opposite direction.

When Lizzy opened her door my jaw fell to the floor.

Holy hell, she was sexy.

I had never seen her in a dress. Well, that wasn't true. As a child, she wore dresses all the time. I had seen her in sexy get-ups when we went out clubbing, but she always wore jeans, sexy jeans, but still jeans, paired with a tight top.

This was something else.

Her dress was all black. It had no sleeves, so it showed off her sexy arms and shoulders, but had something like a turtleneck that wasn't a turtleneck. It looked hot as hell. And it was short. Extremely short. I hoped to God that it covered her ass. It was clingy in all the right places and left nothing to the imagination.

It took me a second to recover from that view. I couldn't tear my eyes away from the body that was now mine to explore. My dick twitched in my pants in anticipation, impatient.

Yeah, buddy, I know exactly what you're feeling right now.

But I had told myself that I would not have sex with her until she was absolutely sure she could trust me with her body. When I took her for the first time, I wanted all of her. Holding nothing back. Having no doubts.

Looking at her now, I could tell I was going to take a cold shower tonight. A very long, very cold shower, or maybe a hot one where I would jerk myself off again and again thinking about her in that dress.

My dick was straining against my fly. I took a deep breath to rein him in as my eyes travelled up her body to meet her dancing ones.

"You done?" she asked me teasingly, her eyebrows raised.

"Nope," I said and let my eyes wander again. That made her laugh out loud. A grin spread across my face. I had it back. Her laugh. *My* laugh.

She stepped back from the door to invite me inside, but I shook my head.

"No, baby. Right now, I want to rip that dress off of your hot body so I can explore every inch of you. I don't trust myself enough to not ravage you, so you need to come out here where you're relatively safe."

She pressed her lips together to keep from laughing, grabbed her purse from the little table by the door, then turned around to pull the door closed and locked up. At the sight presented to me when she turned, I groaned. And my dick stood at full attention.

Her back was completely bare.

Naked skin from shoulder to just above her ass.

No bra.

My hands had a mind of their own when they gripped her hips and squeezed. I closed my eyes and took a deep breath through my nose, trying to tamp down my instant arousal.

Jesus! I had never been this turned on by a dress. Or anything for that matter.

She was going to be my undoing.

Breathing in and out slowly, I rested my forehead on her shoulder.

"Cole?" Lizzy's soft and amused voice called me. I lifted my head to see that hers was turned and she was looking at me over her shoulder. Her eyes were beautiful and sparkling, the green surrounded by thick lashes.

"Don't let me come in tonight," I all but growled at her.

"What?" she asked, confused now.

"Don't let me come in, no matter how much I beg. I promised myself I wouldn't touch you tonight and I need you to help me out with that."

"You won't touch me tonight?" Disappointment. This was gonna be harder than I had imagined. I deserved a medal for this.

I shook my head at her.

"Oh." Her voice was small now and she turned her head away from me to finish locking up. Something other than disappointment was laced through her voice. Was it rejection? With my hands still at her hips, I turned her body to face mine and looked into her eyes, searching. Yes, she thought I was rejecting her. Crazy woman.

"Honey, I'm not rejecting you." I gave her a small peck on the lips in reassurance then kept my lips touching hers.

"Believe me, I want you more than I have ever wanted anyone. My body is screaming at me to take you." To emphasize this I pressed the proof of my body's reaction to her into her belly. "But I need to prove to you that this isn't just about sex. It's so much more than that. It's everything." I kissed her again, short and quick, so as not to lose control. "When I take you for the first time, I want you to have no doubts about us." Another kiss, this one longer and deeper.

"Okay," she breathed when I released her mouth. It was cute. She was in kind of a daze and it looked good on her. I reveled in the fact that I had been the one to put my little no-nonsense-spitfire into this state with just a few kisses and some frontal body contact. My chuckle seemed to snap her out of her daze and she took a small step back.

"You're right. You know I trust you, but it's probably a good idea to take things slow, give either of us a chance to back out if things aren't going the way we expected before we ruin something that's important to us."

What the hell! There would be no backing out!

I closed the short distance she had gained and framed her face with my hands, so that all she could see were my eyes.

"I'm not backing out. Neither are you. I won't let you. All I'm doing is giving you time to get used to us before I take what has always been mine. Get this, Liz, if you run from me, I will follow you and drag you right back where you belong, and we will work out whatever it is that made you run." My voice was rough and growly. The thought of her backing out, of leaving me, had me shaking.

Lizzy's eyes had gone big at my statement, and I could see she was gearing up to give me the what for. My little spitfire.

"Excuse me? You won't let me? You'll drag me back? What? You're a goddamn caveman now?" Yeah, from soft and breathy to hot and spitting fire in under five seconds. That's my Liz. I grinned at her.

"You heard me."

She narrowed her eyes to slits and opened her mouth to blast me, but I stopped her by putting my mouth to hers and sliding my tongue inside that hot mouth. God, she tasted good. I wondered if the rest of her tasted just as great as her mouth, knowing and fearing that she would probably taste better than anything that had ever touched my tongue. I couldn't get enough and delved in deeper, tangling and twisting and exploring. This was all the exploring I would get tonight, so I made it last.

When I tore my mouth from hers, we were both breathing hard.

Jesus! But she could kiss!

She was again in that daze and was staring at my mouth, her lips still parted, her breath ragged. Damn, that was a good look on her. I drew on my last reserves of control and kissed her nose, then pulled back and took her hand.

"As much as I would love to make out in your breezeway all night, I'm starving. I need food, woman, and we need to talk. Let's go."

I couldn't blame anyone but myself. I had asked for this. Had told her to dress sexy, that I wanted to show her off. And holy hell, did she follow that instruction to a t. She was killing me and she knew it. Sexy little devil was smirking at me from across the table right now. My answer was a low growl, which made her press her lips together and look down at her plate so as not to burst out laughing, I suspected. Fucking hell. I didn't deserve a medal, I deserved a fucking trophy.

"I should have taken you to Chuck E Cheese. At least there, nobody would be ogling you all night long. Though, scratch that. All those horny dads would just get fodder for their spank bank," I growled across the table at her, my eyes narrowed on her smile.

"You're being ridiculous, Cole. Nobody is ogling me."

"Oh, believe me, baby, they are. Every man in this restaurant knows that you're not wearing a bra and is glad that their boner is hidden under the table."

Her shoulders were shaking in silent laughter while she was shaking her head. There was nothing even remotely funny about this situation. I growled at her again, which made her silent laughter not so silent anymore as she burst out laughing. Fuck! Now every man's head within a five-table radius was turned her way and I was starting to see red. If she didn't tune it down, I was going to end up in jail tonight.

"Liz," I called her name.

"Yeah?"

"Honey, if you don't want me to face assault charges in the very near future, do me a favor and at least try to be less sexy. That means no sexy smiles, no laughing, and we gotta do something about that fucking dress. What the hell were you thinking not bringing a coat?" I saw her eyes narrow through my little speech.

"Cole, stop. It's been entertaining, but now you're starting to piss me off. It's a dress. Get over it."

"And no attitude, either."

"What about breathing? Am I allowed to do that?" That was it. She didn't want to make this easier for me? All right. She wasn't giving me any other choice then but to stake my claim openly and publicly. I got out of my chair, pulled her out of hers, and laid a long, deep, wet one on her. One of my hands was tangled in her hair while the other was pulling her in close at the small of her back. She didn't resist and kissed me back, spurring me on even more. It took someone clearing their throat close to us to make me break the kiss. *Yeah, that should do it.* It was me who gave her the dazed and turned-on look she was now sporting. None of these assholes were allowed to touch her. Only me. That thought eased my raging jealousy as I helped her back into her chair before I sat down again. The waiter served our food and I started eating.

"What was that?" Lizzy asked me, still out of breath from our kiss, but she also sounded a little annoyed.

"That, baby, was me staking my claim."

"So you just pissed on me in the middle of a fancy restaurant?"

Yeah. She was definitely annoyed. "Yeah." I answered nonchalantly and motioned for her to start eating her food. Her glare made me give her a grin, which made her growl. That was so cute that now *my* shoulders were shaking with silent laughter.

"Liz, cut me some slack. I've always been possessive of you, but now that you're mine, it's even worse. I don't like it when men stare at you like that, because I know exactly what they're thinking."

"No, Cole. You've always been overprotective, but—"

"Not protective, Liz, *possessive*. There's a difference," I interrupted her.

Her head tilted to the side and her eyebrows went up, asking me for an explanation.

"Like I told you this morning, I have always considered you mine, but wouldn't let myself touch you. You have no idea how many fights I got into in high school because of you. With jackasses who wanted to get in there or who talked shit about having had you. Thank God I never actually had to see you make out with some guy or I would have killed him.

Nobody touches what's mine."

"So what you're saying is that all this time you wanted me, didn't do anything about it, but wouldn't let anyone else have me either, while I had to watch you make out with all those girls, knowing you fucked everything that moved?"

Yeah, I was an asshole and a hypocrite. She was right to be angry.

I leaned over the table and took her hand in mine, stroking the back of her hand softly with my thumb.

"I'm sorry, Liz. I know it wasn't fair to you, but I never looked at it from your perspective. All I could see was my jealousy. I also didn't know that you were into me like that. I thought for a while you had a crush on me, but you were young and pure and I was a total bastard. I never thought you could really want me."

"You're an idiot, Cole. Do you have any idea how many times you broke my heart? How many times I had to watch you touch other girls when all I wanted was you to touch me like that? How many times, when you were screwing around and giving every other woman a piece of you, I felt like I wasn't pretty enough for you? When all those girls in high school talked about how good you were in the sack? When I thought I would never be anything but a little sister you had to protect? You could have saved both of us a lot of pain, Cole."

Jesus, she didn't beat around the bush. I normally loved that about her, but the torture she just revealed that I had put her through made my heart ache and regret spread through my body so hot that it was hard to breathe. She wasn't looking at me, but instead was staring down at her plate, the hand I wasn't holding clenched in a fist under the table. I could tell her fingers were clenched even though I couldn't see them. I wasn't sure if she was mad I had wasted years for both of us, or if she was trying not to cry. I needed to see her eyes.

"Look at me, Liz." I urged her. It took her a few seconds before she complied, but when she finally gave me her eyes, I could see that they were as torn as her body language had suggested. There was pain and sadness, but also accusation and remorse beside a whole lot of anger.

I squeezed the hand I was still holding and leaned further over the table.

"You're right. I have wasted a lot of time and caused you a lot of hurt, disappointment, and embarrassment. I take full responsibility, but I swear I will do anything I can to make it up to you, if it takes the rest of my life. I know it's hard to believe that I could go from hooking up with random girls to being in a committed relationship, and I would agree with you. But this is you and me. You know me better than anyone else and I know you. I screwed up, baby, but I'm fixing it now. You trust me. You know I don't make promises I can't keep. I wouldn't pursue this if I weren't serious about us. I can't ever lose you. Give me a chance and I *will* make you happy." I was begging at the end. I needed her to believe in me, in us, to give me a chance to build on what we'd always had between us.

Chapter 7

Lizzy

I wanted him to mean what he said so badly. For as long as I could remember, this was what I had hoped for. Even when I had given up on that dream, somewhere deep inside me there was still that little part of me that wouldn't give up, wouldn't lose hope. Until last night, when I had thought he was screwing someone in the bathroom and losing his shit on me.

I had given up then.

Not even twelve hours later, he had again turned my world upside down, had turned it on its axis when he said he loved me and had kissed me like it was his first and last kiss merged into one. It was overwhelming. Getting what you always wanted was not as easy to deal with as you might believe. It was downright terrifying.

But what was the alternative? Saying no to him right now, letting him go and watching him hook up with random women over and over again? And what about me? Would I settle for some guy who would never be Cole? No. That was something I knew I wouldn't survive. It had gotten harder and harder over the years and now that I knew what his kisses felt like, what his arms around me felt like, and how he reacted to me, I couldn't go back.

I wanted what he promised.

I wanted *us*.

His eyes were glued to mine, imploring, slightly panicky as I was thinking through what he had said. I returned his squeeze and nodded at him. He closed his eyes and exhaled in relief, then brought my hand to his mouth and pressed a light kiss on my knuckles. That was sweet.

"Thank you, Liz," he whispered there, "I promise you won't regret it." I believed him. But we still needed to clarify what being in a committed relationship meant.

"Cole," I called him quietly. He opened his eyes to look at me. "Your words are beautiful. And I believe you mean every single thing you said. I do. What concerns me is that you are used to women throwing themselves at you. I wasn't allowed to act on my jealousy before, but if you're mine, you need to know that I will not stand back and let them touch you. I get just as jealous as you do, but it's worse. I *had* to watch you with other girls, whereas you have never really seen me with another guy. I don't have to imagine. I have the visual, probably in more detail than you think I do. So I think it will be harder for me to keep my shit together when those skanks go after you. What I need you to do is make it clear to them that you are off-limits. Don't get me wrong, I can fight my own battles when it's necessary, but I won't tolerate you giving them mixed signals or the wrong idea. You need to make it very clear that you are not interested and won't ever go there again. And you need to tone down your jealousy of other men. Going out with you is not gonna be fun if you're this growly beast who does nothing but stare down other men and piss all over me."

His face was serious while he listened to me. When he answered, he squeezed my hand in his again.

"I can promise you I will make it clear to everyone I'm off the market," he said without hesitation, "and I'll try to control my jealousy, but I can't make any promises there. You're right. I never had to watch you with another man and I'm very grateful for that, but I've got a vivid imagination when it comes to you." His serious face turned into a teasing one when he continued, "Maybe once I've claimed you completely and made love to you, that will help, but I doubt it."

I shivered at the thought of him making love to me. I didn't like the idea of waiting, though I did understand why he thought it was necessary. His smile was almost predatory now and it made my womb flutter in anticipation. That was also something that concerned me, though, and I had to be honest with him about it.

I took a sip of my water with my free hand and realized that it was shaking. This was embarrassing.

"Baby?" Cole asked. He must have noticed my nervousness.

"Uhm..." I didn't know how to say this. *Just rip it off like a bandaid.*

"I'm not good at the sex thing," I blurted a little too loud, the words tripping over each other. Cole startled and looked at me in shock.

"You're not good at the sex thing?" he asked like that was a foreign concept to him, which it probably was. All I could do was nod.

"Liz, I have no idea what you're talking about. I need a little more than that," he prompted. I took a deep breath. I didn't want to go into detail. This was embarrassing enough.

"You know. Sex." That was all I said.

"Yeah, beautiful, I know what sex is," he was trying to suppress a smile.

This wasn't funny.

"Sex, Cole. I'm not good at it." I was being clear. What was there not to understand?

"That's hard to believe." He thought I was joking? Guess I had to spell it out for him.

"Okay, I'll be *clearer*. I've had orgasms during sex, but it always took a lot of work, and in my experience, men get impatient with that. It has been indicated to me that I can be cold and stiff, that I'm not active enough, nor can I let myself go enough to enjoy sex and make my partners enjoy it. There, is that enough detail for you?" I was annoyed and pissed that he had made me say it.

"Hold on a second." I was so absorbed in my snit I hadn't seen the change in his demeanor. He wasn't amused now. He was angry.

"Nobody has ever managed to make you lose yourself during sex and then they blamed that shit on you? Are you kidding me?" Confused by his question and his obvious anger, I shook my head. Cole swore under his breath then focused on me again.

"Liz, if the way you kiss is any indication as to how hot you are going to burn for me, sex with you is going to be off the charts. Those guys you had sex with were assholes and shit in bed. I'm not gonna lie. I like the fact that you have never burned hot for anyone. That means you're gonna be mine even more. What I don't like is that you took that shit on yourself. If a man can't make a woman let go enough to enjoy herself, it's on him. Not on her. Shit, Liz! You are off the charts hot and you don't even know it. When I saw you in that dress tonight, my dick was about to explode. Nobody has ever turned me on like you do, Liz. And you haven't even touched me yet."

Wow. That made me feel kinda proud. But he wasn't done.

"Shit! Now it makes total sense. You really don't see it when men look at you, do you?"

I shrugged my shoulders. "Not really."

He studied me. I could see the wheels in his head spinning. Then it looked like it clicked and he swore again under his breath.

"Fucking hell, baby, your fucking mother really did a number on you. And me being an asshole with my head up my ass probably didn't help matters."

What the hell was he talking about? His hand was squeezing mine hard as he was looking down at the table, shaking his head. I had no idea where this was coming from or where it was heading. "What do you mean?"

He looked up at me and lost it a little. "Your fucking mother and those fucking bitches in that fucking town. How they treated you like trash and told you that you were worthless. How many times did I find you crying because they were mean to you? How many times did the other kids in town make fun of you? I thought I was protecting you, helping you through it, but I see now that they still got to you. And then me being a jackass led you to believe you weren't pretty enough for me. Fucking hell!" His voice was getting a little loud and people were starting to stare. I hushed him and he talked more quietly.

"Liz, you are the most beautiful woman I know, inside and out. You are honest and loyal and brave and strong. God, you're so strong. You're a fighter. A survivor. Nothing and nobody can beat you down. It makes me so fucking proud of you. Outside of our shitty hometown, has anyone you ever met not loved you? You don't have a lot of friends, but the few you have, you are close to, your colleagues love working with you, the kids you work with are protective of you. That boy that interrupted us today in your office to check on you?" I nodded when he didn't proceed. "He saw me when I came in and clocked me right away. He knows I can take him easily, but he didn't care. He would have taken me on if I had upset you in any way. Lizzy, don't you see? I know you had a shit childhood, but that's not on you. It's on your mother. She is a selfish bitch who was too drunk or stoned to realize what she had in you. People weren't mean to you because you were trash, honey, they were mean to you because they knew you were better than them. You were better than them even though you grew up the way you did, and they hated that. And those guys you were with knew you were out of their league, but they blamed their shortcomings on you to make themselves feel better. And I know you don't believe me, but wherever you go men notice you, notice your class. There aren't a lot of women out there who are the total package, but you have it all and men see that and want it. I've got it now and I swear to God I will make you see it, too."

I was speechless.

Completely and totally speechless.

Did he really think all that about me?

Was that how people saw me?

Strong? Loyal? Classy? Good?

That couldn't be.

There were a lot of people I rubbed the wrong way. True, they usually had a problem with my being straight-forward and blunt to the point of being rude. I hated it when people played games and didn't want those people in my life anyway, but still. It kinda stung when they talked about me behind my back. Were they mean to me because they thought I was better than them? That was something I couldn't fathom. I had never seen myself as being better than anyone, had always thought that I was just different and maybe not good enough and that's why I didn't fit in. And my mother. Yes, it hurt when she told me I was worthless. It still did. Of course, it did. Your parents are supposed to love you, no matter what. Mine didn't love me. I don't know who my father is. He took off before I was born. And my mother had always hated me. There must be something wrong with me if they can't love me. Right? It was confusing. I didn't understand, couldn't make any sense of it.

"I don't get it," I told Cole.

"No, honey, you don't. But you will. I'll make sure of that."

Okay, we needed to change the subject. I was done with the heavy. But Cole apparently wasn't.

"One more thing, Liz. You told me what you needed from me, so now I'll tell you what I need from you."

Oh, boy.

"You're strong. And I am proud you are. What I need you to promise me, though, is that you don't retreat into your head when something is wrong. I know you and have watched you do it hundreds of times. When you're hurt or confused or upset, you lock yourself in that head of yours to not feel anything. It's almost like you have a switch in your brain that shuts everything out and pushes it far down. I'm not gonna let you do that. I want you to talk to me when something is wrong so we can figure it out together. Don't push me away or freeze me out."

I nodded hesitantly.

That's exactly what I did, exactly how I dealt with difficult situations that threatened to overwhelm me. Shut everything out so I didn't have to feel. I had done that since I could remember. All my life. I could see that that was something I would have to work on, though. To let Cole in.

"I'll try," I assured him. I would, but I couldn't promise him that it would work. But I would try for him. I didn't want to freeze him out when I got my feelings hurt, but I had never learned any other coping mechanisms. I knew they existed. Had studied all the theories in college. Hell, I made my kids at the shelter talk to me, and they did, and I gave them advice and steered them in the right direction, but it's different when it's yourself. Guess that makes me a hypocrite as well.

Cole nodded in understanding. "All right," he said, "that's all I can ask. Enough with the heavy. Let's eat and then maybe get a drink somewhere and then make out on your doorstep."

That made me smile.

Something to look forward to.

I wanted more, needed more, but the stubborn ass wouldn't budge. I tore my mouth from his and went to work on his back, roaming my hands over his muscles under his jacket while I kissed and nibbled his neck. His head fell back and he groaned. Yes! I was getting somewhere. His hands had been at my hips the whole time during our make-out session and it was frustrating. My body was longing for his touch. My nipples were hard, my breasts were swollen and heavy, and my panties were wet. All that just from kissing. And from his body pressed into mine.

Incredible.

I was determined to make him break his no-sex-on-the-first-date rule when my hands wandered down to his behind and pulled him into my heat at the same time I lifted my left leg to wrap it around his thigh. For one glorious moment, I could feel his hardness against me when he ground against my sex as he grabbed my thigh and pulled it up higher.

Then he was gone.

I blinked in shock, feeling the coldness he left behind on my exposed skin.

He was standing three feet away from me by the railing, hands at the back of his neck, head leaned back, face towards the sky, eyes closed tight, breathing hard.

I waited.

And waited.

But he didn't move other than his inhaling and exhaling making his chest puff out.

I was breathing hard, too, but stopped altogether when he tipped his head down and opened his eyes to look at me. There was a need so desperate I felt it touching me. A want so frantic it bordered on dangerous. But instead of it scaring me, it only aroused me further and I let out a small whimper.

Cole cursed. "Fuck, baby, I want you so bad it hurts."

I whimpered again.

His hands let go of his neck and landed on his hips as he started pacing for a good minute, then stopped again in front of me. He was close, but he wasn't touching me. When I lifted my hands to touch him, he intercepted them, pulling them straight down my side, our fingers interlaced.

"I can see you want this just as badly as I do. But I need to walk away tonight. It's important to me, Liz." He was asking for my help. Asking me to not push him. I think if I did, he would give in. But I didn't want him to have any regrets about our first time together, so I relented. I rested my forehead against his chest and nodded in silent agreement.

"Thank you," he breathed, then planted a soft kiss on the top of my head. I liked it when he did that. I always had. His forehead kisses were great, too. They had always made me feel special, had made me believe they were something that was his and mine, but now it was more. That thought spread warmth through me and made me sigh in contentment. He let go of my hands and his arms came around me, hugging me to his warm body. I tilted my head back and gave him a smile.

"Tomorrow is Friday. I have to work late, but I want to take you away for the weekend. Somewhere nice. Maybe to the coast."

My smile widened at the idea of having him to myself for a full weekend. "I would love that." He kissed me softly, lovingly, then let me go and took a step back.

"Okay, I'll see you tomorrow. Be ready at seven and we'll leave right away."

"Okay. I'll be ready."

"Night, Liz."

"Night, Cole."

Then he turned around and walked back to his car. I went into my apartment and locked the door behind me.

God, I was a lovesick mess. It was kind of ridiculous.

But I also kind of liked it.

Chapter 8

Lizzy

Twelve years ago.
Lizzy is thirteen. Cole is fifteen.

I am shaking. My whole body is trembling. Tears are streaming down my face, but I can't feel the cold wind turning them into ice on my cheeks. All I can feel is that man's hands on my legs as he is pushing up my shorts, his hot breath on my neck, then the pain as he grips my thighs roughly as he tries to push them apart when I start to struggle.

I'd been asleep. My mother was having another one of her parties. The kind of party where she got drunk and high and forgot that I existed. Not that she gave much of an indication that I was a living and breathing person with feelings and needs any other time. She was a drunk and saw me as a burden. Always had. The burden she'd been settled with when my father left us before I was even born. Almost every day, she told me that if it weren't for me, my father would still be there, would never have left her. That hurt. My own mother was telling me that I was the reason that he left us, that he didn't love me and didn't want me. That I was unwanted and that my existence had destroyed my mother's life.

"I should have never had you. If I hadn't gotten pregnant, your father would have never..." That's usually how far she got before she drowned her sorrow in another bottle of booze and I either locked myself in my room or hid in my spot for hours until I knew she would be out cold and it was safe to go back home.

But the nights she had people over to get drunk and high with were worse. Lately I had noticed that some of the men she had over were giving me leering looks. I wasn't stupid. I knew what that meant. I knew why they came here every week, sometimes more than once. I knew that my mother used her body to pay for her addiction to alcohol and drugs. Everyone in town knew. But until a few months ago, those men had left me alone. They knew I was up in my room, but didn't pay me any attention. That had changed when I had started to fill out, when my body was starting to go through the changes that would turn me into a woman. I had mentioned it to Cole and he had instantly gotten mad and worried, and had made me promise to always make sure that my door was locked. Always. Not just when my mother had company. Always. Just to be safe. I had promised him I would as I reveled in the fact that there was someone who loved me and cared about me.

I stumble but catch myself before I fall. I'm barefoot and in my pajamas. It's cold.

"Come on, sweetheart, don't pretend you don't like it. I've seen the way you look at me. You're dying to give it up and I'm only too happy to show you what it's like to have a good time."

Bile rises in my throat as I hear his words replay in my mind. I cough. Then I sob again. I can't stop sobbing.

I know I was lucky. Lucky that he had been too drunk and high to overpower me. That I got free and ran before he had a chance to pull my shorts all the way down.

I shiver thinking of what would have happened. And in that moment, I hate my mother. Truly hate her. For not loving me enough to make sure I was safe. For not caring what happened to me. When I had stumbled down the stairs, intent on getting away as far and as fast as possible, she hadn't even roused. I saw her lying on the couch, with two men, all three of them in some state of undress, passed out, just like I had seen her so many times since I was six years old.

I shiver again.

Disgusted.

Heartbroken.

Terrified.

It isn't far now. I'm almost there. Almost to Cole's.

Just get to him and he will make it better. That's the only thought I want to hold on to.

Get to Cole. He'll make sure you're safe.

Through the woods. Around the pond. Up the small incline.

There it is.

His house.

His window is dark.

I have to wake him.

I find small rocks and throw them at his window.

One. Two. Ten. Twenty. I don't know how many.

All I know is that I need Cole.

So I keep throwing rocks at his window until I hear him ask, "Lizzy? That you?"

All I can do is nod. I don't realize that it's too dark outside for him to see me, but it doesn't matter. A few minutes later, his back door opens and he is there. I run to him and cling to his body, my face in his chest, holding on tight.

That feels so good.

I start to sob again. Loud, body-wrecking sobs. They hurt my throat, but I can't stop. Cole hugs me back and rubs my back, soothing me.

Up and down.

Up and down.

It helps. I calm down a little.

"Wait here," Cole whispers, then lets go of me and goes back into the house. Not two minutes later, he comes back to me, a blanket rolled up under his arm. He takes my hand and heads towards the trees. I know where we're going.

To our special place.

When we get there, he opens the blanket, moves me to sit on it, then sits down beside me and wraps the blanket around us, cocooning us in.

It makes me feel safe and I take a deep breath and slowly relax my body.

This is why I went to Cole. He makes me feel safe.

"Now, Lizzy, tell me what happened."

I don't want to. He's going to be mad. But I know he won't let it go until I tell him.

"My mother had a party tonight," I feel his body tense at my words. He knows what that means, knows all about my mother's parties. The alcohol. The drugs. The fights. I had promised him to lock myself in my room and not open the door until the next morning. I had listened to him. But tonight, I must have forgotten to make sure the door was actually locked. "There were a lot of people at our house. More than usual. Lots of new people. I went up to my room like I always do. I thought I locked the door, but I must have...I went to bed and fell asleep."

My body starts trembling now at the thought of having to tell him what happened next. Cole holds me tighter in his arms and starts rubbing my back again. I can feel his body is still tense.

"When I woke up, I was confused. I could feel someone was in my room, but it was too dark for me to see." I'm crying again. "Then I felt someone touch my leg," Cole's body locks beside me. His hands on my back go still. I stop talking, afraid that he will get really mad at me for not locking my door. I hold my breath and wait.

"Please tell me you got away," Cole says. He is angry. Very angry.

I nod my head and whisper, "Yes. I kicked and screamed and scratched until he let go. He was drunk. I ran as fast as I could to your house."

Cole slightly relaxes and starts rubbing my back again. "Thank God." Is all he says for a while. Then, "From now on, when your mother throws a party, I want you to come to my house. We'll sneak you in the window and you stay with me where you're safe. Promise me, Lizzy. As soon as you know people are coming to your house, you leave and come to me."

"I promise," I say, grateful that he will keep me safe.

We are again silent for a long while.

"I'm sorry, Cole. I should have checked to make sure the door was locked."

"Don't be sorry, Lizzy. It's not your fault. It's your bitch of a mother who invites those people into your home, making you unsafe." He was still very angry. We sat for a little while longer until Cole got up from the blanket and held his hand out to me.

"Let's go. You're staying with me tonight."

That was the first night I stayed in Cole's room, in Cole's bed.

But not the last one.

From that night on, I crawled through his window on a regular basis, at least once or twice a week, so he could protect me from my mother's filthy friends.

Chapter 9

Lizzy

I was standing on the deck of our little cottage, looking out at the ocean. It was beautiful. I loved the water. It had a peaceful and tranquil quality to it, which made me want to stand here watching it move and sparkle in the moonlight all night.

Cole had taken me to one of those little seaside towns just South of Boston. It was a cute little town with a main street straight out of a romantic comedy or a TV show, lined with shops and restaurants that I wouldn't mind exploring at some point this weekend.

In the back of my mind, I was still thinking over the situation with Jesse and Chloe. During the meeting this morning with Taryn, we had discussed our options of how to get them off the streets into someplace safe. Jesse had mentioned that he was worried their father might be looking for them. I know this was how the system worked, but there was no way I would support Taryn in trying for a reunion, which was usually the first step. We had no evidence of abuse other than Jesse's and Chloe's statements, but the sad story was that sometimes that wasn't enough. The system was terribly flawed and it wasn't surprising that so many kids preferred living on the streets because most of the time they couldn't get the support they needed. I had given Jesse my word that I would make them safe and I intended to keep it. Foster care was the other option. With Jesse being sixteen, it was still a long way until he was legal and could take responsibility for Chloe, so foster care was our best bet. Finding a good one was the tricky part. Another flaw in the system. Most foster parents didn't care about the kids much, but were only interested in the money they got from the government for taking them in. So I needed to make some phone calls to see where we could place them. But for now, they were safe and sound. They were staying at the shelter and had agreed to meet with a counselor and start tutoring sessions next week.

When Cole had knocked on my door to pick me up, I had been on the phone with Jimmy to make sure they were both there and hadn't taken off. Jimmy had checked on them while I stayed on the line and assured me he would keep an eye out for me over the weekend and call me with updates every night. Rainey, one of my full-time colleagues, and Marie had promised to do the same thing during the day shift. So everything was under control. But for some reason, I was anxious, as if somehow I knew something was going to happen, as if there was something I had overlooked. On our way down here, I had told Cole the whole story. He knew how much I cared about my kids, how much of myself I involved into their fight for a better life. He understood why I did it. Why it was my calling. He hated it when some cases didn't work out that great, when kids disappeared, or I couldn't gain their trust, or I couldn't help as much as I wanted, because he knew how much it took out of me. When that happened, he never complained, though. He always supported me when I needed to talk things out or needed him to get my mind off things. And I loved him for it, for being such a good friend. Now it felt even better when I told him how worried I was about Jesse and Chloe, how much it had hurt when they had told me their story, and he took my hand in his to softly brush his lips over my knuckles or squeeze my hand in reassurance. It felt natural and familiar.

On that thought, I felt arms snaking around my waist from behind and lips at my ear softly tracing the shell. That felt natural, too. It was odd that even though neither one of us were used to being in a relationship, these little displays of affection came to us naturally. It didn't feel awkward, but instead felt easy and almost instinctive. Maybe it had to do with the fact that we had known and trusted each other for so long. I didn't want to overthink it, though. I wanted to enjoy it.

"What are you thinking about?" Cole whispered as he was nibbling my ear.

"You actually," I said on a giggle.

"Yeah? What about me?" His hands started moving on me over my shirt, stroking my belly, one hand going up my side almost to my breast, the other going down to the edge of my shirt then lifting it just enough for him to touch the skin there. I tipped my head back to rest it on his shoulder and reveled in the full-body shiver his touches caused.

"How natural it feels when you touch me. How easy it is to touch you back," I breathed on an exhale.

"You're damn right it is. Now that we broke the seal, all I wanna do is touch you, all I can think of is kissing you." I lifted my head a little and reached for his mouth. When our lips connected, we both groaned in relief. His hands were getting serious, exploring, touching, feeling, gently groping. Both were under my shirt now. The skin-to-skin contact there for the first time jolted me into action and I opened my mouth to him, snaking my tongue out to touch his. His hand had found my breast and squeezed lightly, his thumb caressing my hard nipple, causing me to moan against his tongue.

That's when things got out of control. Cole broke the kiss just long enough to turn me in his arms so that I was facing him, then he lifted me up with is hands at my behind, leaving me no choice but to hold on to his shoulders and wrap my legs around his waist. Without breaking the kiss, he shoved his hands under my shirt at my back and walked us inside, straight to the bedroom. He sat down on the edge of the bed with me straddling his lap and kept on kissing me. Deep searching kisses, leaving no part of my mouth untouched. It felt like a branding, a claiming, a promise of more to come. My hands were all over him, were seeking as much contact as possible, but not finding enough. As quickly as possible, we divulged each other of our shirts.

It was frantic.

Desperate.

Utterly delicious.

When Cole's hands went to unclasp my bra, he leaned back to look at me. "Let me see, baby. I need to see you," his voice was strained with need. His eyes were roaming across my now naked chest, which, it sounds silly, made my nipples harden even more.

"God, Liz. You're so beautiful." He leaned down and took me in his mouth. He wasn't gentle, but I didn't care. It felt great. No, it felt fantastic. He licked and sucked and nibbled, stimulating me, turning me on so much that I started moving on him, grinding my sex against his hardness. By the time he focused his attention on my other breast, my panties were soaked and I needed him inside me.

"Cole," I urged. But he didn't stop. He kept right on devouring my breast. I started undoing my pants. I needed them off. I needed him to touch me there.

Now.

Cole took my hands in one of his and held them behind my back, making me arch and practically shoving my breasts in his face in the process. "Soon, baby. I promise. You'll get my cock soon. I need to claim every inch of your body first." I wasn't sure I could hold out that long. Watching him ravaging my breasts, unable to touch him, was hot, so hot I couldn't do anything but watch in fascination as I kept moving on him, rubbing my heat against his hardness, seeking friction. I was close. So close.

God, how ridiculous. It was like my body had been waiting for his touch to come alive.

The pressure kept building and building. My breaths were coming in short puffs and my whole body was tensing in preparation for orgasm.

That couldn't be, though. We weren't in some fantastical romance novel where the hero educates the inexperienced heroine in the art of being pleasured. I was no innocent damsel in distress that had never been touched.

All of a sudden, Cole's mouth was gone and I was on my back in the bed. His hands were working on my pants, taking them off in one swift move. Then his mouth was on me again. Not on my breasts. On my sex, pressing his mouth against my clit over my panties. I threw my head back in ecstasy and clenched my fists in the sheets. There was no way I would be able to hold out. It felt too good. I couldn't believe it myself, but I was going to come.

"Cole, I can't..." I moaned.

In a flash, my panties were gone and his mouth was on me. His tongue gliding through my folds, finding my clit, flicking and rolling and pressing and sucking.

God! That felt even better! My eyes were rolling to the back of my head it felt so good. "Let go, honey." He thrust his finger into me and explored while putting pressure on my clit with his thumb, giving me no choice but to give in, to let go and come. Hard. Stars were exploding behind my eyelids. My body was shaking and a deep moan escaped my mouth. Cole kept working me, not letting up, his finger stroking inside me, his mouth at my clit and sucking, prolonging the orgasm.

When I came down, my body felt sated and languid. I didn't think it had ever been this relaxed before. Cole was making his way up my body and let me taste myself on him when he reached my mouth. That was incredibly hot, too, and made my body shiver once more.

Cole

"That was the most beautiful thing I have ever seen. You're amazing." The beauty that lay beneath me was taking my breath away. I was staring down at Liz in utter adoration, not believing that I could be this lucky, that I was able to call her mine. The urge to claim every single part of her was still strong, stronger than ever actually. It was all encompassing. "Let me make you mine, Liz."

"Yes."

That did it. There was no holding back now. She was going to be mine. All mine. In a frenzy, I pulled off my pants and settled between her legs. "I want to take you bare, baby, I want nothing between us. Are you on the pill?" She hesitated. With good reason. "I have never gone without protection. You will be the only one." Relief washed over her face and she nodded at me. Yes! I rubbed my bare cock through her wet heat, spreading her juices. "This is gonna be hard and fast, baby. I don't think I'll be able to hold back. You okay with that?"

"Please, Cole. Don't make me wait any longer."

She was ready for me and I couldn't restrain myself from filling her with one hard thrust. God! She felt good. A perfect fit. I felt her heat spreading through me. Her muscles were gripping me tightly, skin on skin, urging me to move, and I obeyed all too willingly. I couldn't hold back. I started thrusting in and out. Shit! I wouldn't last long. I refused to close my eyes to let me concentrate on holding myself back, though. I needed to see her face, needed to see she was enjoying this. She was looking up at me with love and wonder in her eyes.

And lust.

A whole lot of lust.

Christ! She was gonna be my undoing.

I thrust faster, deeper, holding her hip in place, grinding, searching for her spot. When her loud gasp and shocked face indicated I found it, I repeated the motion, rubbing against it over and over again. I needed her to find it, needed to show her what sex was supposed to be like, needed her to find pleasure in it with me, to let go. She was hot and wild for me, moving with me, her hands all over me, touching me, stroking me, scratching me. My thrusts became almost violent.

I was losing it.

I could feel the tingles in my spine, my balls starting to tighten and pull up.

I was going to come.

But she needed to come again first. I wasn't gonna be one of those assholes she was used to, who took their pleasure but didn't return it.

I found her clit with my thumb and started rolling and pressing, helping her find her climax again. Her eyes got big and I could see that she was close. "Show me!" I demanded, then thrust deep and hard, once, twice, three times, before she convulsed around me, causing my dick to explode inside of her. I came on a shout, bucking uncontrollably, filling her with my seed until the last drop had left me.

I collapsed on top of her.

Holy hell! That was the hottest sex of my life.

I was completely gone for this girl. There was no turning back for me, no going back after this. I thought it would scare the shit out of me to bind myself to someone, but all I felt was contentment and pride. This beautiful creature was mine.

I lifted my head and slowly kissed her. My dick was still deep inside of her, far from done. Feeling her body still twitching underneath mine, feeling her little aftershocks inside, had him ready to go again in no time. I started gliding in and out of her, reveling in the feeling of absolute rightness.

"Wow," Lizzy breathed when I released her mouth and looked down at her. "So this is what everyone's been talking about."

I chuckled.

"Not sure about that. That was absolutely amazing. I'm not sure anyone else has ever experienced it quite like this."

"Really?" God, she was cute.

"Really, honey. Told you we'd be off the charts. Best I've ever had."

She liked that. A lot.

Her eyes were shining brightly when she pushed up to kiss me. I was ready to take her again, slowly this time.

So that's exactly what I did.

I felt strangely content when I woke up the next morning with Liz's body curled into mine. She was lying half on top of me, her legs tangled with mine, her head on my shoulder, hand and my chest. Never. Never, had I spent the night with anyone. It was one of my rules. I never let anyone sleep at my apartment and I never spent the night. Too intimate. Sex was a bodily function for me, one I enjoyed a great deal, but it never involved emotion. Until now.

Seeing my parents' fucked up marriage, both my mother and father being cold-hearted and selfish, and seeing everyone else's twisted relationships and especially Liz's mom, I had never been interested in more than release and a good time. I hadn't wanted anyone constant in my life, thought that needing a partner was bullshit, a myth created by Hollywood and authors who created a lie in order to make money. Relationships were either a nightmare or didn't last.

But now, lying in bed with Liz after the night we shared, after *feeling* something for the woman I had sex with, those beliefs had been shattered. Fuck me, but it was true. Sex *was* different when you had it with the person you loved.

Vastly different.

So different it wasn't sex. It was something more. Something I hadn't believed existed. And I wanted to kick my ass over and over again for not giving this to both of us years ago.

So many feelings were churning inside of me I had trouble identify them all.

Happiness.

Contentment.

Protectiveness.

Excitement.

Fear.

But the prevalent ones were love and possessiveness. Liz was mine. She always had been and she always would be. I was going to make sure of that. If I had to lock her up and tie her to my bed. I would never let her leave.

Yes, she was right. I was a total caveman. But I didn't give a fuck. I would do whatever was necessary to bind her to me. Which meant I had to pay my parents a visit. My mother in particular.

At that thought, apprehension and fear seeped in. My mother was a bitch. A manipulative, fake, sneaky, backstabbing bitch, who would *not* approve of me being with Liz. She was one of those stuck-up bitches in town that had always treated my girl like trash. Worse actually, she had always pretended Lizzy didn't exist, had only acknowledged her when she forbade me to see her and locked me up in the basement to keep me from meeting her. Though that had never stopped me and she knew it. But once she figured out I wasn't going to introduce her as my girlfriend, she had backed off. Still, that hadn't stopped her from making snide comments about her and 'people like her'. She was going to hate us being together and would make that abundantly clear to not only me but Liz as well. And that was something I was not going to tolerate. Liz had had to endure enough abuse in her life and she was not taking any more by being with me. It was my job to protect her from that. Which meant I'd have to make it very clear that Liz was going to be in my life and I didn't give a shit if they liked it or not. That would be first on my agenda Monday morning.

The weekend was Liz's and mine.

On that thought, I felt my girl stir beside me. She tensed in my arms for a second before she relaxed and moved closer into me, nuzzling my chest and kissing me there. It looked like she wasn't used to waking up beside anyone, either, and that gave me a deep sense of gratitude and contentment.

"Morning," she mumbled sleepily. Her being adorable and sweet made this waking up-with-her business even better. I was a man and seeing as it was morning, my dick was already hard, but her sweetness combined with her naked body pressing into mine made him twitch and demand attention. I was all too eager to give it to him.

I rolled into her, taking her to her back, my hips automatically settling between her legs. "Morning, baby," I mumbled, my mouth resting on hers. "Ever had morning sex?" The answer better fucking be 'no'. Her sleepy eyes smiled at me when she shook her head.

"Me either," I said before I kissed her lightly, "let's remedy that." The light kiss turned into something else when I saw her eyes flash hungrily. I took her mouth with abandon while my hands started roaming and teasing, touching and gripping, until I found her wet and ready. I lined myself up with her swollen entrance and slowly pushed inside, enjoying every single inch until I was seated to the hilt. Then I started rocking slowly but deeply, drawing out both our arousals with every thrust, teasing her, testing her, giving, but not giving enough, watching, waiting, giving a little more, then retreating. Liz's pants and sexy little moans were driving me insane with the need to pound into her, but I wanted to drive her crazy first, wanted her so out of her mind with pleasure and need that she would light up for me and take over. So I kept on teasing her, going faster, then slowing down, grinding, then pulling out; all the while I tasted her mouth, her neck, her throat, her breasts. When I looked into her eyes, I could see the fire there. Yeah, she wanted it and she would go for it. Any moment now she would have enough of my teasing and take over. I bent my head again to kiss her, but instead only rested my lips on hers and moved back when she asked for a kiss. That did it. She put one of her feet in the bed, pushed and rolled me to my back, sitting up astride me, and started moving immediately.

Fuck, yes!

Liz in all her glory was riding me, hard and fast. Harder and faster than anyone had ever ridden me. It was phenomenal. *She* was phenomenal. I reared up and bucked into her, holding her steady at her hips, over and over again, until her pants turned into moans.

God, this was good! Watching her grab her breasts and pinching her hard nipples while she was bouncing up and down, her slick heat gripping my dick, was going to undo me. I thrust faster and deeper, wild for her now, needing her to find it so I could let go. I used my thumb to press and roll her clit until I felt her explode around me, squeezing me tight and taking me with her, making me erupt inside her.

When we were both done, Liz collapsed on top of me, still connected to me. I started to lazily run my fingers over her back, drawing circles. Something else that I had never done, would have never thought of doing, but came natural with Liz. Exactly like she said last night. Us being together was natural. It felt right. And I would do anything in my power to keep it that way.

Chapter 10

Lizzy

Our drive home was quiet. I think we were both lost in our own thoughts. Neither of us wanted to leave our little bubble behind and return to reality.

The weekend had been perfect. Well, almost perfect. It gave me hope that Cole and I really had a future together. After our morning in bed we had a late breakfast at a nice little cafe in town before we went exploring. I was excited to see what this picturesque little town had to offer. Those quirky little towns along the seaside had always been my favorite places to discover. Every once in a while when I needed a break, I would just get in my car and see where I ended up. Almost always I would find myself in one of these charming little towns, which I would then walk around in for a few hours. Exploring. Discovering. I wasn't a fan of those touristy stops but preferred the towns that had personality. This town was a mix of both and definitely one of those that wanted you to unlock its secrets, find the local hangouts, and meet interesting characters.

All day long Cole and I strolled through town either hand in hand or in each other's arms. It was kinda weird, but also kinda awesome and exciting. We had always had fun when we went out together, teasing and bickering and driving each other insane, but always laughing and happy in the end. Now that we were a couple, it was no different. But it was better. And I was glad that that part of us hadn't changed. We still bickered. We still teased. But it was all good-natured. Both of us were passionate, and I was sure that at some point there would be arguments and fights. We would clash. It was unavoidable. Cole could be bossy and there was no way I was going to give in to him and do whatever he asked me to do. I had my own head and I was stubborn. He knew that about me. I also didn't talk in code. That was too exhausting. But hopefully, seeing as men didn't do code either, that wouldn't be an issue.

The only time we argued during the last two days was when he closed down on me after receiving a slew of text messages that seemed to piss him off. We were sitting outside at a pub, having lunch, when he narrowed his eyes at his phone before he dropped it on the table and started cursing under his breath. I was worried that maybe something was going on at work and we had to head back home early.

"Everything okay?" I asked him.

Instead of answering me, he just stared out at the water. I wasn't sure if he was ignoring my question or if he hadn't heard me, so I tried again. "Cole? Is something wrong?"

He looked at me and it was clear that he definitely had something on his mind. Then his face gentled and he lied, "No, baby, nothing's wrong." He took my hand in his for a second, gave me a quick squeeze of what I am sure he intended to be reassuring, let me go, leaned back in his chair again, and looked back out across the water. I wasn't reassured. Not in the slightest. I knew him better than he probably knew himself. The fact that we had been *together* together for only two days and he was already lying to me instead of confiding in me or at least admitting that something was wrong but he didn't want to talk about it, disappointed and pained me. I stared at him, waiting. Then I waited some more. Then I tried again.

"Cole, babe?" But he didn't react. He seemed lost in his thoughts, so I decided to leave him to it. If he wanted to shut me out and brood, then I would darn well let him brood. By himself. This wasn't me being bitchy. He had asked me not to shut him out when something was on my mind and now he was the one shutting me out. I had to admit it didn't feel great and I was gonna try and learn from being on the receiving end, but that didn't mean that I was going to let him get away with it.

When I got up to go to the restroom, he didn't even move or make any indication that he knew I existed. I went to the restroom, hoping that when I came back out he would have snapped out of it, but when I saw him from the door, I could tell that he was still sitting in the same position, contemplating. So instead of watching him and waiting, I decided to stay inside to play a round of pool. That should give him enough time to sort through things.

I joined some of the locals and played a round with Sean, a tall, dark-haired guy in his mid-twenties, who had a really nice smile and warm eyes. About fifteen minutes into the game, a loud bark of "What the fuck!" coming from the doorway made my head snap up in the middle of taking a shot. Cole was standing there scowling at us, his arms crossed on his chest. "Hey," I said casually, then leaned back over the table to take the shot that he had interrupted. The sound of his boots on the floor told me he was approaching, but I didn't look his way. He had no reason to be angry. I took my shot and felt him crowding me. When I straightened to look at him, his scowl had turned into a glare. My eyebrows went up in question.

"Again. What. The. Fuck!" He growled in my face.

In order to give him a chance to be smart and back down, I tipped my head and asked, my voice calm, "What the fuck what?"

But he didn't back down. Instead, he seemed to get more incensed when he leaned into me to ask me with barely controlled anger, "What the fuck means, baby, what the fuck are you doing?" I looked at the pool table, then back at him and raised my eyebrows once more, in answer this time.

"Liz—" he started warningly, but I interrupted him.

"You were brooding and forgot I existed, so I went to the restroom." Now his eyebrows turned up.

"You're not in the restroom now, baby. You're in here playing pool with some guys while I'm sitting out there waiting for you."

Oh really? I leaned into him as well so we were nose-to-nose to inform him angrily, "I went to the restroom, Cole. Almost half an hour ago. You forgot I existed, proven by the fact that it took you this long to realize I was gone." That shut him up. I turned back to the table. Sean had taken his shot and I was assessing the balls to take my turn. I was so focused on ignoring Cole that I didn't realize he had followed me to the other side of the table until I felt his hands at my hip trying to turn me to face him.

"Liz, honey—" but I yanked my hip from his grip and took a step back to glare at him. He knew my glare, knew not to mess with me when I was this pissed. I wasn't just pissed, I was disappointed in him and hurt that he would actually forget I even existed, but being pissed was easier than being hurt, so I decided to go with that emotion.

"Don't, Cole. Don't expect me to be all hunky dory now that you remembered my existence. I'm playing pool with Sean. You can either go out there and brood some more or go back to the cottage for all I care." He gave Sean a glance then closed the distance between us until he was again only an inch away from my face. I expected him to growl at me and be all bossy and command me to get my ass in gear or some shit like that. But he surprised me. With both hands holding me on the sides of my neck he said in a low voice laced with remorse, "I'm sorry, baby. You're right. I shut you out and I shouldn't have." He closed his eyes, then pulled me into him more. "I promise to tell you what that was all about once I have you in bed snuggled close." He kissed me softly. "I'll wait right here until you're done hustling this guy, okay?" He ended on a small smile and another soft peck on the lips.

I was stunned speechless, completely surprised by his apology. But also grateful that he realized his mistake and owned up to it. In my experience, not a lot of men or people in general are capable of doing that. And anyways, when someone apologized in earnest it didn't say much about you if you didn't forgive them. So I had no other choice but to give in.

I leaned up to kiss his lips lightly, then murmured, "Let's go," against his lips before I dropped my queue on the table, looked at Sean to give him a wide grin, and thanked him for keeping me company.

"You were gonna hustle me?" he asked, his eyebrows lifted in bafflement and disbelief.

"Absolutely," I confirmed through my grin. Sean shook his head at me, grinning, and Cole chuckled by my side, then he took my hand and led me out of the pub back to our cottage.

Lying tucked to his side on our bed, he told me that one of the girls he used to hook up with wouldn't stop texting him, although he'd made it more than clear that he was not available. I had frozen solid at the mention of her name. I knew that name, but hoped to God that it was a different Courtney.

"Courtney?" I asked.

"Yeah," he said.

"Courtney from home, Courtney?" Now it was his turn to freeze solid. His voice was wary when he repeated, "Yeah."

"Courtney, the meanest bitch in town you hooked up with during senior year in high school, Courtney?" No response. "You've been hooking up with her since high school?" He could not be serious. That meant he'd been going back to her for years.

Cole sighed a deep sigh then he turned onto his side so we were facing each other. His arms stayed locked around me. The look on his face made me brace, telling me I would not like what I was going to hear. "I didn't hook up with her every time I went home, but apparently enough for her to think she has some kind of claim on me." I was right. I didn't like what I was hearing. Courtney was a bitch with a capital B. A conniving, mean bitch, who had ridiculed me whenever she had a chance, had played mean tricks on me and taunted me. I knew Cole had screwed her because she was all too happy to tell me all about it in detail when she had me pinned against the wall in the locker room of our high school gym, with her friends egging her on. She had been mean to me because Cole had never made a secret of being protective of me and she had considered him hers. It was almost like she had singled me out of all the people she considered losers.

Even when she had graduated, she hadn't let up torturing and embarrassing me whenever she got a chance.

Fucking hell!

I turned away from him to my back and stared at the ceiling. This was not good. If he had been going back to her for all these years, then she would still consider Cole hers. She was not someone who would give up easily. And she hated me, which would fuel her anger only more.

"Did you tell her why you are not available any longer?" I asked the ceiling.

"Yes. I told her we're together. That I love you and am committed to you. That I want her to lose my number."

Okay. That made me feel better. But she sure as hell would *not* accept that and let me have him without a fight. Good thing I didn't intend to ever set foot in Ashford again. I'd never gone back home even once since I started college. Nothing for me to go back to. I wouldn't have to see her and deal with her.

"She didn't like the fact that you committed to me of all people, did she?" I was still talking to the ceiling, trying to come to terms with the fact that Cole had been in a relationship with her for years. A very, *very* casual relationship, but it was still a relationship in my eyes, and Courtney was the type of woman who would see it as something more than what it was. I couldn't put my finger on why exactly, but his revelation worried me more than I wanted to admit.

Cole's hand on my stomach started stroking me soothingly. He could tell this was a blow and he was being cautious.

"No. She wasn't," he paused, then, "she keeps calling and texting me. I turned my phone off." I nodded. What else could I do?

"Baby, you have nothing to worry about. I'll deal with her." I sighed. He thought I was jealous. Granted, I had been extremely jealous of her before, since she had been one of those girls lucky enough to get attention from Cole, but I was not jealous now.

"I'm not jealous if that's what you're thinking. Is that what you were brooding about for an hour?" I felt him tense beside me, but then he relaxed and pulled me closer to him. "Yes. And the fact that by now she'll probably have called my mother since they run in the same circles. Though, why she would think she has any claim on me, I have no idea. I never promised her anything but a good time. Like all the other women who came before you, she was nothing but a fuck. She knew the drill. I wanted to enjoy this weekend and was gonna tell my parents about us on Monday, but Courtney likely has jumped the gun, seeing as my mother is also calling me non-stop." I closed my eyes. Right. I had forgotten about his mother. She despised me. Hated me. Hated what I represented. I knew in her eyes, I was never going to be good enough for her son. Not because she loved him and she thought I would break his heart. Oh, no. Simply because I would tarnish the family name and status, because I was born on the wrong side of town, was trash. Having to deal with his mother would understandably make him zone out. They didn't get along. He put up with her to avoid an argument, but this argument he wasn't going to be able to ignore.

"Liz, baby, look at me." I did. "You have nothing to worry about. I don't care what my parents think. They never gave a shit about me, so it's none of their business who I'm with. And I'll deal with Courtney." He was right. There was nothing I could do anyway. His mother would always hate me, and Courtney came before I was in the picture. I couldn't concern myself with every single woman that came before me. I had to trust him to deal with it.

"Okay. But just so you know, she shows up and gives me shit, I'll take her down." And I would. She had tortured me as a teenager, but I was now a grown woman and would not take her shit anymore. Those times were over. I had left all that behind when I left for college and it sure as hell was not going to fuck with my new life in Boston. Granted, I hadn't gone that far, only an hour's drive away, but for me, it felt like I lived in a different universe now.

Cole chuckled and nuzzled my neck. "I know you will. And I won't stop you. The opposite. I will cheer you on," he said and started to kiss me, taking my mind off all the crazy bitches in his life and giving me better things to focus on.

We spent the rest of our mini vacation in bed before we had to pack up and head back to the city.

Now was now.

Back to reality.

Cole parked in front of my apartment building and killed the engine but didn't make a move to get out of the car. Instead, he turned and faced me. I could tell by the look on his face that he wasn't all fired up to end our weekend, either. He also seemed conflicted about something as he studied me in the dim light of the parking lot. Then determination replaced indecision as he seemed to make up his mind. He cupped my face with his hand and pulled me closer across the console.

"This is gonna sound crazy, but I don't care. I don't want this weekend to end, don't want to drop you off at your place, go home, and sleep without you beside me. I know we are new and in normal relationship terms, this is going really fast. But you and I are not normal, Liz. I want you with me. Every night. I don't care if we stay at your place or mine, as long as we are together. Though I have to say, I would prefer my bed, seeing as it's bigger and closer to work." The last he said through a smile while his thumb was stroking my cheek.

I smiled back at him but wasn't so sure. I'd had roommates before, during college, and it had never really worked for me. Yes, anything was better than living with my alcoholic drug-addict mother, but still. I preferred to live alone. Not that he had asked me to move in with him, but at the speed we were going, I wouldn't be surprised if that was what was really on his mind. I wasn't an expert in relationships and no relationship was the same, but I knew me. I was kind of a loner and needed time for just me sometimes. I was afraid of feeling smothered and disappointing him. But then again, wasn't this exactly what I had always wanted, what I had dreamed about my whole life since I was ten years old? Having Cole? Him wanting me? Wanting me so much that he couldn't be without me? God, I was confusing myself.

"Liz, don't overthink this. I know what's going on in that head of yours. You're taking everything apart, overanalyzing it. It's simple. I want you with me. You want to be with me. Let's act on that and be together whenever we can. We've lost enough time as it is and I'm not willing to waste any more. We'll spend tonight at your apartment, seeing as we're already here, and tomorrow night we'll try mine and see how it goes. Deal?"

He was right. We had lost enough time. I took a deep breath and pushed my anxiety and insecurities aside. "Deal," I answered on a small smile. Cole grinned at me before he pulled me all the way across the console to give me a quick but deep kiss. "Deal."

Chapter 11

Cole

Things were going great with Lizzy and me. I knew she had been concerned about how fast everything was happening with us, and for a few brief hours on our way home, the intensity of my feelings for her and my need to have her with me whenever I could had scared me. But I had powered through it and my reward was a contentment I had never before felt in my life.

Lizzy and I had not slept apart since our first weekend together. Most nights we spent at her apartment, the reason being that I'd had to work late a lot these past two weeks and she didn't want to be in my apartment by herself. Totally understandable. I wanted her to feel comfortable at my place, but I knew where she was coming from. Liz wasn't the type of person who would sit and wait for me to come home. She wasn't a social butterfly. She was content to be by herself, but my place didn't feel all that homey. I was a guy and my place reflected that. It looked exactly like you would imagine a bachelor's pad. A loft-like space with a big screen TV, huge comfortable leather couch in front of it, hundreds of movies on my shelves, a kitchen off the living room with dirty dishes stacked in the sink, not much more than beer in the fridge, and a bed in the far corner of the vast room with a matching dresser and wardrobe for my clothes. Yes, all of it was high end, but it didn't feel like a home. It felt like a crash pad. Or a fuck pad. Which is exactly what it had been since I moved in. And Liz knew that. So I wasn't surprised that she preferred to stay at her place, especially when I had to work late. Still, it might be caveman behavior, but I wanted her at my place, wanted to take care of her like a man. But I knew I had to tread carefully in that respect.

Lizzy was an independent woman who didn't want to rely on anyone else to take care of her. Her father had left her and her mother before she was even born. Her mother wasn't a person Liz had been able to rely on, the opposite actually. More often than not, Liz had had to escape that house to be safe from her mother's pedophile friends. So I didn't blame her for being the independent person she needed to be to escape her childhood.

With any other woman, I had been annoyed when they were clingy and treating me like their property, but with Lizzy it frustrated me that she *wasn't* like that. I wanted her to consider me hers, needed her to rely on me to be able take care of her. Oh, she was possessive. When we went out and other women tried to make a play for me, or when someone she knew I had fucked got too close, she always staked her claim and it was hot as fuck.

The sex was phenomenal. Every time we touched each other was like a fire coursed through our bodies, melding us together with a need that was indescribable. I'd had more than my fair share of women in my life, but what Liz and I had was something else. When we weren't having sex, we were comfortable around each other, teasing, nagging, fighting, just like we always had. It was easy being with her. Natural, like she had said our first night together. I was proud to have her on my arm when we went out, proud that she was mine. All those fucktards that ogled her would never touch her. She never paid them any attention. Even after I had laid it out for her how much attention she garnered from the men around her, she seemed not to notice. Or she didn't care. And I loved it. Loved it that she didn't need to play games, didn't try to make me jealous, didn't need other men's attention to make her feel good about herself.

So things were great. We were happy and for the first time in my life, I was looking forward to my future seeing as it was filled with Lizzy. There was only one thing happening in my life right now that I could do without. Or two things actually: Courtney and my mother.

As promised, I had called my mother to tell her the news of Lizzy and I being together, informing her that she should expect her as my partner at the next dinner party. Just like I expected her to, she had lost her mind, guilt-tripping me about ruining the family's reputation, her reputation, by being with the daughter of the town's slut.

"Why you would lower yourself to be with trash like her I will never understand! Is it to spite me? Do you hate me that much that you'll do anything to get back at me?" Typical for my mother, she made me being with Liz all about her.

"No, mother. I am not with Lizzy because I am using her to get back at you and ruin your oh so holy reputation. I know you have no frame of reference, will never understand what I am talking about, but I am with her because I love her, because I cannot be without her. We belong together. She is mine and I am hers, and if you can't respect that, then neither of us will ever set foot into your house again. I will not tolerate you and your friends treating her like a second-class citizen.

Accept it or lose me in the process, mother. Your choice." Not much came after that. She huffed and puffed, but I was done. She could let me know when she was over it or I wouldn't go back there.

Courtney was another matter altogether. I hadn't mentioned it to Lizzy since that day at the coast after lunch, but Courtney had not let up with her harassment. She was hard to shake. Her behavior was escalating. It had turned from incessantly text messaging and calling my cell to her trying to contact me at work. I was going to have to deal with her face-to-face. And soon. I had promised Lizzy she didn't have to worry, I would make her go away, and I intended to keep that promise. When Courtney had called my office today, demanding to speak to me because of an emergency, my assistant had interrupted me during a very important meeting, which my boss had also attended. This could not happen again or I could lose my job. So I had agreed to meet her after work to talk. Not that I would let her talk much. I would go in there, tell that bitch to get it through her head that there would never be anything between us again, and leave. It would be quick. In and out in five minutes' tops. I wouldn't even order a drink. So why did I feel guilty that I hadn't told Lizzy about it? She knew I was working late again, so she didn't expect me at her apartment until later, and I didn't want her to worry or get mad because there was nothing to worry or get mad about. Courtney didn't factor into my life, so there was no reason to share the situation with Lizzy. I was just doing what I had promised her I would do, making Courtney go away.

Nothing to feel guilty about.

Right.

Shit.

I left my office and walked the two blocks to the bar I was meeting Courtney at. As soon as I walked through the door, I could see her sitting in a dark, quiet corner. Great. She was dressed and made up to the nines and was staring at me—with what I'm sure she intended to be seduction in her eyes—as I walked towards her table. My gut twisted in disgust at her blatant display. This is what I had usually gone for before I let myself have Lizzy: over-the-top women who dressed like skanks and threw themselves at me to enjoy for a night or two. I felt dirty and disgusted with myself.

Courtney rose from her seat in an attempt to kiss me, but I moved away before her lips could touch mine. Her sweet perfume was overwhelming and made me want to gag. I needed to get this done fast and get the hell out of here. She pretended she didn't notice my rejection and smiled huge at me while sitting back down. I sat across from her and glared at her. She started laughing. Crazy bitch. *Let's get this over with.* I leveled my glare at her and jumped right in without preamble.

"Courtney. Get me right now. There is nothing between us. All there ever was, was sex. You're a good lay, but I've had better before you and definitely better since. I am with someone now and I will not be contacting you ever again. Now, tell me you get what I'm saying to you." I could see her flinch slightly at my harsh words, but I didn't give a shit. I had tried to be nice when I told her I was off the market. After her shenanigans during these past two weeks, I was done with nice. She had proven that she was a bitch, meaning I would treat her like one.

"Now, now, Cole. We both know that's not true. I have had my hooks in you since high school. You've been coming back to me for eight years, Cole. A girl knows what that means. I understand I have to let you be you, let you sow your wild oats before you're ready to commit to me. I'm a patient woman, baby. Fucking that trash is just another need you have to fulfill before you'll let yourself love me, just like fucking all those other skanks over the years. But don't worry, baby, I'll wait for you." God, this woman was crazier than I thought. Was she serious?

"Woman, you are one of the skanks I have been fucking. I will never commit to you, there is nothing to commit *to*. You are delusional if you believe any of the shit that just came out of your mouth. We are done." With that I gave her one last glare and got up to leave, hoping she got the message.

"Your mother agrees with me. We talked."

I stopped and turned around to face her. "I bet you did. I also don't care what my mother thinks." She smiled a dangerous smile at me. Almost predatory. As if she knew something I didn't. It made my gut clench. "I'm not a quitter, Cole. I always get what I want." Fucking unbelievable. There was nothing more to say. Meeting her had been a mistake.

I should have known.

Without saying anything else, I turned away from her, left the bar, and headed to Lizzy's apartment.

Lizzy

Thank God this day was over. Don't get me wrong. I absolutely loved my job, but today was one of those days where I'd rather be somewhere else. Anywhere else. Being a social worker at a youth shelter in a big city like Boston came with its daily frustrations. But today had been like a kick in the gut. I was still trying to find a suitable home for Jesse and Chloe. Finding a family that was willing to take on siblings was always tricky. But separating them was not an option. I wouldn't even bring that up for discussion. Jesse would pack up his sister and bolt. Guaranteed. I couldn't risk that. Over the last few weeks, they had come to be important to me. Yes, I knew all about keeping my distance, how not to involve my emotions, blah, blah, blah. But honestly, whoever advised you to keep your emotions locked up when you worked with children had never worked with children. It was impossible to not feel anything when a sixteen-year-old boy tells you the reason he and his sister are living on the street is because their father is sexually abusing both of them. How could anyone stay detached? If you didn't feel anything for these kids, then you couldn't be the kind of social worker they needed. At least that's what I think. So I was sick and tired of some higher-ups with their fancy-ass degrees telling me I was too involved, that I cared too much. That if I distanced myself, it wouldn't hit me so hard every time I hit a brick wall or there was nothing at all that could be done for the kids. Are you shitting me? What I wanted to do right now was snatch up all my kids and kidnap them, take them to live with me in the jungles of Costa Rica, far away from this city and its budget meetings where it was decided how many hours of counseling an abused child needed, if tutoring really did them any good since they chose to live on the streets, and how many fucking pudding cups we were allowed to hand out every day. Okay, maybe I was being a bit harsh since it was only one person that acted like a stick-up-her-ass-penny-crunching bitch, but she had pushed me too far today, suggesting I concentrate on the cases that had the promise of success instead of trying to save every child I meet. Seriously! She was a social worker in a different district of the city, and I had called her for information on any new foster parents in her area, seeing as all of our trusted ones were full.

I thought it was my job to do everything in my power to help, to work together in making the kids' lives easier, to try and make them realize that there is a future for them out there. *Every* child that needs my help. Not just the ones that I know I can save or are 'easier' or looked 'more promising'. And why did that bitch try to enlighten me about how best to do my job? Because I had dared to question the system of sending kids to the first available foster home without making sure it was actually a right fit. Apparently I was taking too long, I was too picky, I asked too many questions. I was so mad after that phone call that Taryn had asked me to see her when my ranting got so loud that everyone in the common room could hear me. She had tried to calm me down. I knew she felt the same frustrations, but her hands were tied. We had to follow procedure. Taryn encouraged me to hand in a proposal for a better procedure of networking and had suggested I get Rainey on board. "The two of you seem to agree on pretty much everything anyway and regularly give me a hard time about the limitations you have to work with. Might as well partner up in your bullheadedness," she had said, almost making me smile. Or if I wanted to file a complaint, she was even going to support me in that. I was treading on thin ice though, I knew. If people started talking about me being difficult to work with, it would make it harder not only for me but the kids I handled. But I couldn't help it. I was passionate about my job and sometimes that passion got the better of me.

On my way home, I decided to stop at the bookstore, get a hot chocolate, and hang out for a bit. Cole told me this morning he would be working late again, so I had lots of time to kill. Funny how things worked out that way. At first, I was afraid we would be spending too much time together, would smother each other, but spending every free minute with him had instead balanced me somehow. Instead of thinking and overthinking and going to bed frustrated or pissed off after a bad day at work, I now had someone to vent to, to bounce things off of, to get a different perspective from, to call me out on stuff, and do the same in return. It was nice. Yes, before we became a couple, Cole and I would talk on the phone almost daily and do the exact same thing, but having him with me every day made it more personal somehow. Sometimes all you needed was a hug or a smile from the person you love to make things better. It had always been like that with us. Tonight, I would probably earn a reproachful look after I told him how mad I got in front of everyone.

My favorite bookstore was down by the pier. It was more than a detour from my way home but so worth it. Sitting in one of the store's super comfy armchairs with a good book, slurping a hot chocolate, and looking out over the water was very calming and serene. It was a good spot to relax and go into my head without anyone bothering me. I still needed that sometimes. Not as often as I used to now that I was away from Ashford and everything that was supposed to be my home, but from time to time I needed to get my head straight and I did that best when I was by myself. Even when things were good and I was happy, I took those breaks to think, to appreciate what I had, how much I had accomplished, how far I had come. So that was my plan. To stop and take a break and let everything that happened in the last few weeks run through my head, let my thoughts wander, and just enjoy a quiet moment or two or five. I could also use a new book. My life had been so busy and eventful lately that I hadn't had time to stock up on anything new.

So that was what was on my mind when I crossed the street

in front of the bookstore. I'd had to park a few blocks away. The pier area was always busy and I had some trouble finding a spot. When I was trying to navigate through the pedestrian traffic without bumping into anyone, I saw Jesse about twenty feet in front of me. This wasn't a popular hangout for street kids, so seeing him here took me off guard. And anyway, Jesse should be back at the shelter. I was heading toward him when I realized that a man was holding him by the arm, stopping him from getting away. *What the hell?* I started running, wanting to get there as fast as possible to see what that was all about. I could hear the man's low voice, but couldn't make out what he was saying. What I could make out, though, was that he was angry. Very angry. Right before I got there, Jesse wrenched his arm out of the man's hold and took a swing at him.

"Jesse!" I shouted, which made both of them look in my direction. "What the hell is going on?" The relief on Jesse's face at seeing me made my gut clench. Relief at seeing your social worker when you've been caught in an altercation with an adult is not the usual reaction street kids had. I expected anger or arrogance, but Jesse's reaction told me that something was wrong here, that he didn't want to be anywhere near this man and saw me as his rescuer. I took a good look at the man while stepping closer to them, angling my body in a way that Jesse was standing half behind me on my left side. The man in front of me was a big guy with dark brown eyes that were glaring at me with contempt. They were Jesse's eyes. His hair was dark blond and needed a cut about six weeks ago. There were only certain men who could pull that look off. He was definitely not one of them. His clothes looked like he had been sleeping in them and smelled worse. This was Jesse and Chloe's father. Anger so raw it clouded my vision ran through me as soon as I realized who he was.

"Bitch, this has nothing to do with you. Run along," he disregarded me in a voice filled with condescension. His eyes were locked on Jesse and they were filled with hatred. When I pulled Jesse further behind me, trying to block him from view, his father's eyes came to me and narrowed. He took a step closer to me and glared down at me. That didn't intimidate me, though. I was too angry for that.

"Step back," I hissed at him. He leaned in closer and smiled an ugly smile at me. Bile rose in my throat at what I could tell he was thinking behind those dark eyes. I raised my voice to get the attention of the people around us. Witnesses. "I said, step back!" He still didn't give in. Instead, he inhaled deeply, then closed his eyes and hummed low in his throat. Gross! When his eyes opened again, he said in a low voice, looking at Jesse over my shoulder, "She smells even better than your sister, son. Maybe I should take this one home as well to keep me entertained. What do you think?" I froze. So did Jesse behind me. Then I could feel the rage and hatred waving off of him right before he lunged at his father, shouting, "You fucking piece of shit!" I was caught in the middle and tried my damnedest to keep them apart, but didn't stand a chance. One of them threw me out of the way and I landed on my ass, watching in horror as they started to beat the shit out of each other. I got up and called Jesse's name over and over again, but he wouldn't listen. I didn't blame him. I wanted to beat the shit out of that man myself. Instead of joining the fray, I called the police, hoping that my and Jesse's statement were enough to make him leave his kids alone. By the time I ended the call, Jesse's father had him flat on his back, holding him by the throat, choking him. We had an audience now of about twenty people staring down at the scene. Typical. Everyone enjoyed a good show, but nobody jumped in to help. I kept screaming for him to let go, yanking at his arm, but I was no match for him. Instead of releasing his son, he reared his free arm back to punch me in the face. I let go of his arm and stumbled back, my hands going to my nose and feeling blood there. Stars were dancing at the edge of my vision and I had to sit down so I wouldn't pass out.

Shit, but that hurts.

Someone was kneeling beside me, holding me by the shoulder, talking to me, but I couldn't make out the words. I was too busy fighting the nausea and the overwhelming feeling of passing out. In an effort to fight off unconsciousness, I blinked my eyes repeatedly until my vision started to clear little by little until I could take in the scene before me.

"Miss, are you okay? Can you hear me?" an older man was asking me. He was the one kneeling beside me, shaking my shoulder slightly to get my attention. I nodded, but kept my eyes on Jesse lying on the ground a few feet away from me. His face was a bloody, swollen mess and he wasn't moving. I shook off the arm still holding me and crawled to Jesse's prone body. "Jesse," I whispered, "Jesse!" *Please don't let him be dead.* Hot tears were running down my face. Two people were checking Jesse over, one of them kneeling by his head, holding his neck straight, the other one checking for a pulse and breathing. I reached for his hand and squeezed it, not taking my eyes off his face. "Please, please, please," I chanted through sobs.

"He is breathing and his pulse is steady. Just knocked out cold," one of the men assured me. "We'll wait for the ambulance. Don't worry, he'll be okay." Oh thank God! Relief washed through me at his words. Then I heard a girl shrieking and seconds later, I saw Chloe running towards us. I let go of Jesse's hand and got up to intercept her. No reason for her to see her brother like this, unconscious and covered in blood. I caught her and wrapped my arms around her as tightly as I could while I whispered in her ear, "He's going to be fine, Chloe. It looks bad, but he is going to be okay. I promise. I promise, baby." Her body was shaking and she was crying so hard it broke my heart. "Hold on to me, Chloe. Just hold on tight." Her arms came around me as she buried her face in my neck and kept on crying while squeezing me so tightly it actually hurt a bit. But I didn't let her go. She needed me to be her lifeline right now, to assure her that things would be okay, that I would make them okay. As we kept holding on to each other, we heard the police and ambulance arrive. Over Chloe's shoulder I could see that the EMTs were checking Jesse's injuries, talking to each other quietly. Jesse was slowly coming to. I could see his eyes flutter open and closed a couple of times before they stayed open and he looked up at the EMT in confusion. A police officer approached me and took my attention from Jesse when he started talking to me.

"Ma'am, you should get checked out as well," he said in a quiet and comforting voice. "Let me lead you over to the ambulance and we'll have someone see to your nose, make sure nothing's broken." I nodded at him and let him lead Chloe and me to the ambulance. Jesse was fully awake now. I could hear his voice as he answered the EMT's questions. Chloe was still shaking and crying in my arms as we walked over to the ambulance. Another EMT cleaned me up and checked my nose, asked me if I passed out at all.

"No. I saw stars and had to take a few deep breaths so I wouldn't vomit, but I didn't pass out."

"Okay. That's good. Your nose isn't broken, but it's swelling and there's already a bruise under your right eye. You might have a mild concussion. I'd like to take you to the hospital to make sure we're not missing anything."

I nodded at her and closed my eyes. Now that the fight was over and the adrenalin was leaving my body, my face hurt like hell. Chloe was sitting beside me on the back of the ambulance, wrapped in a blanket. She grabbed my hand and held on tight. I looked over to her and gave her a small smile, which I meant to be reassuring but wasn't sure didn't look like a grimace. I gave the police officer my statement while the EMT finished cleaning me up.

"Do you mind if Chloe rides with us in the ambulance? She's Jesse's sister and I don't want to leave her behind," I asked the EMT.

"Sure, no problem," he said.

"Do you mind letting him know that his sister is with me? I know he is going to be worried." He nodded then gave me a blanket before he walked over to where they were loading Jesse onto a stretcher.

On our way to the hospital, I called Taryn to let her know what happened. She was beside herself with worry about all three of us and promised me she would get on Jesse and Chloe's case right away to make things happen with Child Services. Their situation of being street kids had now changed to a case of physical evidence of assault and abuse witnessed by a social worker, meaning they would be taken in by the state to make them safe.

"I don't want Chloe going to an emergency foster home tonight, Taryn. She's gone through enough. She is scared out of her mind and worried about her brother. Let her stay at the shelter until Jesse is released. She needs people around her she knows and trusts, not thrown into a new situation without her brother at her side." I felt Chloe's body tighten next to me in the ambulance at hearing me talk.

"I hear you, Lizzy. I won't do anything tonight. You're with her, so that gives us time to see how Jesse is doing in the morning to come up with a plan. But I'll have to call it in tomorrow first thing. I'll do my best to talk them around to letting her stay with us until her brother is released, but I can't guarantee it, Liz. For now, let's worry about Jesse and we'll deal with everything else tomorrow. You gonna bring her back here or do you need someone to pick her up?"

"I'll call Cole to come and get us. My car is still at the pier, but we'll make sure to drop her off once she has seen Jesse and I've had a chance to talk to both of them. Let Jimmy know it might be a few hours, though."

"Alright, Liz. Will do. I'll talk to you tomorrow." Taryn paused, then added in a low voice that was laced with concern, "And Liz, I know you'd do anything for those kids, but I swear to God if you ever try to take on a parent in a physical altercation again and get hurt in the process, I'm gonna kick your ass." With that she hung up. Huh. Guess I should prepare myself to get seriously reamed out tomorrow morning when she saw my face. I might have downplayed how hard Jesse's father had hit me.

My next call was to Cole. We had arrived at the hospital and were being led through the hall to the emergency room. This was not going to be fun. He would lose his shit when he heard someone had punched me in the face. He answered on the third ring.

"Hey, honey, I'm just on my way home. I was gonna pick up dinner. I thought we could cuddle up on the couch and watch a movie. You want Indian or Pizza?" That was sweet and considerate, and I so wanted that right now, but instead

I had to burst his bubble of takeout dinner and a movie.

"That sounds really good, babe, but unfortunately, you're gonna have to turn around to pick me up. I'm at the hospital."

"What? Why? What happened? Are you okay?"

"I'm fine. I'll tell you everything when you get here. One of my kids got beaten up by his father today, and I kinda got in the way when it happened, but I'm fine." I didn't think it was a good idea to tell him about the punch in the face while he was driving. Better disclose that information when he was not behind the wheel.

"You got in the way when it happened? What does that mean? They must have reason to worry if they took you to the hospital, Liz. Tell me what's going on!" He was shouting now. Worried and panicked about me not being okay.

"I got pushed around a little and they want to check out my head just in case," I downplayed, "I'm okay, Cole." Shit. I was right. He was absolutely going to lose it when he saw my face.

"Liz, I know you're lying to me. Tell me what happened. Now." Great. He was being bossy. I knew what that meant. He wouldn't let up until I told him and if I didn't, he would be even angrier by the time he got here.

I took a deep breath before I told him what happened. "Fine. I was pushed and fell to the ground, then when Jesse's father wouldn't let up and beat the shit out of Jesse, I tried to pull him off and he punched me in the face—"

"He did WHAT?" Cole roared into my ear. Oh yeah, he was mad.

"Babe, I'm fi—" I tried to calm him down, but was interrupted again.

"A grown man punched you in the face, Liz! Stop telling me you're okay! He better not have broken your nose!"

"No, it's not broken. I just have a bruise—"

"Fuck, Liz. Fuck! I'll be there in ten minutes!" Then he hung up on me. I looked over to Chloe who gave me big eyes. Guess Cole had been shouting loud enough for her to hear everything. I gave her an eek-face to lighten up the mood and earned a small smile in return.

"Can we go see Jesse now?" She asked me after the nurse had taken a look at my nose and a doctor had come in for some simple tests and to ask me a few questions. Turned out I had a mild concussion. Nothing serious. But the swelling of my nose looked horrendous and I had a purple bruise under my eye. I looked like Rocky Balboa after fighting Apollo Creed.

"Yeah, Chloe. We're gonna go see him now." I threw my arm around her shoulders to give her some support when we walked down to hall to where they were taking care of Jesse. When we got there, his doctor assured me that his injuries were minor. He had some cuts and bruises and a split lip, but nothing was broken. We would be quite the pair for a few days with matching black eyes and swollen faces.

"He has a full blown concussion, so we'd like to keep him here overnight, where we can keep an eye on him to make sure there is no swelling in his brain. But other than that there is nothing much we can do. He'll have to take it easy for a few days." Okay. That was good news.

Chloe was sitting by Jesse's bed while I was talking to the doctor, and I could hear them talk quietly. I walked over to them and sat down on Jesse's other side. It was time to talk and let them know what was going to happen now.

Before I could start, though, I heard someone call my name. Cole was here. I turned around just as he was reaching our little curtained-off cubicle. One look at my face and he froze. The muscle in his jaw was ticking and he clenched both his fists at his sides. I got up and walked to where he was standing, stopping right in front of him. Cole didn't take his eyes from mine, but also didn't make a move toward me. He was trying to control his anger. I could tell it took everything in him not to charge out of there and make Jesse's father pay for what he had done to me. When I tentatively leaned my forehead against his chest, his arms came around me and I could feel his lips against my hair. Slowly, his body relaxed into mine.

"How much pain are you in?" He asked me after a few minutes. His voice was calm and controlled.

"Not much. They gave me something. I just feel some pressure." I mumbled into his chest. Cole leaned back to get another look at me. His hands came up to cup my face gently. He closed his eyes and inhaled slowly, concern and anger warring on his face. I knew his concern for me won out when he leaned in and kissed me gently on the lips. "It will be a lot worse than pressure by tomorrow, baby," he murmured there. "You ready to go home?"

"Uhm... not really." I moved to his side so he could see Chloe and Jesse across the room. Both their eyes were fixed on us.

"Right." The anger was back, as was the muscle twitching.

"They're keeping him overnight to monitor his concussion. I was about to explain to them what was going to happen next, now that their father has been charged and arrested."

"He's in jail?"

"Yeah. Some people came to help us when I got hit and held him until the cops arrived. I gave them my statement and they arrested him. Not sure how long they're gonna be able to hold him, though. I need to talk to them tonight. They need to tell their story so he can be locked away. Then we need to take Chloe back to the shelter before we can go home. I don't want to leave her right now. She's scared out of her mind and apart from her brother, I'm the only person she trusts right now."

Cole looked down at me with a warmth in his eyes that surprised me in the current situation. His next statement explained it, though.

"You're gonna make a good mom to our kids someday. I knew you felt deep, but if you feel this responsible and protective of other people's kids, I can only imagine what you're gonna give our babies." Holy hell. Where did that come from? Not that having babies with Cole had never crossed my mind. It had. A lot. But his pronouncement still blindsided me. My body locked and my eyes got big. I wanted to say something, but couldn't hold on to one coherent thought. Cole chuckled then kissed my temple and gently pushed me towards the bed, saying, "I'll leave you to it. I'll see if I can hunt down some decent coffee and be back." Then he was gone. I still stood there, looking at the space where I had last seen him, and couldn't make myself move. So many feelings were warring inside of me. Shock. Fear. Worry. Excitement. Elation. I couldn't settle on just one.

"Lizzy?" Chloe's quiet voice snapped me out of my daze. I turned around and took a deep breath. Then I sat down and talked them through everything that was going to happen now. There was a lot of anger and fear and tears, but in the end, we agreed that they would give a statement to the police about their abuse the next day. I promised them I would be there if they wanted me to and they both nodded. What a relief. They were done living in fear. Now they could start to heal, start their new lives, and I was immensely happy for them.

By the time Cole and I got back to my apartment, it was almost midnight. The pressure in my face had changed to a dull pain that I could tell would be excruciating soon if I didn't take more painkillers. Cole made sure I ate something before I took more meds, then we cuddled up in bed and he held me until I fell asleep.

Chapter 12

Lizzy

The smell of coffee woke me the next morning. The pain in my face was killing me. Who would have thought that a punch in the nose would hurt that bad? I got up and slowly walked to my kitchen to see Cole leaning against the counter in his pajama pants, a cup in his hand, staring at his feet. When he heard me, his head snapped up and he gave me a small smile that didn't reach his eyes. He walked toward me and kissed my forehead. "Morning, baby. You sleep okay?" his lips mumbled against my skin. I nodded then looked up at him. Something was wrong. He was too quiet.

"Everything okay?" I asked.

His eyebrows shot up at my questions. "No. Everything is not okay. My girlfriend took a punch to her face by a man who has a hundred pounds on her. She is standing in front of me with a swollen and bruised face. That, baby, is not okay. I want to hurt him so bad I can hardly control the urge to drive down to the station and beat the shit out of him." Oh. That's what was wrong.

"Oh," I said stupidly.

"Yeah. Oh."

He turned to the coffee machine and poured me a cup. I walked up close to him and wrapped my arms around his waist from behind, resting my cheek carefully against his naked back. I wasn't sure what to say. I loved it that he was so worried about me, but at the same time I hated that he had reason to be worried in the first place. He had been worried about me since the day we met. The angriest I had seen him was that night when I barely escaped being raped by one of my mother's friends and ran through the forest to get to him. This anger was different. This time, someone had actually succeeded in physically hurting me and Cole was the kind of man who needed to do something about it. And I loved him all the more for it.

"I love you, Cole." He turned in my arms then held me tightly to his chest.

"I love you, too, baby. More than you can imagine. Nothing can ever happen to you. You can't ever leave me. Don't ever scare the shit out of me like that again."

"Okay." Really, what else could I say?

"I'm going in late today so we can go and get your car. Promise me you'll take it easy today. I know there is no chance you'll let me talk you into staying home to rest. I get you have a lot to deal with and figure out today, but please don't overdo it. You'll be in pain and I'll worry about you. I wanna see you at lunch today if at all possible, and I'll be home early tonight. And don't freak out, honey, but I want to move in together as soon as possible. We'll have to decide who's gonna make the move or if we're looking for something new. No more moving back and forth. I want us to settle."

"Cole—" I started, but he wouldn't have it.

"No, Lizzy. You being out on the streets saving kids has always worried me. Your shelter is in a bad enough part of town that anything can happen to you. Yesterday proved that and that wasn't even anywhere near as bad as what could potentially happen. I'm smart enough to know that I won't stand a chance to talk you into changing jobs. Your job fulfills you, it's who you are and I love that about you. That you can be so passionate about something, that you would do anything in your power to help people in need. But this is me making sure you are safe and with me whenever possible. I also want you to take up some classes. Self-defense would be good or some kind of fight training. We'll look into that so you can start as soon as you're healed. I know you're tougher than you look, but you don't stand a chance if someone wants to actually hurt you. I need this, Lizzy, and you're going to give it to me."

Wow. There was a lot there. I got it that he was worried about where I worked and how easily I could get hurt. And he was right. There was no chance in hell I would give up the job I loved. Taking up fight training or self-defense was probably a good idea, but moving in together? It had only been two weeks!

Cole was watching me as those thoughts flitted across my face.

"Let me ask you this, baby. You think you're gonna fall out of love with me?"

No. Absolutely not. I had been in love with him all my life, and now that I had him, I couldn't imagine being without him again.

"No," I whispered.

"Then what are we waiting for? You are the one I want to be with for the rest of my life. The only one I can imagine my life with. Let's start our future now, not in six months or a year. Move in with me."

It made sense when he worded it like that. We weren't going to fall out of love with each other, so why not move in together? And if I were honest with myself, having him with me every day was exactly what I wanted. These past two weeks had proven that. It had been better than I had ever imagined, actually. And I had imagined a lot and had come up with some good stuff. What I didn't want to do, though, was move into his fuck pad. I didn't think I could get over how many women he had brought back there and I definitely didn't want any of his past flings to show up at our door. That would not be pretty.

"I'm not moving to your place. You can move in here or we'll find something else. And we're donating your bed." He chuckled then crushed his mouth to mine in a fierce but still careful kiss so as not to hurt me before he pulled back and grinned at me.

"Done. I'm getting rid of it today. Tonight, we'll start looking for a new place. Don't get me wrong, I like your place, but it's too far from work and it's too small."

"Deal." He gave me another kiss, this one long and deep before he took my hand and pulled me into the bathroom to take a shower with him. That was definitely something I could get used to: daily morning showers, which meant daily morning orgasms for me.

Eight hours later, I stumbled into my apartment in search of the pills in the kitchen. The pressure in my face was gone. Instead, there was this constant dull pain that made me think my head was going to explode any second. The painkillers I took this morning had worn off by lunch, four hours ago. Since then, every movement or loud noise or actually any noise at all had intensified the nonstop throbbing. I was ready to call it a day. Take the meds, change into sweatpants, and collapse onto my couch. Good plan. Time to follow through. The day had been successful. Jesse was released around noon and we settled them in at an emergency foster home after we sat down with Child Services so they could tell their story. That had been hard on both of them, as was to be expected. There had been a lot of tears on Chloe's side and coursing on Jesse's side. They still seemed shocked and pained by the time I left, but also relieved that it was finally over.

"Will we still see you around?" Chloe had asked me at the door. She was nervous about staying at a stranger's house, I could tell.

I touched her cheek gently and assured her, "Of course, honey. I'll come to check in on you tomorrow and keep you in the loop about getting you into a more permanent home. And you are always welcome to stop by at the shelter. Actually, I demand that you visit me often," I said, smiling at her.

She smiled back at me then leaned into her brother next to her, who was looking at me with grateful eyes. He didn't need to say anything. I knew. So I nodded at him and gave him a smile as well.

"Tomorrow, guys." I waved from the car before I drove off and headed home.

Now I deserved a break.

I dropped my purse on the kitchen table and completed my task of drugging myself so I could take a nap. Not even five minutes later, I was curled up on my side, fast asleep.

Soft fingers stroking my cheek woke me up. I blinked a few times before I could keep my eyes open long enough to see Cole sitting in the space by the crook of my hip. His warm, dark eyes were following his fingers' slow movements on my cheek. There was a tenderness there that I had never experienced before. Tenderness and love that made warmth and contentment spread throughout my body. I watched him for a few seconds before he realized I was awake and his eyes came to mine.

"Hey," he whispered in a voice as soft and tender as his touch.

"Hey yourself," I whispered back. He smiled.

"How're you feeling?"

"Better."

"That's good." We stared at each other silently for a few moments. His fingers kept softly stroking my skin.

"How was your day?" I asked.

"Long, but good. Yours?"

"Same." Another smile. More staring.

"You need more sleep or can I show you something?"

In answer, I leaned up and touched my lips to his in a barely there kiss, which he deepened when I started to retreat. Our lips were moving against each other lovingly, tenderly. There was no tongue, just our lips brushing and pressing, not leading to more. Just enjoying each other's closeness. This kiss spoke more than any words could ever convey. It spoke of commitment, of possession, of passion, of sweet, true love. It was a promise. It branded me as his and him as mine. When he ended the kiss in a soft nip to my lower lip and opened his eyes, the emotions in them took my breath away. I'm not sure what he read in my eyes, but he must have liked what he saw because his face spread into a wide grin before he reached out for me and pulled up my body to sit in his lap.

"Okay, baby, I've got news." Still in a daze from our moment, I looked up at him in confusion. Cole chuckled and kissed my forehead.

"Wake up, honey. This is kinda important," he murmured

there. I blinked a few more times, then sat up a little straighter in his lap and focused on him.

"What's up?"

"I sent my assistant on a quest today."

"What quest?" I prompted when he didn't continue.

"A quest to find the perfect place for us that is somewhere in the middle between your work and mine." Boy, if I had doubted his seriousness about moving in together as soon as possible, I sure as heck couldn't doubt it now. He didn't waste any time.

"Don't you think that is something that you and I should be doing together? I don't even know your assistant."

"You're right. And we will. All I asked her to do was find a few places that fit the parameters I gave her and set up appointments for viewings." Okay, that sounded good, actually.

"And?" I prompted him again.

"We have four viewings this Saturday. Two apartments and two houses. From what she's shown me, they all look great on paper. I've got the printouts right here for you to take a look." He reached over to the table and handed me four sheets of paper. I looked through them one by one. The first two were apartments. Good location, good size, great amenities, but nothing special. They were high-end like Cole's current apartment, but they didn't do much for me. The third one was a house. One of those Brownstones with Victorian architecture that Boston was so famous for. It had a short brick path that led to the concrete stairs going up to the wooden double front doors, framed by two small flowerbeds. Inside there were big bay windows in the half-turret style front living room, hardwood floors, wood burning fireplace, farmhouse kitchen, two bedrooms with lots of sunlight upstairs, gorgeous bathroom.

I couldn't tear my eyes from it.

"Looks like we've got a winner," I heard Cole say with a smile in his voice.

"It's beautiful," I breathed, my eyes still fixed on the pictures. It was the most beautiful house I had ever seen. But it was also very expensive. And it wasn't a rental. It was for sale.

"Cole, I thought we were going to rent a place?" Before answering me, he studied my face for a few seconds.

"I was gonna start looking for a place to buy soon to make an investment. Now with us building something that's leading to everything, buying a house is not gonna be a strictly financial investment, but an investment in our future." His voice was careful and a little hesitant. He wasn't sure how I was going to react.

"Cole, I'm a social worker. I'm doing okay, but I can't afford—" a squeeze of his arms stopped me.

"I can. I've made a few profitable investments and then there is the trust fund from my grandfather that I haven't touched. It's more than enough to buy that house upfront."

"Cole, I can't—" I tried again, but was again interrupted.

"You don't need to. I'm the one who wanted us to move in together right away. I'm the one who suggested we move. Means that I'm the one who's taking care of us." I was getting ticked now. Gone was the calm, sweet, mellow mood from moments before. In its place was irritation. I jumped up from Cole's lap to stand in front of him, arms crossed, totally peeved.

"I'm not a gold digger, Cole. You want us to move in together? Great. I want that, too. But I'm not gonna let you pay my way. We either split it two ways or we're staying in separate apartments since you don't want to live here."

"We agreed on moving in together, Lizzy, and we're not going back on that. There is no way I'm gonna let you pay half. You're gonna let me take care of you."

"I am not!"

"Liz—"

"No, Cole! That is not gonna happen! I have taken care of myself for as long as I can remember. I started taking odd jobs when I was thirteen to buy stuff for school and clothes that didn't make me look like a homeless person. When we didn't have food in the house, I used that money to buy peanut butter and bananas so I didn't go hungry for days. I fought my way out of that and have a good job that pays decent enough money so I can live a moderate life. I never strived for luxury. All I ever wanted was a good and simple life and I made that happen. I won't let anyone take that from me! Not even you!"

"I'm not trying to take anything from you! I'm trying to give you something! Don't you know how hard it was for me to watch you go through all that? To know you had no decent clothes unless you bought them yourself? To know you were going hungry but not being able to feed you without you feeling like a charity case? All you ever let me pay for was ice cream cones and cake on your birthday! Even as a kid you were so damn proud and stubborn!"

"I'm not stubborn!" Though I knew I was. His raised eyebrows indicated his disbelief at my words. He hung his head and shook it in a show of male incredulity and reflection. All that shouting had made my head start to throb again and I pressed the palm of my hand to my temple. When he looked back at me and saw me in pain, his anger dissipated instantly. He walked over to me and held me loosely against his body.

"Liz, seeing you struggle and fight every single fucking day of your life broke my heart. I'm so proud of you for being strong and making it on your own. But you're not on your own anymore. You are part of a unit now. We are a unit. Does it really matter which one of us makes more money and pays a bigger share of our expenses? What if it were reversed and you were the one with the trust fund? Would you let me pay my way even though that meant I would have to keep struggling?"

Well, shit!

Did he have to put it that way and make sense?

He paused, gauging my reaction to what he had said. My silence told him that he was getting somewhere, that I started to come around, because what he said made sense. When I didn't say anything, he moved in closer and his arms tightened around me.

"It's you and me, Lizzy. This is it for us. From now on, we'll share everything. That includes our finances. Please let me do this for us." God, he made it hard to resist him when he was like this. What he was saying made sense. Would I let him pay his way and watch him struggle if I were the one with the money? No, I wouldn't. I would think it silly and unnecessary. I didn't care about money, so I wouldn't care if I were the one paying the bigger portion. So what did not letting him do the same thing say about me? It said I was a hypocrite. That I was too stubborn and proud to let him take care of us.

Shit!

He was going to buy us a house.

My forehead fell to his chest. "Shit," I mumbled there. He read that as what it was, me agreeing with him—if begrudgingly—and giving in, and hugged me tighter in response as he kissed my temple.

"So we're going to look at the Brownstone?" I nodded my head against his chest.

"Good." Another squeeze and a kiss to the temple. "Now, dinner?"

"Pizza."

"Okay, honey. I'll order a pizza. You go lie down and rest." He let me go and went into the bedroom to change out of his work clothes before he ordered a large meat pizza, then grabbed himself a beer and me a pop before he joined me on the couch. We cuddled while watching a movie until the pizza arrived, then cuddled some more until I feel asleep in the middle of the movie.

Cole

I was standing in line at the coffee shop, waiting for my Americano. The meeting at the bank had gone well. Not that I had expected it to go different. I was using some of my trust fund money to buy the Brownstone that Liz had fallen in love with at first sight. I will never forget the light that shone in her eyes when we had first walked into the house last Saturday. She had stood in the middle of the living room, slowly turning around, taking her time to take everything in. Happiness and excitement gave her eyes a sparkle that made her normal beauty even more powerful and shoot straight up to stunningly marvelous. She literally took my breath away. We spent a good hour in the house, looking at every little thing, arranging furniture in our heads and out loud, creating scenarios like Sunday morning breakfasts or lazy winter afternoons in front of the fireplace. It was perfect for us. Even if I hadn't liked it just as much as Liz, I would have bought it for her just to see her eyes sparkle like that every day. I had humored her and we had looked at the other places Sam had found for us as well, but there was absolutely no contest. They were nice enough, but compared to the Brownstone they didn't even rank.

An hour ago, I had made things final and had signed the papers that would let us move into our home in just over three weeks. Time to pack. I was impatient to start our lives together, living in the same space, making her mine that much more. The sooner we moved in, the sooner I could move on to the next step and put a ring on her finger. I would give her a couple of months to get used to the idea before I proposed, though. Then a wedding by next summer and pregnant by fall. I had it all planned. Liz had no idea I intended to move this fast, but for me it was a given. Nothing and nobody would come between us. I would give her the life that she deserved and be grateful every day that she allowed me to share that beauty with her.

My friends had been relentless in their request to meet the famous Lizzy who did the impossible and chained me to her. They were idiots. It was the other way around. I wanted her chained to me as much and as fast as humanly possible. They had a bet going about Liz being pregnant and that being the reason why instead of being out on the prowl I looked at houses and discussed paint colors and furniture. If I had it my way, I would knock my girl up tonight, so she would always be bound to me in some way. That would also speed up us getting married. Nobody but my oldest friend Steve understood my, what seemed to them, sudden change of heart. Steve had met Lizzy once, and I had had a hard time keeping my cool and not ripping his head off when he started flirting with my girl. That had been the only time I had let any of my friends near her. They were all pigs. Steve had known, though, and had ribbed me ever since. He had also known why I wouldn't let myself have her and had been in my face about that as well. Once I introduced her to the rest of them, they would understand. One look was all it took and they would be goners, just like I had been. We were all going out this weekend with some of Lizzy's friends and coworkers. I still had a hard time not pissing all over her—as she called it—when we went out, so I wasn't really looking forward to having her anywhere near the guys who would undoubtedly flirt their asses off just to aggravate me.

I grabbed my Americano when I heard my name called at the end of the counter and turned around to head back to my office when I bumped into someone. I looked up to apologize but clamped my jaw shut when I saw who it was. Courtney. What the hell was she doing here? I had been glad when I hadn't received any more phone calls or text messages from her since I laid it out for her at the bar, but the look she gave me right now and the determined proximity of her body to mine told me that I had been too quick or stupid in the assumption that she had given up. I tried to step around her, but she stepped with me and put her hand on my arm. I moved the other way, but again, she moved to stay in front of me. I lost my patience and, not caring about the other patrons overhearing us, I snarled at her.

"Bitch, get out of my way."

"Relax, Cole. As hot as you are, I'm not going to jump you in the middle of the coffee shop. All I wanted to do was say 'hi'."

"You've said it. Now move."

"Fine. Be that way," she said as I stepped around her and dislodged her hand from my arm in the process. Without looking back or paying any attention to the shocked expressions on the faces around me, I walked out the door and left, putting her out of my mind before the door had even closed behind me. I wasn't going to waste any more time trying to convince that bitch. She wasn't worth it.

But over the next week, I had to admit to myself that the game she was playing was concerning. Twice more she ran into me. The first time was during a business lunch with one of the company partners. Clive had excused himself after our meal. He wasn't gone for ten seconds when none other but Courtney sat down in his chair across from me. She gave me some stupid excuse of having lunch there herself with one of her girlfriends. Not that I cared, but I could smell bullshit when sitting across from it. I was waving the waiter over to pay the bill and get the hell out of there, sticking to my new strategy of ignoring her. My eyes were on the waiter, so I didn't see it coming when her hand landed on mine or I would have pulled away before she made contact. My head whipped around and I pulled my hand out from under hers. We were in a fancy restaurant with lots of high rollers in the business world in attendance, so I couldn't exactly make a scene. Calculating bitch probably knew that all too well. I leaned across the table and rumbled too low for anyone else to hear.

"I'm not sure what game you're playing, but I'm not biting. Save yourself the trouble and give up."

"That, my dear, is never gonna happen," she said in a smooth but determined voice. I should have known then that she had every intention of making my life hell.

The waiter appeared at my side and I gave him the company credit card to pay the bill before I rose from my seat. I caught Clive's eye on his way back into the room and nodded that I was ready to go. Without another word to Courtney, I left, hoping that she would eventually give up, but knowing deep down that she wouldn't. Something needed to be done. Who knew what vindictive, spurned bitches like Courtney were capable of? I, for sure, did not want to find out. First order of business would be bringing Lizzy up to speed, though honestly, I didn't want her to know. I wanted her to feel safe in our relationship, not have to deal with my past mistakes. She trusted me and I wanted to deserve that trust.

By the next time Courtney made an approach, I still hadn't filled Lizzy in. I was leaving my office at the end of the day, my thoughts on my girl and how I was going to show her how much I'd missed her and needed her. The elevator doors opened to let me out to the parking garage and there she was, leaning against my car. Annoyed, I stalked toward her. I was done with this shit once and for all. Obviously, she needed to be persuaded in a more serious manner to leave me the fuck alone. If I had to hire someone to do that job, I would.

Annoyance turned into fury when she started taking her coat off and I realized that all she was wearing was sexy lingerie underneath. Fucking hell! Did this woman have no shame? Sure, the old Cole would have taken that invitation without blinking, but I was not that man anymore. Her offering her almost naked body to me in all its glory didn't stir me in the slightest. Nobody could compete with what I had at home. I would never risk that and betray Liz's trust, and I was glad that my dick and I were in absolute agreement about that.

"Put your fucking coat back on!" I growled at her. She didn't move to do so, but instead turned around to lean over the hood and offer me her ass, looking at me seductively over her shoulder. I ignored all that was her and went straight to the driver's door, intent on leaving. Before I could get in the car, she pressed her body to my back, her hands reaching for my dick from behind. I pushed her off me with such force that she fell and landed on her almost naked ass. But I didn't give a shit. I got in my car, started the engine, and roared off before she even got up.

Fuck!

That bitch was demented.

There was no way I could tell Liz about this. She was going to go apeshit not only on Courtney, but also on me for letting it escalate to this degree without telling her what was going on. Fuck! I had to get this sorted. Now. There would be no other encounters. She would go away and Liz wouldn't have to know anything ever happened. I made a few calls until I got the number I needed and made arrangements to have a message delivered to Courtney that should make it crystal clear how serious business just got.

"I want her out of my life, to lose my number, to forget I ever existed. And she can't come near Liz."

"How far you want me to go if the scare tactic doesn't do the job?"

"Make her life hell. Whatever it takes for her to not ever mess with my relationship again."

"You sure about that?"

"Absolutely. I'm not losing my girlfriend over this bullshit."

"Alright. I'm on it."

Max was a PI who worked for our company from time to time to get information we needed. He promised me he would set the plan in motion that night.

For the next two weeks, everything was quiet. No phone calls, texts, and thank fuck, no more run-ins. It looked like some big bulk of man appearing on Courtney's doorstep giving her a firm talking-to had worked. Upon checking in with Max, I learned that indeed all the guy had to do was show up at her house and scare the shit out of her and she backed off.

"Looks like a scare is all she needed. Pity really. Was looking forward to throwing some dirt at that rich bitch."

"Good. You've been monitoring her?"

"Yeah. Been following her for the past two weeks. Hasn't gone anywhere near you or your girl. All she does is meet other bitches for lunch, get laid by three different guys, and go to the salon. Got pictures and notes as proof for you."

"Okay. Thanks, Max."

"Was a pleasure doing business with you."

Grateful I had dodged that bullet without having to escalate things further or bringing the situation into Lizzy's life, I hung up. Now it was time to focus on moving my girl into our new house this weekend.

Chapter 13

Lizzy

Ten years ago.
Lizzy is fifteen. Cole is seventeen.

Cole and I are walking down Main Street, talking and laughing. We don't usually stroll down the sidewalk like this. It makes me uncomfortable, knowing that people are looking at us, disapproving of him spending time with the white trash girl from the wrong side of town. Cole said it's just my imagination, that they aren't looking, but we both know that he's lying. The glares he gives them when he thinks I can't see only confirm that.

People in town hate me.

They always have.

Well, at least the women do. They give me withering looks and turn up their noses at me. I know why. I'm not stupid. We live in a small town where everyone knows everyone. I know, for example, that the woman who is giving me the death glare from across the street is Mrs. Evanston. I also know that Mr. Evanston comes to our house to see my mother. Frequently. And not just to have a chat from townie to townie. Oh no. As soon as he walks through the door, my mother starts unbuttoning her jeans while his eyes grow needy and wanting before he pulls her up the stairs and has his way with her. Our house is old and in bad repair. I can hear them through the walls. Neither of them care that I'm there and know what's going on. It's like I don't exist. But that's better than the alternative. At least Mr. Evanston isn't one of my mother's friends who stare and leer at me. He completely ignores me. I prefer it that way.

I'm trying to make myself small, hunching as my eyes move from Mrs. Evanston and land on a group of men who are standing outside the town's garage. There are three of them and all of their eyes are trained on me, grinning, looking at me lasciviously, almost carnally.

I know them.

All of them.

They are some of the men my mother has over when she's in the mood to party. They are the ones who make me escape through the back door and run to Cole's house. Before I can avert my eyes, I see one of them lick his lips as if in anticipation. I shiver in disgust, remembering his hands on my thighs as he tried to push them apart, remembering the smell of his foul breath on my face, remembering the panic that coiled in my stomach. It has been almost two years since then, but I remember everything as if it happened yesterday. Cole's arm comes around my shoulders and he pulls me into his side. I look up at him to see his eyes on the men, his jaw clenched, his look fierce and challenging.

He's protecting me. Again.

I look back down to the sidewalk, feeling embarrassed and guilty.

"Hey." Cole's arm around me tightens. I say nothing and don't look at him as we keep walking along Main Street. I feel his lips at the side of my head and am about to look up at him when I see two pairs of low-heeled shoes come to a halt a few feet from me. I look up and stare into hard eyes.

Cole's mother's eyes.

And right next to her is Courtney's mother, her eyes equally cold and hard on me.

Cole tenses beside me but doesn't let me go. I try to move away from him, out of his embrace, but he won't have it. His mother's eyes narrow on me, giving me chills, before they move to her son.

"I can't believe you," she hisses at him.

"What is it you can't believe, mother?" Cole's voice is hard and unyielding. He knows exactly what she is talking about.

"I can't believe that you are still hanging out with this whore. I forbade you—"

Cole lets go of me as he moves into his mother's space, intimidating her, and standing protectively in front of me at the same time. "Careful, mother. I've told you before and I'll tell you again. Lizzy is my friend, my best friend, and I will not abandon her because you want me to. You and your reputation with your stuck-up friends can go to hell for all I care. One more nasty word out of your mouth and I will make sure the whole town will get a show they won't soon forget."

I look around nervously. It's Sunday afternoon, people are out and about, a few of them already stopped, curious to see what's going on.

God.

How I hate this town and the people in it.

I can't wait to get out of here.

Cole and his mother are in a stare-down, neither of them giving in. I'm about to just leave to make it easier for him when I hear Courtney's mother hiss, "Home wrecker." My eyes fly to hers and I freeze at the hatred I see in them. My heart starts beating rapidly. I try to think. Had her husband come to our house? Is he one of my mother's fuck buddies? No, he isn't. At least not that I know of. And my mother doesn't keep any of them a secret, so I would know. I would have seen him at some point. She must be referring to one of her friends' husbands. Not that that makes me feel any better.

"What did you just say?" Cole's voice is lethal as he directs it at Courtney's mother.

"I called her what she and her mother are. Home wreckers. No good white trash slutty whores of home wreckers." The hatred rolls off of her as she glares at me, unblinking. I hate myself for it, but tears are starting to pool in my eyes. I have sworn over and over again to not let anyone's hatred get to me, but for some reason I can never seem to manage to keep that oath.

Cole takes a threatening step toward her, but I grab his elbow and he stops. I see a muscle jump in his cheek as he clenches his teeth.

"Let's go," he says to me without taking his eyes from her. "They're not worth it." Then he takes my hand and pulls me behind him.

"Don't listen to them, Lizzy. They're mean bitches who thrive at making others feel worthless."

I say nothing, just let him pull me along as I stare at the sidewalk.

I'm embarrassed and hurt and mad at the same time. I wish the mad would win out. It would make things so much easier. But it's always the hurt that has the upper hand. I want to be strong and stand up for myself. Tell them to go to hell like Cole just did, and I'm embarrassed that I always fail. They get to me. The hatred and the disgust and contempt get to me.

It cuts me deep that people would think that way about me, would call me a whore and a home wrecker and worse. That they think I'm useless just because I was born to a woman who cares about nothing and nobody but herself. I hate, hate, hate that I let them get to me.

Angry tears wet my eyes and I take a deep breath to swallow them down.

Cole's hand around mine is firm and unyielding. I wouldn't be able to let go even if I wanted to.

Which I don't.

I might hate the fact that I'm weak and that he always has to protect me, but I can't help but cling to him. It gives me strength. I already dread the moment he has to leave for college and leave me behind.

"Hey," his voice is low as he squeezes my hand. I squeeze it back.

"Look at me, Liz." He stops us on the sidewalk, away from all the Sunday afternoon strollers and shoppers.

I take another deep breath and look up at him as I try to put on a brave face even though I know I won't be very successful. Cole knows me too well.

"Don't listen to them."

I shrug. "I try, but it's hard."

My eyes wander over his shoulder. His mother and Mrs. Miller are still watching us with contempt as they talk to each other. Nobody else is looking, but I still feel everyone's eyes on us.

I feel Cole's hand squeeze mine and my attention snaps back to him.

"Don't, Liz. Ignore them."

"It's not that easy, Cole. No matter what I do or don't do, I will always be the town whore's daughter who everyone despises just by relation. Nothing will ever change their minds." My mind went back to Courtney's mom and all the other women who knew what their husbands were really doing—or should I say whom they were doing—when they claimed to have to work late or be stuck in a meeting or in traffic. It wasn't just other drunks and drug addicts who frequented our house. Oh no. Upstanding town citizens stopped by on regular basis as well. Usually during the week, making it easier for them to lie to their wives about their whereabouts. I had never told Cole who they were, but I suspected he knew. As I said, we live in a small town. And if you really wanted to know what was going on, it was easy enough to find out.

Shame and guilt run through me once again. I am trash, born into it, and nobody in this town will ever let me forget it.

"I know. And it pisses me the fuck off. Who does that shit? Condemn someone because of the circumstances they're born into. Fuck. I fucking hate those people." His voice is low but I can hear the absolute anger vibrating in it. He closes his eyes and takes a deep breath through his nose before he opens them again. "Not much longer now until we can get out of here."

I huff and murmur, "Only three years," under my breath. I keep the fact that two of those years I will be alone, without him, to myself. I don't want him to feel guilty. I don't want to become a burden. But I can see that he can read the words on my face, that he is thinking the same thing, and that he is worried.

"Promise me you'll stay strong. Promise me you won't let them break you."

That was the plan. To hang in there until I could follow him to Boston. I planned on sticking to that plan, no matter what.

I nodded.

"I promise."

"Good." Cole exhaled in relief and gave my hand another squeeze. Then he brushed his lips softly against my forehead. I closed my eyes and savored the moment. These were the moments I lived for, the moments when I could pretend that we were a couple. It made the wait until we could actually be together easier. We had never actually talked about what would happen between us when I followed him to school, but I knew, I just knew he was biding his time until he could make me his.

Just like I was.

Chapter 14

Lizzy

Thanksgiving weekend. Usually, I would work at the shelter all day, but this year, Cole and I invited some of our friends without family in the city for dinner at our place. It would be our first family holiday in our new house and I couldn't wait.

My mother and I never celebrated Thanksgiving, or any holiday for that matter, so I usually sat at home reading a book or, after Katie had become my best and really only friend in town during my junior year in high school, I would spend Thanksgivings and Christmases with her and her family. Cole had never invited me over to spend a holiday with him, not that I had ever expected him to. Other than sneaking into his bedroom when things got out of control at my house, I had never even been to his house.

And after I moved to Boston to go to college, Cole stayed with me whenever he could weasel his way out of going home for a holiday, which wasn't very often, almost never actually, but I never blamed him. So I mostly just stayed in my dorm room and read or studied all weekend, even though both Katie and Cole repeatedly tried to talk me into staying at Katie's.

This would be the first year that Cole didn't go home for Thanksgiving weekend. He didn't go into details, but apparently his mother had not come to terms with the fact that I was in his life in the capacity I was and would stay there. Refusing her demand to come alone, he instead wanted to celebrate with friends at our house.

"I'm telling you what I told my mother. If she can't accept you being as the vital part of my life and welcome you to the family, then I want nothing to do with them. I'm not going home to celebrate a family holiday without you there."

"Are you sure? I don't want to be the reason you distance yourself from your family."

He chuckled. "Baby, seriously? There isn't much to distance myself from. My mother has never been a nice person, you know that. That's probably the only thing my father and I ever agreed on. We are family by blood, but that's about it. They refuse to accept you, which means they refuse to accept me and my happiness."

That was true, but still. At least he had family to spend time with.

"What about your cousin Daniel? You guys always got along fine."

"How about this? Daniel dislikes those family gatherings just as much as I do. We'll invite him to come to dinner here. He can bring his girlfriend, who by the way, my mother also won't accept but can't do much about, seeing as my aunt and uncle adore her. Ask some of your friends and colleagues to join us and we'll celebrate our first holiday with the people we actually like to be around. Okay?"

"That actually sounds great. I would love that."

"Then it's done. I'll call Daniel and Steve. You call your friends."

And so we planned to spend Thanksgiving with our chosen family of friends. I couldn't be happier. Everyone was coming at noon and I couldn't wait.

It was early in the morning when I pulled into the shelter to help with the food prep until I had to head home for my own prep. Jesse and Chloe were now living at a foster home with an amazing couple that only took in older kids nobody else seemed to want. I had worked with them before and had practically begged them to take them in. They had only had one spot open after one of their wards had started college in the fall, but agreed to take on both kids after I told them their story. Both Chloe and Jesse had settled in fine and often stopped by the shelter after school to spend some time with me. We had developed a fairly deep bond and I cared about them immensely. They wanted to be home for turkey dinner, but were coming to help with the Thanksgiving preparations at the shelter today before I was going to drop them off at their house on my way home.

When I walked into the common room, Marie was already in a tizzy trying to get everyone organized. All the staff and volunteers were there today to make this holiday something special for the kids. The only one coming over to Cole and my place was Marie. She had worked closely with me during the past few months and we had become friendly. Rainey was staying at the shelter until early afternoon then was going to head home to spend Thanksgiving with her mother and a family friend. Everyone else was here for the day. Seriously, I loved my job and the people I was working with.

"Lizzy! Thank God you're here! There is so much to do!" Marie advanced on me as soon as she saw me walking in.

"Relax, Marie. It'll be fine," I tried to calm her down then turned to the kids. "Kids, listen up! Girls, grab those decorations and put them up. Boys, go to the basement and grab enough tables and chairs to seat about thirty people, then set them up. Once that's all done, the boys can start vegging out in front of the TV and hang with Rainey and Jimmy and the girls can meet me and Marie in the kitchen and we'll put you to work."

Everyone started buzzing around to do their respective jobs. Marie followed me into my office so I could drop my coat and purse.

"It kinda annoys me sometimes that they all listen to you and not to me, you know," she mumbled under her breath. I gave her a small smile.

"Don't worry, Marie. You'll get there. With these kids you have to earn it. Took me a good year until everyone knew I was kind of a ball buster and would follow through on my threats. You've only been here a few months. They are hard kids on the outside, Marie. They have to be to survive and you have to earn their respect before they let you in even an inch, but you'll make it. I'm sure." Marie nodded and gave me a hesitant smile in return.

"If you say so."

"Exactly. Now, what do we need to do first?"

"The turkeys and potatoes are being delivered at three. Taryn, Jimmy, and Rainey know, so they should be fine. We'll have to start on the veggies and pies to have them ready on time. Jimmy is currently setting up the screen in the back room so everyone can watch the game, and Taryn brought a bunch of new games and stuff for the kids that are not interested in football. Rainey brought her camera to take pictures. We'll need to make up the rooms. All our regulars agreed to spend the night and it sounded like some of the not-so regulars intended on staying as well."

"Alright. Sounds like everything's under control then. Let's head to the kitchen to get a start on those veggies and pies. We'll get the boys to set up the rooms for everyone once they've finished with the tables and chairs."

We got to work. The girls joined us in the kitchen to bake a variety of pies while the boys enjoyed a holiday tradition and spent most of the morning in front of the TV. It was getting close to crunch time and I had to hustle my butt back home to get ready for my own guests. I sent Chloe in search of Jesse so we could get a move on and went into the common room to make sure everything was ready. The girls had done a fantastic job with the decorations. The room actually looked kind of home-y and cozy. I was proud of them. I poked my head into the back room to wish everyone a Happy Thanksgiving before I left. A chorus of Happy Thanksgivings from the girls echoed back at me. The boys were too immersed in the game to pay me any attention.

"You did good," I heard a low voice utter beside me. I looked over and gave Jimmy a smile.

"We all did."

"Yeah, we all do our piece, but you go above and beyond the call of duty, Liz. The kids see that and respect you for it. They trust you. Look at them. Since you started working here, our numbers of kids who actually stay and accept our help has more than doubled and that's all you." Tears started pooling in my eyes at his words.

"Stop, Jimmy. Crying like a baby is gonna make me lose my street cred." He chuckled, then gave me a quick hug and wished me a Happy Thanksgiving before he rejoined the group on the couch to watch the game. I took a deep breath to control my girly tears then grabbed my stuff from the office and met Jesse and Chloe by the door.

Cole was sitting on the couch watching the game when I came home. When he heard the door open, he turned his head to look over the couch and smiled. "Hey, baby." He got up and walked towards me.

"Hey," I replied, then lifted up on my toes to give him a small kiss on the lips.

"What was that?" Cole asked, amused, when I stepped back.

"What was what?" I was busy taking my boots and coat off and going through my to-do list in my head, so I didn't see him getting close. He hooked an arm around my waist and gently pulled me to him until he could wrap both arms around me. I looked up at him in confusion.

"Baby, kiss me like you mean it," he murmured before his head descended toward mine and he took my mouth in a long kiss that left me a little dizzy.

"Everything good at the shelter?"

"Yeah. They have a lot of kids there, but they've got it under control. Marie is on her way over. I should probably get started on the turkey," I informed him while extricating myself from his arms and moving toward the kitchen. "You stay out of the way and go follow Thanksgiving tradition. I'll be slaving away in the kitchen. You're on door duty." I heard him chuckling behind me and smiled to myself, happy and content, then I got to work immediately.

The turkey was almost ready to go in the oven when Cole came in to get a beer. He stopped in the doorway and looked at me, then smiled and came over to where I was standing at the counter. When he got close, he leaned down to murmur in my ear, "I like this. Watching you work in our kitchen to make a holiday dinner for our friends. It's very sexy." I giggled.

"Watching me with my hands up a turkey's butt is sexy,

huh?"

He chuckled low. "You have no idea." I giggled again.

"You happy?" He looked deep into my eyes.

"Yeah," I whispered.

"Good. Me too," he whispered back then headed to the fridge to get himself a beer. I watched him as he did this so I could appreciate his butt as he walked out of the room, and felt so very, very lucky that that ass and everything attached to it was mine.

Marie showed up ten minutes later and Katie and her boyfriend, Chris, five minutes after that. The women came straight to the kitchen, where I poured us all a glass of wine.

"Good God, woman. Now I know why you've been hiding that hunk of a man. Please tell me he can be an asshole or is really bad in bed," Marie said, fanning herself and making me laugh.

"Yes to the first, no to the second," I informed her through my hilarity.

"He can be an asshole?"

"Yes, but he's never one to me. At least not on purpose."

"It's about time he got his head out of his ass. I honestly didn't think he had it in him," Katie chimed in.

"What do you mean?" Marie asked.

"He's been in love with Liz since they were kids but was too busy screwing around to see what was right in front of him all these years."

"Ah, here comes the asshole part."

"It wasn't like that, Katie," I tried to defend Cole.

"No? What was it like, then? Every party he was at he hooked up with a new random girl, but made sure that no guy ever came near you, or God forbid, touched you. Every guy in town was too afraid to even ask you out on a date, scared they would have to endure the wrath of Cole, even after he left for college. Tell me, how many dates exactly did you go on during high school?"

"Boys didn't ask me out on dates because I lived on the wrong side of town. It would have tarnished their reputation."

"That's bullshit, Liz. Every guy in high school had the hots for you, but Cole kept a close eye on the situation. He was the school king even after he graduated and made it very clear to everyone that he considered you his. Nobody wanted to mess with him. That's why no guy dared to come near you." I stared at Katie, completely dumbfounded. My whole life I thought the boys I went to school with treated like a pariah because of where I came from, because of who my mother was. I couldn't wrap my head around what Katie just said.

Boys had been interested in me?

Katie saw the shocked expression on my face and her tone gentled. "I confronted him about it once. He told me he was just looking out for you, that he didn't want any of those pigs using you or breaking your heart. I'm sure that's what he was telling himself he was doing. But not all of those guys were bad news. There were a few good ones that would have treated you right, given the chance. Like Scott, for example."

She was right.

Scott had been one of the good guys. After that fateful night at the party when my world came crashing down, when I knew that Cole and I would never be a couple, I had opened myself up to the idea of dating and had hoped that Scott would ask me out. He was the nicest guy in school, good looking, always helpful and friendly, polite. We had been partnered up for one of our science assignments and had spent a good amount of time together, just the two of us. He had made me laugh and seemed to be genuinely interested in me and what I had to say, which made me forget about all that crap that was going on in my life. I had caught him staring at me a few times during class and in the cafeteria, and had thought he might be into me, but when he never made a move on me, I thought I had imagined it or read too much into a friendly look. We had stayed friends during high school and still sent each other messages and talked from time to time. Now Katie was saying that the reason he hadn't gone for more was because he was afraid he'd have to deal with Cole?

I narrowed my eyes at the living room.

"Yeah, I see it's sinking in," Katie murmured.

Yes, it was definitely sinking in.

"Well, the way I see it, if they didn't have the balls to go for it despite Cole, then he was right and they weren't worth your time in the first place." This came from Marie. I turned my head to look at her.

"What do you mean?"

"I mean, a man or a boy who will be a man, at any age, if he wants something, he'll go for it, no matter if someone is threatening him or warning him off. He'll take the threat head-on if he thinks what waits for him at the end is worth the effort. And seeing that none of them went for it proves that Cole was right. They weren't good enough for you if they didn't think you were worth the effort of taking him on."

"Huh. I've never looked at it that way. That kinda makes sense in a roundabout way," Katie mumbled, then took a sip of wine and looked towards the living room with a thoughtful look on her face. My irritation with Cole dissipated at Marie's words. I agreed with Katie. They did make sense in a roundabout way.

"Anyways, from what I've seen and heard, he has claimed

you now and has no intention of ever giving another guy a chance of even considering making a play for you. He's gone whole hog and made you move in with him after a few weeks of dating. No man does that unless he's found what he wants and is going for it, no matter the consequences. Actually, after what you've been telling me, I'm surprised he hasn't tattooed his name on your ass to show his ownership."

"Whose name tattooed on whose ass?" Cole's voice came from the door. I lifted my eyes over Marie's shoulder to see Cole waltzing into the kitchen with empties. Marie turned around and filled him in.

"Your name, her ass," she said, pointing first at Cole, then at me.

Cole's eyebrows shot up, then his face split into a grin. "I like that idea."

"See? Told you," Marie looked back at me and gave me a pointed look.

I looked over at Katie and watched her take in what Marie had said. Her eyes were on Cole, still thoughtful, while she twirled her wineglass in her hand. They followed him as he got close to me to softly kiss my temple, and kept following him as he retrieved more beer from the fridge, until he disappeared back into the living room. Then her eyes came to me and she gave me a small nod and a smile.

"Marie is right. Doesn't mean I won't still keep an eye on him," she said as she put her wine aside and went to work at rolling out the dough for the pie. Fair enough. Still a little shocked by what I had learned, but also, strangely, even happier than I was ten minutes ago, I went back to work.

Our dining table was filled to the max with eight people around it. Dinner was delicious and conversation was constant and filled with laughter. Katie and Chris entertained us with tales about their last vacation to England, where apparently they'd had some difficulties conversing with the locals, believe it or not. You would think that English would be English no matter where you were in the world, but according to them you needed a dictionary if you wanted to understand any of their slang terms, like 'dog's bollocks' meant something great, or how when someone said, 'have a butcher's' at something meant to go and look at it. Marie, Sophie, and I were in tears the more Katie and Chris got into it.

Sophie was Daniel's girlfriend and she and I bonded over Cole's mother's hatred for us. The stories she told me about how she had been treated by her were kind of intimidating. Daniel had refused to ever have anything to do with his aunt again for any reason, that's how bad it was. I wasn't looking forward to ever officially meeting her as Cole's girlfriend.

"Don't worry, Liz. What can she really do to you? Cole will have your back and she won't go up against him, especially now that he is actually richer than them," she tried to reassure me.

"What do you mean?"

"Well, you know, because his grandfather left all his money and assets to Cole instead of his own son when he died last year. Shocking, but apparently, he never liked his son or his daughter-in-law very much, but Cole he was close to. So he left everything to him." That was news to me. Wow. I just stared at Sophie, not knowing what to say. Her eyes grew big at the realization that I hadn't known any of this.

"You didn't know, did you?" she asked, concerned now. I shook my head at her. I wasn't sure what to make of this. I didn't care about money, Cole knew this, and neither did he. We had that discussion when he wanted to buy this house.

So did it really matter that he was even richer than I thought? Not really. But he could have told me. I hadn't been able to go with him to his grandfather's funeral last year, but I had known he had been very upset. His grandfather had always supported him and taught him the life lessons that his father had been too busy to teach his son. They had been close; I knew that, even though they had only seen each other a few times a year because he lived in California. When Cole was fourteen, he spent his whole summer break there. It had been the longest and loneliest summer of my life. But when he came back, he had told me how awesome his grandfather was. How he was different from his own father and that he wished he could live with him all of the time. That thought had terrified me.

But I hadn't known that he had left all his money to Cole. That must have caused some serious tension with his parents. I couldn't imagine they liked the idea of being skipped over in favor of their son who was so different from them and whom they didn't like very much. I wondered why he hadn't told me about it. I would have to ask him about it. But not now when we had a house full of guests.

Determined to put his family out of my mind for now, I gave Sophie a small smile to let her know it was okay and changed the subject.

Daniel and Sophie had to leave right after dinner. They had promised his parents, who also lived in Boston, to stop by their house for dessert and a nightcap. Sophie had her arm hooked through mine as we followed Cole and Daniel to the door.

"You okay after what I dropped on you earlier?" she asked in a low voice that only I could hear.

"I'm fine. It's not really a big deal. Don't worry about it."

"Okay. Let's get together soon. I have a feeling we're going to be great friends." I would love that. Sophie was great and lots of fun. It would be nice to have another girlfriend. I didn't have too many of those. We made arrangements to meet up for coffee the following week.

"Glad to see you finally got your shit together, bro," I heard Daniel say when he gave Cole a man hug. "You're lucky nobody snapped her up before you came to your senses."

"Believe me, I know exactly how lucky I am," Cole replied after he released Daniel and looked at me. Daniel nodded. When he hugged me, he whispered in my ear, "He's been in love with you all his life, you know?" Yes, I was starting to believe it. Cole had said it when he came to apologize after our fight and again when he took me out to dinner; Katie said it tonight; and now Daniel. "I love him, too," I whispered back. Daniel gave me a squeeze before he let me go, but held on to my shoulders, studying me closely. "I see it." Then he turned to get Sophie's coat and Sophie moved in to hug me goodbye.

Katie and Chris left shortly after. They were going home to Katie's parents for brunch the next day, so they had to get up kinda early in the morning for the drive out to Ashford. After some more TV for the men while Marie and I cleaned up the rest of the dishes and shared some more wine in the kitchen, our last two guests called it a night as well. Marie had had too much to drink, so Steve volunteered to give her a ride home. She would come and get her car tomorrow.

I was undressing in the bedroom when Cole came upstairs after closing down the house. Too tired to worry about my clothes, I dropped them on the floor, crawled to bed in only my panties, and collapsed on my stomach. Soft kisses on my naked back made me shiver and I sighed contentedly.

"Tired, baby?"

"Mmh."

"This is what I've been thinking about all day. Having you naked underneath me to do with whatever I please. Completely at my mercy." One of his hands was joining the action and wandered up and down my side, lightly touching the swell of my breast before it went down and over my hip to my ass, all the while his lips kept slowly and softly exploring my back. His hands felt like magic on my skin, making every single cell of my body come alive with need. His fingers found my sex and started playing, gently gliding through my folds. I tipped my ass slightly up to give him better access. He chuckled.

"Never too tired to play. Always so hot for me. I can't get enough of you, Liz." His words in that low raspy voice turned me on, and I started circling my hips with the movement of his fingers. Then one finger entered me, left me again, and went back to circling, spreading the wetness his movements caused. I moaned and pressed into his finger. A few minutes of playing and he already had me where he wanted me.

Needy and ready to take him.

I started to turn around to face him, but his body came down on mine, keeping me in place.

"No, baby. I want to play a little longer. Be good and don't move." He lifted up off me. I stayed where I was and was immediately rewarded with two fingers entering me, stroking lazily a few times, then leaving me again to press and circle. His other hand moved my hair over my shoulder so that his mouth could explore the back of my neck with soft kisses and gentle touches, driving me absolutely crazy. I wasn't very good at submitting, so we both knew I wouldn't be able to hold still for very long. The feel of his jeans against my almost naked ass was unbelievably sexy when he leaned into me, letting me feel his hardness against my backside.

"Cole," I whispered. I wanted him so badly that the need of feeling him inside me made my body shiver.

"Shh, baby, soon. Just a little longer. I love your back, your ass, your neck," he whispered, his lips on me, fingers playing, hips gently thrusting against me. I clenched my fingers in the sheet and held on, breathing hard. Finally, I could feel his other hand between us at his jeans, unzipping them, pushing them down, and then he was there, rubbing his hard cock through my folds, coating it, before he slowly entered me from behind, inch by slow inch, holding me in place with his weight on top of me, so all I could do was wait for him to give me all of him.

Torture.

Slow torture until finally he filled me completely.

"God, Liz. Every time. You feel so good every time I take you. Gripping me so tight. I'm gonna take you slow, baby, so slow. Gonna drag it out until you can't take it anymore and beg me to fuck you hard. You feel this, baby? This is you and me. Perfect. Absolutely perfect." He took me slowly, making love to me, pushing in a bit then pulling back out, back in a little more, then grinding, in a bit more, back out. Over and over and over again. I could feel his body shaking above me with the effort of holding on to his control. His mouth kept at my back and my neck, making me shake and shiver all over while he kept slowly thrusting and grinding. I wanted to push back into him, demanding more, but his hips held me firmly in place.

"Liz, baby," his breathing was labored now, his voice growly. I couldn't take it anymore.

I started begging, "Please, Cole. I need more."

He thrust in a little harder and faster but it was nowhere near hard enough.

"Cole, please!"

With almost brutal force he slammed into me, hard, fast, driving me up to climax with a speed that left me reeling. His hands were pulling my hips back to meet his thrust for thrust. After only a few minutes, I was there, and my sex started spasming around him. I knew there was no chance of holding it back and I came on a loud groan, bucking my hips against his until he groaned my name with his own release.

He dropped his weight on top of me for a few seconds, breathing hard, then rolled off me and took me with him so I ended up on top of him, front to front. We stayed like that for a while until both our heartbeats slowed down. I slid off his torso until I was lying pressed to his side, my head on his chest, his arm around my shoulders, our legs tangled, and fell promptly asleep.

Chapter 15

Lizzy

"Let's play hooky," I said against his neck, where my mouth was busy exploring. It was Monday morning after Thanksgiving weekend. We hadn't left the house in three days. It was glorious and I didn't want it to end. I was sitting naked in Cole's lap. He was already dressed and ready to go to work and had pulled me in his lap for a goodbye kiss.

"I wish I could. But I have important meetings first thing this morning and one of my projects is starting up today and needs my attention." His hands were lazily running up and down my naked back.

"Let's compromise then. You can be late." I kept kissing and licking his neck while my hands were loosening his tie and unbuttoning his shirt. He grabbed my hands with his to stop me.

"Sorry, baby. I can't. I'll make it up to you tonight." He kissed me long and deep and lovingly.

"I'll do that thing you like so much," I gave it one last try and pulled out the big guns when he ended the kiss. His body stilled under mine. Heat burnt in his eyes. Then he closed them and dropped his head so that his forehead rested on my shoulder.

"God, honey, you're killing me. I'll be running around with a permanent hard-on all day thinking about that." He tipped his head back to look at me. "That calls for punishment tonight, baby." I shivered. I liked his idea of punishment. It always ended in an amazing orgasm for me. Cole felt the shiver and his eyes got heated again.

"I see you like my punishments," his voice had turned sexy growly. All I could do was nod before he crashed his mouth to mine and gave me a kiss filled with lust and anticipation.

"Hold that thought. I'll try to skip out early so we can play."

"Okay," I breathed.

Then he gently pulled me out of his lap and deposited me in the bed, pulled the covers over me, kissed my forehead, and he was gone. I cuddled into the blanket, smiling to myself, and fell back asleep until my alarm went off an hour later.

My desk was a mess. I had a ton of messages and files piled up high in front of me, and had no desire to pick up the phone and start my computer. My head was still with Cole and all the things he would do to me tonight. It was ridiculous, really. I had always made fun of all those couples that couldn't spend a few hours apart without calling each other, and look at me now. Cole had left me in bed only two hours ago after three full days of being in that bed with me and all I could think of was the way he touched me. It wasn't just about the sex. I wanted him close all the time, to hear his voice, make him laugh, smell his musky scent, have him hold me in his arms.

I was like a lovesick puppy.

Disgusting.

A knock on the door snapped me out of my reverie. Marie came in carrying more files and envelopes. Looked like today would be a day of being stuck behind my desk, catching up on paperwork. I sighed in resignation and held my hand out for the files and mail. Marie dropped them on the already threateningly high pile in front of me, making it almost topple over.

"What's with the grumpy face?"

"It's Monday. I hate Mondays. And looking at all of this, I'll be stuck in my office all day."

"Yeah, that's probably true. You'll have to come out of your torture chamber after lunch, though. The tutor wanted to talk to you about something." That was never good. This Monday was shaping up to be even worse than I thought. I hoped Derrick wasn't going to quit. He had only been with us for a couple of months and the kids were just getting used to him. From what I had seen, he was doing a great job. Didn't take any shit from the kids, had a firm hand, but wasn't too strict to make the kids not want to come back, was patient, and had no problem explaining things a hundred times until the kids got them. I thought the kids liked him and things were going great. If he quit, I would have a hard time finding a replacement.

"A courier dropped off an envelope for you early this morning. It's at the bottom of the mail pile. I'll go get you a coffee and then leave you to it," Marie told me before she disappeared only to come back two minutes later with my coffee, then she left again and closed the door firmly behind her.

I was looking through the pile of mail first and organized the letters according to priority: one pile for budget forms and updates, one pile for bills that needed to be paid, one pile for correspondence with foster homes. The last envelope must be the one Marie mentioned was couriered this morning. It was a letter-sized brown envelope with my name written in Sharpie, no return address, no indication whatsoever of where it came from.

Weird.

I opened the flap and looked inside. Looked like a stack of smaller papers or cards. I pulled out the first one and looked at it. When I realized what it was, my heart stopped, then started again at a much faster pace. It was an ultrasound picture with Courtney Miller's name on the top. Courtney Miller, Cole's ex-fuck buddy and my childhood arch nemesis. My hands were shaking so hard I dropped the photo. With a lump in my throat that was threatening to choke me, not wanting to know what else was in the envelope but needing to at the same time, I upended the envelope to see what else she had sent. More photographs fell out.

Of her.

And Cole.

Together.

At a coffee shop. A restaurant. A parking garage.

In almost every picture she was touching him, smiling at him. The worst one was one of her leaning over the hood of Cole's car in nothing but high heels and sexy lingerie with Cole stalking towards her, what looked like in a hurry to get to her.

I couldn't believe what I was seeing.

This couldn't be true. It had to be some kind of ploy or bad joke.

Courtney was a vindictive bitch who was definitely capable of something like this. I needed to talk to Cole, needed to see his face when he looked at the pictures, needed to see the truth in his eyes. I needed him to tell me that this was a lie, that Courtney was scheming against us somehow, that those pictures were not what they looked like. I grabbed the letter and the photographs with shaking hands and shoved them back in the envelope, then grabbed my keys and ran out to my car. I heard people calling my name as I ran through the common room, but I didn't stop.

I had to get to Cole.

Only he could make this right. Only he could take away the pain that was waiting at the sidelines, waiting to overwhelm me, to drown me. And he better do that quickly or I would rip his balls off if any of what the pictures implied were actually true. Who was I kidding? If any of that turned out to be true, I'd curl up into the fetal position, lock myself away somewhere, and drown in self-pity.

I got in my car and raced across the city to Cole's office building. I parked in the garage and had to close my eyes at the realization that this was the one from the pictures.

Get to Cole. You promised you wouldn't shut him out. Talk to him. He'll explain everything.

I raced toward the elevators, got on, pushed the button for his floor, then stared at the numbers on the screen until I finally got out on his floor. I had only been here once, but had no problem finding his office in my determined single-mindedness. Again, I could hear someone talking to me, but I again didn't pay them any attention. I opened the door to Cole's office, eyes going directly to his desk and stopped dead.

There she was.

Sitting on his desk.

Naked.

And Cole had his hands on her hips.

I blinked. This couldn't be true. My mind must be playing tricks on me, being in panic mode. Having just seen the photos of her with him, I must be confused, my mind conjuring up images of my worst fears. But after I blinked a couple more times, she was still there, sitting naked on his desk, his hands holding her hips.

I looked from her naked body to Cole. His eyes were on me, filled with terror.

Terror at being caught.

He pushed away from the desk and rose from his chair, not taking his eyes from me.

"Lizzy, this isn't what it looks like," his voice was careful, soothing, like he was talking to a frightened animal or a child. He was walking toward me. I stepped back, staring at him through my tears.

"Liz, baby—" Pain and hatred shot through me at him using that endearment. It killed something inside of me.

"Don't you ever call me that again."

Cole stopped at hearing the tone of my voice. It didn't sound like me at all.

It sounded dead.

Exactly like how I felt.

I tossed the envelope at him, then turned on my heel, ran from the office, and caught the elevator just as it was about to close. I could hear him shouting my name, could hear his running footsteps following me, but he was too late. The doors closed before he could reach me and I was gone with a finality that tore my heart apart. I couldn't breathe. I was choking. Choking on my own sobs, on the betrayal, on the pain slicing through me, on my heart breaking into a million little pieces. So many pieces I knew they could never be put back together again.

I should have known.

Good things didn't happen to me.

Or at least I didn't get to keep them.

I should have been happy with the way things were instead of asking for more. Dreams were just dreams and should stay just that. Every word Cole had said to me in the last weeks, every promise he had made, every gesture, every touch, every kiss had been a lie. I had seen the proof with my own eyes. Pictures that proved he had been lying, that he had been seeing Courtney. Her naked body in his office for some coffee-break action. His hands on her. And she was pregnant. Pregnant with Cole's baby. That hurt so much I had to curl up into a ball to keep the pain from consuming me.

I don't know how long I stayed like that, curled up in my car seat, crying and sobbing silently. I didn't even have the slightest idea how I ended up in my car. I was trying to escape into my head, to block everything out so the pain would go away, so I could be numb and not feel anything. But it didn't work. How could I be so unbelievably happy one second and completely devastated the next? My life was in shambles. In one short moment, I had lost both the love of my life and my best friend at the same time. I wouldn't be able to recover from this, I knew. I would never love again, could never trust again to let myself fall. My mother and all those people in our shitty town had been right.

I wasn't worth people's attention.

I didn't deserve to be loved.

Somehow, I was driving. I must have lost some time back there because I had no idea how I got here or where I was headed. My phone was ringing, but I didn't check to see who was calling me. There was nobody I wanted to talk to, nobody that could help me.

I was lost. So very lost.

Unsure of what to do next, I just kept driving for what must have been at least an hour. I stopped when I realized I was close to the beach. I loved the beach. The soft movement of the water against the sand could give me peace. I could sit there and just be, look out over the water and forget everything else. Yes. That was what I needed.

I parked my car in a deserted parking lot. It was the middle of the day, but too cold and windy for people to want to be at the beach at this time of year. I was grateful for that. It meant I would be left alone. Nobody would ask me if I was okay, nobody would try to interrupt my thoughts. I could sit in the sand, letting it run through my fingers, thinking of nothing but the feeling of the sand crystals on my skin until I was ready to face the facts.

Just like I had done so many times during my childhood.

Escape.

Cole

Fear so raw it threatened to cripple me; that's what I felt when I saw the elevator doors close, cutting me off from getting to Lizzy.

Fuck!

This was not happening! It couldn't be happening!

How the fuck did this happen?

The look on her face when she saw Courtney sitting on my desk... I couldn't think about it without the pain of it piercing my heart.

Betrayal and pain.

Then her eyes had gone dead, as had her voice. My sweet and fiery Lizzy was looking at me with dead eyes. I had seen her hurting before, lots of times throughout the years of her childhood and as a teenager. But never like this. Even when I had been an asshole to her that night at the bar, when my words had cut her deeply, she hadn't looked like she had a few seconds ago. She had looked at me like she was gone, like I had killed a part of her, a part of her soul, the light and fire in her eyes extinguished.

And it was all my fault.

"Fuck!" I shouted as I reached the elevator. I punched my fist against the wall beside the door, splitting open my knuckles. I watched the numbers indicating where she would get off. The parking garage. Shit! By the time I got down there, she could be anywhere. I had to find her and explain. Tell her that Courtney had been a problem for a while now, that she had been stalking and harassing me. I had to tell her how I had taken care of it.

Fuck!

I should have told her. Then all of this could have been prevented. The pain I had caused her because I had wanted to keep her out of it…

It was eating me alive.

I realized I was still holding the envelope Lizzy had flung at me before she ran. This must be important, maybe the reason why she would come to my office in the first place, because she wanted to show me something.

The first thing I saw was an ultrasound picture. Lizzy was pregnant? She had come here to share the most precious news with me and instead of that being one of the happiest moments in our lives she had seen another woman sitting naked on my desk?

Oh God!

That would make her feeling betrayed by me that much more painful. Elation about having a baby with her mixed with dread about not being able to fix this warred inside of me. I looked at the picture again more closely. And stopped short. Courtney's name was printed on the top right, as was a date.

Lizzy wasn't pregnant. Courtney was. And she had sent this to Lizzy to make her leave me. I took out the rest of the pictures and glanced at them. Photos of when she had stalked me. At the coffee shop, the restaurant and, fucking hell! Her lingerie clad body on my hood in the garage of this very building. I was going to kill her!

Fuck!

Lizzy had seen these and had come to me. I could only imagine what she must be thinking right now. That I had kept Courtney on the side. That I had lied to her this whole time. And I didn't blame her. The photos were compromising. They didn't show how I pushed Courtney away, how furious I was that she kept following and touching me. But still, Liz had come to me to show me the pictures and ask for an explanation instead of taking them at face value and running from me. This was a set up. Courtney must have known Lizzy would be on her way. And someone had been taking those photos of us. This whole thing was a set up from the start to break Lizzy and me apart.

Panic overcame me.

Panic and fury.

Fury at myself for underestimating the situation with Courtney, for letting it get so far that it hurt the one person whom I never wanted to hurt, whom it was my job to protect. And fury at the woman in my office, who had instigated this play to inflict the worst kind of pain on the woman I loved. She would pay. I would make sure she would pay dearly. But first, I had to find Lizzy to make things right.

I found the number I needed and made the call. It connected on the second ring.

"Yo."

"Max. Shit just hit the fan. Lizzy is gone. I need you to find her."

"Talk to me."

"It's Courtney. That fucking bitch had someone take pictures of those times I ran into her I told you about and sent them to Lizzy this morning in the hopes to make her believe I was cheating on her."

"Fucking hell."

"It gets worse. She included an ultrasound picture. Lizzy thinks Courtney is pregnant with my child."

"Is she?"

"No! It's not possible. The last time we had sex was over five months ago. There is no way that kid is mine! But Lizzy doesn't know that! Fuck!"

"Okay. Calm down. I'll run her plates, check her credit cards, we'll find her."

"It gets worse."

"Shit."

"She came to my office, I guess to show me the photos and ask for an explanation, and found Courtney sitting naked on my desk in front of me. That bitch had it all planned. She came into my office only a minute or so before Liz, dropped her coat on the floor, and was naked as a jailbird underneath. I was about to push her away and call security. I had my hands on her hips to do exactly that when the door opened and Lizzy saw us. Shit, Max! I need you to find her!"

"And I will. Where do you think she would go? Does she have any places where she would go to think or hide out? A friend? Family? Anything?"

I tried to think. Who would she go to? Where would she escape to?

"She has a friend at work who she's close to. Her name is Marie. Her best friend Katie is out of town, so she wouldn't have gone there. No family she would turn to. She had a thinking place back home, but I doubt she would go there. Too many bad memories in that town. Fuck! I don't know!" The panic was rising, making it impossible for me to think clearly. All I could see was that hideous look on Lizzy's face.

That and her dead eyes.

"I'll put an alert on her credit cards in case she uses them. I'll go to your house to check if she went home. You meet me at the shelter so we can talk to that friend of hers. See if she knows anything. I have a guy who can run a trace on cell phones and get him started on that, but it could take a while."

"Okay. I'll keep trying her cell. Maybe she'll pick up. I'll see you at the shelter. And Max, a heads up. I want you to destroy that bitch. Dig deep and use anything you can find on her. If you can't find anything, make shit up and throw it at her. I don't care what it costs. I want her to hurt."

"Consider it done. Out." I had dead air. I hung up and called Liz but got voicemail. I tried again. Voicemail again. I left a message.

"Please call me, baby. That baby isn't mine. The whole thing was a set up. I'll explain everything to you. There is nothing going on between Courtney and me. I can prove it to you. Please, Liz, call me so we can talk."

On my way back into my office I turned to my assistant. "Sam, I need you to clear my schedule for the rest of the day. There's a family emergency I have to take care of."

"Okay, Mr. Brooks."

"I'll let you know later today if I'll be back tomorrow." She nodded at me and started making calls. I would get flak for this. Today was an important day, but I didn't give a shit. All I cared about was getting to my girl and taking away her pain, bringing back the light to her eyes.

Courtney was still in my office, lounging on my couch, a self-satisfied smile on her face. Thankfully, she had put her coat back on.

"I see she's gone. That'll teach her not to go after my man." The fury was back in full force at hearing those words. "Now you and I can focus on our family. We'll set the wedding for next summer after I've had the baby. I don't want to look fat in the pictures." I got closer to her as she was getting up from the couch. The fury must have been clear on my face. Her smile was wavering. I didn't stop until we were almost nose-to-nose.

"You made a fatal mistake by going after the person I love. This, I will not forget. Prepare for a world of pain. Now, get out of my face." I turned away from her and, without another look at her, I gathered my things and left the office in search of my girl.

On my way to the shelter, I drove by the marina and the pier, places I knew Lizzy liked, but she wasn't there. I kept calling her cell, but she never answered. Max was already at the shelter when I pulled into the parking lot.

"Any news?" I asked him.

"Nothing yet. But it's only been a little over an hour. Nothing at your house. Doesn't look like she went back home. My guy is working on that trace. He'll call." I nodded then opened the door to the common room of the shelter. Marie was on the phone when we walked in, her eyes coming directly to me.

"Call me," she said into the phone before she hung up and asked me, "What is going on? Where is Liz? She ran out of here with tears in her eyes and isn't answering her phone. What happened?" She sounded concerned, which meant she had no clue where Liz was either.

Shit!

"I'm trying to find her. She misinterpreted a situation and ran without letting me explain. Do you have any idea where she would have gone?" Marie looked at me with narrowed eyes.

"What situation?"

"Marie, I don't have time—"

"What situation?" This came from Jesse, who was standing behind Marie, arms crossed on his chest. I had to give it to him, he looked scary for only being sixteen. He was protective of Lizzy. I had seen that the last time I had been here.

Taking a deep breath, I explained to them about what had been going on with Courtney as quickly as I could, how I had hired Max to get her off my back, and how she had set Lizzy and I up this morning. I didn't leave anything out. Not the photos, not the pregnancy claim, not my stupid decision of keeping Liz out of it and that leading to her believing Courtney's lies. When I was done, Marie was crying silently and Jesse looked like he was going to blow.

"Now, do you have any idea where she might have gone?"

"No, Cole. I don't know. She's closed up pretty tight about personal stuff," Marie said. Jesse shook his head.

"She likes to look at the stars," a timid voice said from the sofa against the wall. It was Chloe, Jesse's sister. Lizzy had told me about her, how they had bonded lately, how proud she was that Chloe was opening up to her. Jesse walked toward his sister and crouched in front of her.

"What do you mean, Chloe?"

"She told me about how she had this place, how when she was a child she would go there to escape her mother and clear her head or go into her head to not feel anything. She told me it wasn't healthy to try and bury your feelings, that eventually, those strong emotions would always fight their way back out." I closed my eyes and hung my head. I knew exactly what Chloe was talking about, had found her there time and time again.

"I don't think she would go back there, Chloe," I said.

"No, she wouldn't. She hasn't been there since she was seventeen. Some childhood friend had done something to make her hate that place, I don't know what exactly."

My heartbeat picked up at her words. She hated her cave? What happened? I was her only childhood friend. Had I done something to make her hate the only place she had always felt safe?

Chloe continued, pulling me out of my thoughts. "Anyways, she told me she likes to look at the stars now to calm herself down when her emotions and thoughts overwhelm her. And she likes the feeling of sand running through her fingers. She told me to find something or someplace where I can focus my thoughts, where I can forget about everything else around me and organize my thoughts and emotions when things get too much."

"The stars and sand. Where could she find that? It's the middle of the day. The planetarium? The science center?" Marie wondered out loud.

"The beach," I said. "She went to the beach."

Chapter 16

Lizzy

Eight years ago.
Lizzy is seventeen. Cole is nineteen.

I'm on my way to a party. Even though I'm a junior now, I usually don't go to these parties. I never get invited. Actually, this is the first party I've been invited to. So far, this year is shaping up to be the best ever, at least considering school. Cole has gone off to college in Boston, so at the end of the summer I had dreaded the next two years until I could follow him there. Then I met Katie; or rather she met me. She was new to our school and we'd become fast friends, something that is more than a little unusual for me. She lives on the rich side of town. That fact alone should have made her avoid me like the plague or, the other option, hate me instantly and make my life a living hell. Those were usually the only two reactions I got from people who know who my mother is, which is everyone in town.

At least when Cole was still here, I didn't have to worry so much about all the assholes and bitches at school. Though I never told him what happened when he wasn't in my immediate vicinity or worse, when he wasn't at school. I never told him how they would taunt me, especially the girls. How they would call me names and shove me. How the queen bee especially, whom he had incidentally hooked up with more than once, would attack me when no one but her posse was watching. I didn't want to become a burden to him. That was my biggest fear—that being my friend and protecting me would become too much for him and he would leave me in the dust and I would be all alone again.

I had dreaded the next two years without him at school, but at least my arch nemesis had gone off to college as well. Still, I hadn't looked forward to going to school without him there. Katie had made it easier for me. Much easier. She doesn't care that I'm from the wrong side of town, doesn't care who my mother is. From the moment she sat beside me during assembly on the first day of school and smiled at me brightly, she had treated me like nothing but a friend. It's new to me and I don't quite trust it yet, but I'm getting there. I like being around her, talking to her, laughing with her. I realized that having a girlfriend made me feel more relaxed, more normal. Being at school is easier now, less threatening. I'm not sure if it's my imagination, but people seem to treat me differently than they did last year. Girls talk to me now, and boys are smiling at me in the halls and sometimes Katie would tell me she caught them looking at me during class. I'm not quite sure what to do with that. I think she's misinterpreting.

The party I'm headed to is her party, kind of like a Welcome Party her parents are throwing for her. Cole is supposed to be there as well. It's Thanksgiving weekend and he said he would come down from Boston for the holiday. For weeks, I had been looking forward to seeing him again. I had turned seventeen in the summer. It wouldn't take long now until we could be together.

Only one more year.

Less than that even.

I walk faster, impatient to see him.

Katie lives just one street over from Cole's house, her house also backing onto the woods, so I know my way through the tress without needing a flashlight. I'm close to passing my cave when I overhear a couple making out. I try to make out the shapes in the darkness and realize that they are right there, just about twenty feet ahead, just a couple of feet away from my cave entrance. I had been so lost in thought that I had almost run into them. Not wanting to be rude, I try to skirt around them when the voices I hear make me freeze mid-step.

It's Cole.

And Amanda.

One of my classmates.

We are friends. Kind of. She's one of the girls who had started talking to me lately, sitting with Katie and me at lunch sometimes.

She's three weeks younger than me.

And Cole is making out with her right by my cave.

The cave where Cole had found me two weeks before my tenth birthday.

Our special spot.

In that moment, my whole life comes crashing down around me. Everything I had hoped for since I had met him was disappearing right before my eyes. My heart is in so much pain I can't breathe and sink down to the ground, wrap my arms around myself as tightly as I can, and try to shut it all out.

How could he do that to me?

What is happening?

It doesn't make any sense!

Here I thought that he had never made a move on me because I was too young and he was waiting for me to catch up to him. But that had been just silly old me hanging on to a dream that would never come true.

Clearly, he didn't have any romantic feelings for me. He's making out with one of my classmates, who is almost exactly my age, so clearly being with someone two years his junior is not a deterrent for him. It's just as all those girls had been saying all my life.

I'm a pathetic little girl whom Cole feels responsible for and nothing more.

I'm sitting on the ground for a long while, trying to be as quiet as possible, afraid that if I try to leave, they will hear me.

I can't face them.

Not like that.

Not while they are making out.

I would completely lose it.

No matter how hard I try, I can't shut out the noises they make, or their words as they start talking again.

"You sure Lizzy won't be mad at me? She really likes you, Cole," I hear Amanda ask in between kisses.

"Why would she be mad at you? Don't worry, sweetheart. Lizzy and I are just friends. She's like a little sister to me."

A knife straight through the heart.

That's what his words feel like.

The pain that I had thought couldn't get any worse multiplies by a million and explodes in my chest at hearing those words.

My whole body goes rock solid.

Everything around me disappears as I drown in anguish, grief, and heartache.

My heart is broken.

Obliterated.

Shattered into a million pieces.

I have experienced a lot of pain and hurt in my life, but I know that this is something that I will never completely recover from.

Those words and what they mean will be burned into my soul forever.

I don't hear anything or see anything after that. I try not to feel anything either. I have to shut it down. I'm good at shutting down my feelings, have had seventeen years of practice. It takes me a while, but I eventually manage and bury everything deep down inside me while I focus on the stars above me.

They are pretty.

So very pretty and peaceful and quiet.

And mesmerizing.

Exactly what I need to get myself under control.

I must have sat there for a long while because when I finally come out of my trance, Cole and Amanda are gone. I have no choice but to still go to the party. Katie is expecting me. And so is Cole. As much as I don't want to see him right now, I know that if I don't show up, he'll come after me, probably worried I got waylaid by my mother or one of her friends. And anyways, I don't have much of an alternative. Going home means locking myself in my room and listening to the disgusting noises coming from the living room since my mother was having yet another man over. No, that would be too much right now. I can't deal with anything else tonight.

So I get up and trudge the rest of the way until I can see

the lights through the trees. The party is in full swing. The crowd of people in Katie's house is spilling out into the backyard, where a big campfire is blazing.

As good a spot as any to sit down and pretend.

A few boys and girls are sitting there already, talking, laughing, drinking.

I sit down across from them and keep to myself as I stare into the fire.

Lucky me, Cole finds me only a few minutes later. He immediately knows that something is wrong and keeps asking me what happened and if I'm okay.

No, I'm definitely not okay. But I will never tell him that I heard him with Amanda.

That will make me look even more pathetic than I already am.

He sticks close to me for the rest of the night and walks me home after a few hours. When we say goodnight, he holds my face in his hands and looks deep into my eyes. I almost can't stand that the hands that only hours ago touched Amanda are now touching my skin. I can't hide the pain in my eyes that comes with that thought, and being so close, he sees it and swears,

"Fuck! Don't listen to her, Lizzy. She's a loser who doesn't deserve to have you as her daughter. Less than two years and you're out of here and joining me in Boston. You promised me you wouldn't let anyone break you. Don't let her get to you now." He assumes that something happened with my mother and her friends and that's why I'm so upset.

I don't tell him any different.

I nod, say goodnight, and head inside, leaving him standing on the sidewalk. I intend on heading to bed and trying to forget all about this day.

I should be so lucky.

Before I can make it to the stairs, my mother calls from the living room. I hang my head and sigh then go and face the music. If I don't, she'll just come after me until she's done spewing her venom. Better take it now and escape after. It's the lesser evil.

When I turn the corner I'm surprised to see that she's alone. What I'm not surprised to see are her glassy eyes. She's high. And the empty bottle on the floor tells me that there's a high chance she's drunk, too.

"You better get out while you can," she slurs, her eyes pointed to the window.

What? Is she kicking me out now?

"That boy will never be what you want him to be. The likes of us aren't good enough for the likes of him. Get out now before it's too late and he breaks your heart beyond repair."

Her words hit too close to home.

I flinch but say nothing.

Her eyes come to me. She's having trouble focusing on my face, but when she does my body locks at what I see.

Pain. Raw and deep.

So raw and deep it takes my breath away.

"Trust me, girl. I know what I'm talking about," she whispers as tears well in her eyes.

I take a hesitant step toward her to...I don't know what. But my movement snaps her out of her sadness and she narrows her eyes at me before I can figure it out.

"Don't. I don't need your pity. I don't need anything from you. I wish you had never been born. Things would have been so much easier if it weren't for you. You ruined everything."

I'm used to those words. I hear them on a daily basis. But tonight, after everything that's happened and after seeing real emotion on my mother's face for the first time in my life, an emotion that made me want to comfort her, they hurt and cut me deeper than ever before.

She's not done.

"You're the reason I am like this. You're the reason I'm nothing more than trash. I take it back. Go fall in love with your boy. Pin all your hopes and dreams on him. Then watch as he breaks your heart."

Too late. He's already broken my heart.

I flinch again.

My mother narrows her eyes on me. "I see." Then an evil smile spreads on her face. "Maybe now you'll stop pretending you're so much better than me. You're just like me. Here's some motherly advice. Build walls. High walls. And never let anyone get close. Not one soul in this world will ever do you any favors. You're not worth it. Just like your mother." The bitterness in her voice makes my stomach churn and bile rise in my throat.

She gives me one last disgusted look before she shakes her head in dismissal and walks into the kitchen.

I close my eyes and fight the tears, then I head upstairs and lock myself in my room.

That night I don't sleep.

I stay awake, staring out my window into the dark night for hours and hours.

By the time the sun comes up, I've made my decision.

I need to be strong.

I will not end up like my mother.

Yes, I lost a lot last night. Cole broke my heart. But I still have his friendship.

He's my family.

My only family.

And I will not let this come between us.

Though, I would never speak to Amanda again.

I would also never go back to my cave.

From that night on, I would use the stars at night to give me peace.

Chapter 17

Lizzy

I didn't know how long I sat in the sand, cuddled up in my winter coat, arms around my knees, my fingers playing with the sand as I stared out at the water. It must have been a few hours at least. My body was freezing, but I didn't feel it. Dusk was coming soon and I'd have to decide what to do for the night. Should I go home and face the music or should I check into a hotel and give myself the night to think some more? I had called Marie a while ago to let her know I wouldn't be back before tomorrow. She had wanted to talk, had asked me what was going on, where I was, but I hadn't been ready to talk to anyone quite yet.

My mind was still wandering. I had calmed down quite a bit since I'd come down here, but my heart was still hurting like hell and I hadn't come up with a plan of what to do next. Nothing made sense. I knew Cole better than anyone. Yes, he had been a pig, going through women like water, but he had never cheated. He had always told them what they signed up for. He wasn't a liar or a cheater. So why had he lied to me? It was clear that he had met up with Courtney a few times. It was proven by those pictures she had sent me. And he had been working late a lot, so there could have potentially been a lot of opportunities for him to cheat. I knew how it worked. Still, I couldn't wrap my head around him betraying me like that. He loved me. I knew that. The way he was with me could not be faked. Nobody could act like that for such a long period of time. It was impossible. Especially for someone like Cole—a complete straight-talker. So what had happened? And why was she in his office? Naked on his desk? With his hands on her hips? He wouldn't be able to explain that away. I knew what I had seen. And then there was the pregnancy. That photo definitely wasn't a fake. I didn't know anything about ultrasound pictures, but it looked like she wasn't very far along. You couldn't make out more than a little blob in that picture. The thought of them having a child together brought the tears back. I wiped at them angrily, tired of being a sorry mess, of hurting and being frustrated. So many emotions ran through me I couldn't seem to decide on just one.

Footsteps were coming down the beach behind me. Probably someone out for a late afternoon stroll along the waves. If I were living by the sea, I would come out here for a walk every day. Maybe even get a dog that I could watch play in the waves. The footsteps stopped right behind me, and I immediately knew who it was. I closed my eyes, trying to prepare myself for what was about to come. Cole's proximity made the pain and the confusion worse, like when you're really sad and someone gives you a hug to console you, but actually makes it worse by touching you and you can't hold the tears back and dissolve into sobs. I kept my eyes closed in an effort to keep the tears at bay. I could feel him rounding me and kneeling in the sand right in front of me. His hands cupped my cheeks, the physical contact making it impossible for me to hold back the tears any longer. They ran freely down my face, getting his hands all wet in the process.

"Baby," Cole breathed in an agonized whisper, "please, look at me."

I shook my head and kept on silently crying. I knew I was being a coward, but I knew I couldn't look at him yet. His thumbs started moving on my cheeks, trying to keep up with the tears that were rolling down my face.

"How did you find me?" I asked in a broken voice.

Cole's hands twitched at hearing my voice. He took a deep breath before answering me. "I hired a private investigator slash badass a few weeks ago to help me with the Courtney situation," my whole body flinched at the mention of Courtney's name, making his hands tighten on my face before he continued. "His name is Max. He found you. Put a trace on your cell phone and located you when you called Marie." He had hired a private investigator? I opened my eyes. Cole gave me a small smile that didn't quite reach his eyes, which were sad besides a whole lot of other things. I could see pain clearly written there, as well as fear and remorse. And anger. There was a lot of that, too.

"Are you angry with me?" Don't ask me why I wanted to know. I shouldn't care if he was angry with me. He was the one who had lied to me.

"No, honey, I'm not angry with you," another flinch from me and another tightening of hands from him. "I'm angry at myself for not talking to you, for making it possible for someone to come between us, to give them an opening and make you believe their lies. I'm so sorry my actions caused you so much pain." I kept looking at him quietly, trying to understand what he'd just said, trying to make his words fit in with what I had seen today. What were lies and what was the truth?

He must have seen the confusion in my eyes. "Let me explain everything from the start," he continued in a quiet voice. I nodded. I needed to know, even if his words would possibly only hurt me more. I needed to know what reality I was going to have to face.

"Remember when we went away that first weekend and I told you about Courtney calling and texting me non-stop?" I nodded again. "I agreed to meet her at a bar, so I could make it clear once and for all that I didn't want her, that I was committed to you, to our future. I thought if I told her face-to-face, she would get it. I wasn't nice about it, was straight up and to the point, but she wouldn't listen. After that meeting, she kept contacting me, but I ignored all her calls and messages. That's when I started running into her. At the coffee shop. At a restaurant where I had lunch with one of the company partners. In the parking garage. That's when the photos you saw today were taken. She must have a partner who was taking those photos. It was all a set up. I didn't meet with her in any of those places, certainly didn't ask her to undress for me in the parking garage of my company," his voice was getting agitated and he had to close his eyes for a moment to get his anger under control. "Liz, baby, I swear to God there was nothing going on between Courtney and me behind your back. I wouldn't do that to you. Not ever." His eyes were pleading with me to believe him. And I did. I couldn't help it and maybe I was being stupid, but I knew that he wasn't a cheater. At my nod, Cole closed his eyes in relief and kissed my forehead. "Thank you," he whispered there.

"What about the baby?" I asked him, my voice breaking on that last word.

"It's not mine. Even if she really is pregnant, which I doubt by the way, there is no chance I'm the father." How could he be so sure? I had to know.

"When...?" I couldn't finish the question. It hurt too much. But Cole knew what I was asking.

"June. My parents' anniversary party," he answered. June. It was November now, which meant she would be five months pregnant by now if Cole were the father. That ultrasound picture was not the picture of a five-month-old fetus. And she would be showing by now. She definitely did not have a baby bump. Which meant that Cole was telling the truth. He was not going to have a baby with that woman. Relief washed through my body. Relief so sweet that I tipped my head back to look at the sky and my breath left me in one big whoosh.

"Oh, thank God," I whispered.

"Yeah," Cole agreed with me on a chuckle.

I tipped my face back down to his to see a small smile there. Then his face sobered and his eyes went serious again.

"Now, about what you saw this morning in my office," my body tightened again at his reminder of seeing his hands on her naked body. He moved his face closer to mine so that all I could see were his eyes boring into mine. "I know what it probably looked like. But you have to believe me, Liz. I only had my hands on her to push her away. It was stupid. I should have just gotten up and called security. But she surprised me. I didn't think. She must have known you were on your way. She wanted you to see us and make the wrong assumptions. It was all part of her plan to drive you away from me."

"Why did you even let her come in?"

"I didn't. Sam thought she was you. Courtney told her she was my girlfriend and wanted to surprise me with coffee. Sam had never met you and had been instructed to let you through if you ever showed up at my office. I was on the phone and focused on my screen when she walked in. I didn't realize it was her right away, assuming it was Sam bringing me my coffee. The next thing I saw was her naked body in front of me. I was about to push her away when the door opened again and you stood there. I panicked. When I saw that look on your face...God, baby, I will never forget that look for as long as I live." He paused and closed his eyes. Pain was written all over his face. I believed him. Call me stupid, but I did. And it made sense. Courtney had always been a crazy bitch. Her recent actions showed that she was probably crazier than I had suspected. What did she think she would accomplish with this? Aside from driving us apart? What could she possibly gain from this?

I reached for him and he welcomed me into his arms, holding me to him as tightly as he possibly could. I had been so stupid. Instead of running away from him, I should have talked to him, let him explain. This whole thing hadn't made sense to me from the start. But Courtney had timed it just right, making me insecure by sending me those pictures and then not giving me a chance to talk to Cole about it before she hit me with another blow. That vindictive bitch.

"I'm so sorry, Cole. I shouldn't have run," I cried in his arms.

Cole tightened his arms around me. "You have nothing to be sorry for. I handled that situation wrong. If I had talked to you before when she was following me around, none of this would have happened. It was my fault. I underestimated her and gave her the opening she needed to infuse her poison. Don't you dare apologize."

I pulled my head out of his neck and looked at him through my wet eyes.

"I love you. So much," I hiccoughed. "I came to talk to you about those pictures. I didn't believe that you would cheat on me. But when I saw you...with your hands on her naked...it hurt so much...it was tearing me apart. I didn't think. All I wanted was to get away. So I ran."

"I know, baby. Don't think about it anymore." He kissed me. Deep and long. He kissed me like it was our last kiss. Or our first. As if my lips on his were all he would ever need to survive. And I kissed him back with everything I had, poured all my love and need for him into that kiss. Promising him that I would never lose faith in his love for me again. When he ended the kiss, he kept his mouth on mine, mingling our breaths, and stared into my eyes.

"I'm not blaming you for needing to get away. I get it. But I gotta say this. Don't ever leave me like that again, Liz. Not telling anybody where you went, not answering your phone. The past few hours have been torture, knowing you were in so much pain and not being able to do anything about it, not knowing where to find you. I thought I had lost you forever."

"I promise."

He nuzzled my neck. "You know, when I first saw that ultrasound picture, I thought it was you who was pregnant."

"You did?"

"I did. And I was happy about it. I want that with you, Liz. I want you pregnant with my baby. I want to marry you and have a family. The sooner the better." For the millionth time today, I stopped breathing. Then my heart inflated and expanded, filling my whole body with warmth. Tears welled in my eyes again, but this time they were happy tears.

"Are you asking me to marry you?" I asked. There was a little bit of teasing in my voice, just in case he had gotten ahead of himself and needed an out.

"I am. Marry me. Please." His face was open and loving, as was his voice. He was serious. One hundred percent serious. My heart surged and expanded in my chest as tears started to blur my vision.

"Yes," was all I could get out before his lips crushed down on mine and he kissed me again, this time for a lot longer.

"I want you to be my wife as soon as possible. Spring, or better yet, Christmas," he said when he broke the kiss. I burst out laughing but stopped abruptly when I realized he was again one hundred percent serious.

"Are you crazy?" I asked. "It's cold and gross in December."

"Then we'll go somewhere else. How about Hawaii or St. Croix? It's warm enough there." That sounded fantastic, actually. A destination wedding at Christmas. In paradise. Perfect. Almost too perfect. I opened my mouth to ask him if he was absolutely sure about this, but couldn't get a word out before his hand covered my mouth.

"Uh, uh. Not happening. You are not letting your insecurities overwhelm you. Not when it concerns us. Not ever. Not as long as I'm around. Which, since you agreed to be mine legally, will be until you die."

I giggled then smiled brightly at him when he removed his hand. "Okay. Deal. We'll get married some place warm. But we'll have to fly out all our friends."

He chuckled. "Nothing would make me happier, love."

"Well, you can afford it. With your grandfather leaving you all those millions last year," I teased him.

His eyebrows shot up in surprise. "Who told you about that?"

"Sophie did during Thanksgiving dinner. I was going to bust your chops about not telling me, but then I realized it doesn't really matter. I knew you were rich so what's a few more millions?" He threw his head back and this time, he was the one who burst out laughing. I had never heard him sound this carefree and happy. It was a beautiful sight to see. Still laughing, Cole picked me up. I threw my arms and legs around him monkey-style and he carried me like this all the way back to the parking lot.

Standing by the side of his car was a big guy in what I guessed was his mid or late forties, with wide shoulders and legs like tree stumps. He had his arms crossed on his wide chest and was watching our approach, his dark eyes lit with amusement. Even though he was huge and a little scary-looking, I liked him instantly.

"Liz, meet Max. Max, this is my fiancée Liz," he grinned proudly at calling me his fiancée. It was cute and deserved another kiss.

"Fiancée, huh? Congratulations." Max said through his own grin as he slapped Cole on the back in male approval. Then he looked at me and his face became serious for a second. "You okay, doll?" I was shocked by the concern in his voice. This guy didn't even know me, but it seemed like he wanted to make sure I was all right.

"Yeah, Max. I'm okay," I assured him. Then I scowled as I remembered the predicament that brought us here. "I'll be more okay, though, once I get to go a round with that bitch and beat the shit out of her." Max's eyes turned back to amused and he lifted his chin at Cole.

"Fiery, this one. Gonna have your hands full."

"Oh, don't I know it," Cole said like he wouldn't want it any other way. I gave him a big grin. He started walking toward my car.

"Are we going home?" I asked him when he put me on my feet by the passenger door.

"Yeah. Unless you want to spend the night here?"

"No. I want to go home and celebrate. And I think I have some phone calls to make on the way home and calm some people down."

"That's probably a good idea." His face turned serious and tentative when he said, "You know, Chloe gave us the idea that you would be at the beach. So when you called Marie earlier, we were already on our way down here. We just weren't sure which beach you would stop at."

"How did Chloe know?"

Something close to sadness and remorse flitted through his eyes. "She said you told her about how you liked the feel of sand running through your fingers while watching the stars. I knew about the sand, of course, but the stars were news to me. Then I remembered how happy and calm you were when I took you to the cottage that weekend and thought that's where you would go." I smiled at him and kissed him. When I pulled back there was still that hint of sadness in his eyes.

"What's wrong?" I asked.

"Chloe also mentioned that you told her about your cave and the fact that we probably wouldn't find you there, because you have hated it since you were seventeen, when your childhood friend did something to make you never go there again." His eyes were boring into mine and I stiffened. "Care to explain that?" He pushed me when I didn't say anything.

"Not really," I whispered. I had been through the emotional gamut in the past few hours. I didn't particularly want to relive one of the worst memories of my teenage years.

"Lizzy." Cole's tone was a gentle warning.

I sighed. Then I closed my eyes and murmured, "The night of the party, Thanksgiving weekend my junior year. I was there in the woods when you made out with Amanda. I heard everything you said."

Now it was Cole's body that went stiff. I opened my eyes

and saw that his were shrouded with confusion. Then I saw it click in his mind as he put the pieces together and he remembered.

"I was a dick, Liz. A horny dick, who only had one thing on his mind. I didn't mean anything I said. I've never considered you my sister. Never. Not for one second. It was just easier to pretend I did, so it wasn't so hard to keep my hands off of you." His voice was firm and sincere. Still, the pain of hearing him say those words had been with me for so long it was hard to let it go just like that.

I bit my lip. "Did you—"

"No," Cole interrupted me, his arms around me giving me a small shake. "I didn't have sex with her. I couldn't go through with it. All I did was kiss her. I swear." I nodded, grateful to finally know that nothing more had happened between them. Those thoughts had kept me up at night at that time more than I cared to admit. But I had to explain to him why seeing him with Amanda had been such a big blow, why it had led to me never wanting to sit in my cave again.

"Before that night, I always thought that you were just waiting for me to catch up with you in age, that you were just waiting for me to become legal, that that was the reason why you never made a move on me. But after I saw you with her...in our special spot...after I heard what you said..."

Cole groaned and rested his forehead against mine. "Turns out I've been an even bigger jerk to you for all these years than I ever thought possible." He leaned back and caught my eyes. "Even back then I was in love with you. I've always been in love with you, Liz. From the first moment you looked at me with those sad, green eyes, I have been yours. Completely and absolutely. I didn't think I'd ever be good enough for you. That's the only reason I never claimed you as mine. The only reason I screwed around. I was young and stupid. So fucking stupid. Causing you all this pain. I promise you, baby, from now on there won't be any more secrets between us. Ever. I won't keep anything from you. I will always share my feelings and thoughts with you. You are my first priority. Always. Forever."

My heart melted at his words and I kissed him as tears were yet again running down my cheeks.

"No more crying, baby. I can't stand it when you cry," he murmured against my lips.

"But these are good tears," I argued.

"Doesn't matter. No more tears for at least three weeks. You can cry again when you walk toward me on our wedding day."

"So bossy and arrogant."

"That's right. And don't pretend you don't like it." Before I could argue, Cole slammed his mouth back down on mine and effectively shut me up. When he pulled back he searched my eyes. "You okay now?"

"More than okay." I touched his lower lip with the tip of my finger. "Thank you for coming after me and setting my head straight. I was having some trouble putting it all into perspective."

"Anytime and anything for you, baby. Never forget that." We kissed for a while longer until Max cleared his throat loudly, making me giggle and Cole growl.

"Let's get you home," he whispered against my lips, then gave me a gentle slap on my behind and guided me towards the car.

Chapter 18

Cole

Lying in our bed with Lizzy's dead weight snuggled into me, the events of the day ran though my head over and over again. It all worked out in the end, but for a few hours there I hadn't been sure if Liz would believe me or if she was too hurt to even listen. Courtney's games and lies could have taken away everything I now lived for. Instead of being happily engaged to the woman I love, I could be lying in this bed alone, worrying about her, knowing I might never get a chance at happiness again. The guilt of causing Liz pain still churned in my stomach. Guilt at having been a complete and total moron this past decade, at not claiming what was mine, but instead screwing around and hurting both Liz and myself by denying us happiness together, at building a life together. If I had gone after what I wanted years ago, none of this would have happened. I wouldn't have hooked up with Courtney at all. Or anyone for that matter. Liz would have been my one and only and I would have been hers. And to top it off, I went and almost blew it all to shit when she was finally mine by letting my past interfere with my present and both our futures.

Guilt.

It's a terrible thing.

I would move heaven and earth to make up for my mistakes, for failing to protect the little girl I had fallen for when I had first laid eyes on her when I was twelve years old and she was ten, the girl who became the most beautiful woman inside and out and was now my lover, who held my heart and my soul, who had the power to break me. Today I realized that that kind of power went both ways. Unbeknownst to myself, I had almost used that power.

Fucking hell!

That look on her face...I hadn't been joking when I told Liz I would never forget it. It would haunt me for the rest of my life. Being responsible for causing Lizzy's eyes to go dead, no matter for how long, for making her look like her whole world had just crumpled around her and she would never find her way back out of the ruins, would haunt me for the rest of my life.

And her tears.

God! Those awful and devastating tears.

Thinking about it now made my heart ache for her. From now on, she wouldn't be shedding any more tears if I could help it. Unless they were happy tears, like when I asked her to marry me. Or when I slid my ring on her finger. Those tears I could definitely live with. From now on, I would make it my mission to save my girl from any more sorrow.

Only smooth sailing from here on out.

Before we had gone home, I had told Max that I wanted this issue resolved before Liz and I got married. Nothing would interfere with giving my girl my name and making her officially mine. I had decided that after that, we would start making babies and building a family right away. I didn't want or need anything or anyone to hinder our happily ever after.

Max had ensured me he would start digging right away. He had enlisted his hacker buddy's help and they were both going to find out who helped Courtney in her efforts to destroy our lives and would dig up any dirt they could find on both Courtney and her unknown partner. Once we figured out who that was, I would take pleasure in turning the tables and destroying their lives, making sure they would never touch ours again. At some point, Liz would need an opportunity to get her licks in with Courtney. I think she needed to have an outlet to vent her frustration and anger, and what better way to overcome those emotions than directing them at the person who had caused them? I would stand at the sidelines and happily cheer her on when she took on Courtney.

My face spread into a grin at thinking how sexy she would look when she got her power back by kicking Courtney's ass, under my careful watch, of course. My future wife was hot always, but she was something else when she was riled up. I was definitely looking forward to that.

My future wife.

The sound of that made me put today's troubles out of my mind. Instead, I thought about her face when she got a first glimpse of the ring I put on her finger as soon as we got home. I had bought her a ring after our first weekend together and had kept it in my nightstand since then, not wanting to overwhelm her after how she had reacted to me wanting to buy us a house. I wouldn't have waited much longer, was impatient to put a ring on her finger so that everyone would see she was taken. It might make me a Neanderthal, but I didn't really give a shit. Having my ring on her finger would scare at least a few of those asswipes who wanted what was mine off from making a play for her, and in turn would make me ending up with assault charges less certain. Showing her the ring and then later, sliding it on her finger, had given me peace, had made my heart settle and a feeling of rightness spread in my gut.

"When did you get this?" she had asked.

"Does it matter?"

"No, not really. But I'm curious as to how long you've had this for. What, you've had this sitting in your nightstand, waiting for the right moment to give this to me for the whole not even two months we've been together?"

My lips had twitched, but I'd stayed silent and watched as her eyes grew wide.

"You have, haven't you?" she asked in an astonished whisper. I had stayed silent and kept looking at her.

"You're crazy, you know that?"

That's when I had broken my silence. "Baby, I keep telling you. I've been yours since you first laid eyes on me, which in return means that you've been mine since then, too. It might have taken me a while to get my head out of my ass, but I know what I want and what I want is you and me, together forever, raising our babies in this house. And I want that as soon as possible."

Lizzy's lips were twitching. "It might have taken you a while?" she asked, teasing me, her eyes glittering.

"Yeah." She shook her head. Then, "You want babies as soon as possible?" The mirth had left her expression and I saw trepidation creep in. Deciding to cut off her panic attack or massive fit—I wasn't quite sure which to expect—before it had a chance to hit her, I gently but firmly grabbed her face with both my hands and vowed, "I will love you forever and I know you feel the same for me. You and I will be the best parents any child could ever wish for. We both had shitty cards dealt to us in the parent department, so we know exactly how not to be. You will be the most compassionate and understanding and caring mother any woman could dream of being, and I will be the most supportive father. We'll both be there for our children, always, I have no doubt about that." I searched her face. The trepidation was less, but it wasn't gone completely. So I kept talking, "And you know what else?"

"What?" she asked when I didn't go on.

"I can't wait to see you heavy with our first child. You take my breath away always, as soon as I so much as think about you, but to imagine you pregnant with our baby...I can't imagine anything more beautiful."

The tears had come again then. The happy kind that made her eyes glitter with joy and excitement and love. That's when I had pulled the ring out of its box.

"When did you get this?" she went back to her original question.

I grinned at her. Of course she wouldn't let this go. "A while ago," I replied as I started to slide the ring on her finger.

"How long a while ago?" I chuckled at her persistence.

"After our weekend at the cottage," I said quietly while looking into her eyes. They grew big and round at my words, making me chuckle again. I lifted her hand and laid a kiss on the ring that was now decorating her third finger while my eyes stayed glued to hers. Her face grew even softer at my gesture.

"You knew then?" she whispered in amazement.

"I've known all my life, Liz. I've just been too stubborn to admit it." Her tears started running down her face in earnest then and I leaned in to kiss them away.

"It's beautiful, Cole," she breathed when she looked down at her hand in mine, at the vintage piece of jewelry sitting on her third finger. I knew it would look perfect on her. I couldn't resist and played with the bottom of her ring, assuring myself that this was really happening.

"Beautiful," I agreed, but I wasn't looking at the ring. I was looking at her. I started kissing her with purpose then and proceeded to show her how beautiful I exactly thought she was to me.

Feeling her warm body pressed to mine, listening to her soft breathing, exhausted after our long love making session, knowing this would be my future until I died, I fell into a contented and deep sleep.

The next morning I got up at the crack of dawn. I couldn't skip out on work again, but before I had to leave, Lizzy needed to be filled in on the Courtney situation and what I had Max do to resolve the issue once and for all.

No more secrets.

I walked into the bedroom with a coffee for each of us and placed them on my nightstand before I slid back under the blankets. I softly kissed and touched her very sensitive back until she started stirring and grumbling. Smiling to myself at her morning grouchiness, I gently coaxed her from sleep.

"Baby, wake up."

"Sleepy. Very sleepy," she mumbled into her pillow. My fiancée was adorable. I kept at her.

"Liz, honey, I need you to wake up. Coffee's ready." That got her attention. She slightly lifted her head and turned it in my direction, eyes still resistant to open fully.

"Coffee?" she asked hopefully.

"Yeah, baby. It's right here." I kissed her nose, then her forehead, then sat up to reach for her mug and held it close enough for her to smell its aroma. Her eyes slowly opened, then focused on the cup, and her hand reached out while she started sitting up enough to take a sip.

"I should agree to marry you more often if this is the treatment I get."

Very funny.

"Sorry to disappoint you, baby, but I only intend to get married once. To you. So you agreeing last night means I will never ask that question again. Though, I wouldn't mind you saying 'yes' to me without a fight or argument more often."

"I don't argue." I raised my eyebrows at that ridiculous statement. "Much," she amended. I chuckled and reached for my own coffee.

"Why are we up so early?"

"I've got to go to work soon. No way I can skip out again today," I stopped when I saw Lizzy's lips turning into a pout. I couldn't resist kissing them. "I wish I could stay in bed with you for the rest of my life, but unfortunately, we've got important things to do today."

"Yeah? What is that?"

"You have to start planning a destination wedding. Decide where you want to go and make a list of people you want to invite. I'll give you Sam's number and she'll help you with the arrangements."

Liz smiled a bright smile at me. "I like that plan."

"Good. I'll get in touch with Max today to see where he's at with the Courtney situation. But before I do that I need to fill you in on exactly what has been going on and what we're planning on doing. I've learned my lesson. No more secrets that can lead to misunderstandings and unnecessary hurt and disappointment."

"Okay." I could tell that she wasn't looking forward to

listening to me reiterate the details of Courtney's actions, but she agreed that she needed to know everything to avoid further confusion and misconceptions. So I told her about every single encounter I had with Courtney after I had told her to lose my number.

Every word that was spoken, every unwanted and unwelcomed touch, every threat.

How I hired Max to get rid of her, what he said to scare her away and what exactly had happened yesterday morning.

Every hurtful and ugly detail.

Then I went on telling her that I had asked Max to dig deep and find anything he could on Courtney, anything we could use to throw back at her, and if he couldn't find anything, to make stuff up. That I wanted her life ruined. I also wanted the life ruined of the person who helped her, who took the photos of us, and who must have kept an eye out to make sure the timing yesterday morning was as perfect as it was.

"Are you sure all that is really necessary?"

"Absolutely. I will not have anything or anyone trying to take you away from me ever again. Getting rid of Courtney in a way that she is going to stay gone is absolutely necessary. I underestimated her once. That's not gonna happen again."

"Okay. I'm just as pissed as you are, if not more. Courtney has been a pain in my ass since she knew I existed. I have no idea why she always had it out for me, but believe me, she has not made my life easy until the day I left that town. She needs to learn her lesson. Definitely. But destroying her life? I think that's going a bit far."

"Baby, after everything she's done, do you really think she is going to give up? That stunt she pulled took a lot of thought, not to say time and determination. She's like a dog with a bone. She won't stop until she gets what she wants.

Crazy bitch still believes that I will come around and make a life with her. She chose this path and went after the woman I love. Now she has to suffer the consequences." No way was I going to back down. The time for mercy was gone. "I love you, baby. We're building a future together and nobody is going to interfere with that. I won't let them. Anyone who tries will have to live with the consequences."

Liz was studying me with an assessing look on her face. She was clearly working through something in her head. Then she came to a decision and nodded. "Okay, I see you have to do this. And if I'm being honest with myself, I love you even more for wanting to protect our future so fiercely. I'll support you in your plan, but I want to be in the loop. I want to know what Max finds and what you're planning on doing so I know what to expect. Don't keep me in the dark. And just saying, if she approaches me, I will kick her ass, if you're around or not."

I pulled her into my side and kissed her temple in gratitude.

"Thank you, baby. You have my permission to kick her ass if the opportunity arises, but please try and do it when I'm with you." I said on a squeeze, "I want to watch."

She giggled. "Of course, you do. Kinky bastard. I'll do my best to get you first row tickets to the showdown at O.K. Corral." Her eyes were smiling at me over the rim of her coffee mug as she took another sip. I burst out laughing then kissed her on the forehead while still trying to control my hilarity and murmured, "God, I love you."

It was time for me to take a shower and get a move on if I didn't want to be late for work. Sam had rescheduled all my meetings for today, starting with the first one right at seven.

"Care for company?" Liz asked me, anticipation and playful seduction clear in her voice. Another reason why she was so absolutely perfect for me. She didn't take herself too seriously, always made me laugh. My sexy, playful, fiery, and stubborn as hell soon-to-be wife would keep me on my toes for the rest of my life.

I couldn't wait.

"It's gotta be a quick in and out for me, baby. I'm already running behind. You sure you're up to it?" I teased her over my shoulder, my eyes hot on her as I got rid of my pajama pants on the way to the bathroom to give her a show I knew she wouldn't be able to resist. Cocky, but true. Sure enough, my pants hadn't completely hit the floor before I heard her throwing back the covers. The quick footsteps of her naked feet as they patted on the hardwood floor after me betrayed her eagerness. I smiled to myself. My greedy little minx. What I didn't expect was her jumping me. Literally.

"I can do quick. Question is, can you?" She asked as she nibbled on my neck after jumping on my back and having wound her arms and legs around me. Her unexpected impact made me stumble toward the shower, laughing. "Oh, Liz, you have no idea." That started an interesting competition that I swore to myself would be repeated at other locations throughout the house.

I was stepping out of the elevator when my phone rang. I checked the display. Max. I answered on the second ring.

"Max," I greeted.

"Cole. Got some interesting news. Derrick dug deep and found something you'll both want to know immediately. It shines some light on why that bitch has gone off the rails and is after Lizzy the way she is. It's a shocker, but this whole thing isn't really about your irresistible hotness or your money. At least not completely. We need a meet. By that I mean you, Lizzy, Derrick, and me. Today."

"All right. We'll have to meet at lunch. Meet me at my office at noon. I'll get Liz to join us here."

"Good." Dead air. I was impatient to know what this Derrick guy had found. It sounded like Courtney's issues went deeper than just plain jealousy or crazy possessiveness. I called Liz right away to let her know Max had some news for us already and needed to see the both of us.

"That was quick," she said, surprise in her voice.

"It better be. I pay him enough."

"You have any idea what he meant? What he could have found?"

"I have no clue, baby, but we'll know soon and then we can deal with her." Silence on the other end. "Liz?" I called her name. "Something wrong?"

"No. I don't know. I don't have a good feeling about this, Cole. She's always hated me. I thought it was because she was jealous of our friendship and felt threatened, but if it's not about that..."

"We'll get to the bottom of this, baby. I promise."

She sighed. "I know."

"So I'll see you here at noon?"

"I'll bring lunch."

"You don't have to. I can tell Sam—"

"No, I want to. I have a craving for Chinese and the place just down the street makes the best Lemon Chicken in Boston. I'll bring enough for a hulking P.I. and a nerdy computer geek as well."

I chuckled. "What makes you think Derrick is a nerdy computer geek?"

"Gut feeling." I chuckled again.

"All right, baby. I'll see you in a few hours."

"See you then."

"And Liz?"

"Yeah?"

"I love you."

"I love you too," she whispered and I hung up, smiling to myself as I walked toward my office.

"Glad to see you're in a better mood today," I heard Sam call to me and looked up. I grinned. She smiled at me. "I assume that everything worked itself out?"

"It did. Well, most of it. The important parts. Other parts are still a mystery, but they'll be resolved soon."

"Glad to hear it."

"Got a job for you." Her eyebrows went up.

"I thought I already had one?"

"Funny. Very funny." I had stopped at her desk when I announced, "Need you to help Liz plan our wedding." Saying those words brought an instant grin back to my face.

"Ah, that explains the shit-eating grin. Tell me the specifics."

I did.

Then I watched, amused, as Sam grumbled under her breath while she picked up the phone and started making phone calls, presumably getting prices and ideas on sunny and tropical destination weddings.

Chapter 19

Lizzy

Loaded with bags of Chinese food, I stumbled off the elevator en route to Cole's office. I had clearly gone overboard. Chinese food was my weakness. Well, one of my weaknesses. There were many. I wasn't sure what the boys liked, so I got a smörgâsbord of Chinese delights that everyone could choose from. The smells wafting off the food made my stomach rumble. I was ravenous today. Due to all the emotional turmoil yesterday I hadn't really been up to eating anything all day. I rarely ever missed a meal. I loved my food, so I wasn't surprised that my body was trying to make up for lost nourishment.

I looked up as someone called my name. A tall, blond, gorgeous woman in her late twenties or early thirties, dressed in an immaculate and sexy pant suit got up from her chair behind a desk and came toward me, a bright smile on her face. Since she was sitting behind the desk in front of Cole's office, I assumed this must be Sam, Cole's assistant. I hadn't expected her to look like she did. I thought—or hoped—assistants were all the middle-aged motherly type.

"You must be Lizzy. I'm Sam," she introduced herself as she relieved me of two of my filled-to-the-brim plastic bags.

"Hi, Sam. Nice to meet you. I'm sorry about all that drama I caused yesterday." I felt I needed to apologize. Looking at her and knowing she worked in close proximity to my man every day, I also needed to do something else.

"Oh, don't you worry about it. Cole told me the gist of what happened and let me tell you, that woman sounds pure evil," she said before I could continue.

"Listen, I don't want to offend you in any way, and if I do, I apologize in advance. You're hot. Extremely hot. And you're working close with whom I consider mine. I'm not really the jealous type of woman, but I need to know what I'm dealing with. I'm sure you know Cole's history of loving them and leaving them. Now, did he shit where he works and are we going to have a problem, or are you as nice and professional as he made you sound?" I couldn't help but be blunt. Sam surprised me by bursting out laughing.

"I like you, Lizzy," she stated after she controlled her amusement. "Nope, I am not one of his conquests. I'm not saying I've never experienced the slam bam thank you ma'am, but I try to keep the number of times I'm treated like meat low, which in today's times is frighteningly hard to do. I'm almost convinced men are all pigs and am this close to swearing off them." I couldn't really argue with her there. I had my fair share of experiencing asshole maneuvers myself. "So, I would love to be friends if you don't mind. Those are hard to come by. Most men are pigs and most women are bitches, as proven by scary crazy bitch number one yesterday." I giggled. She had no idea. Cole's office door opened just as Sam reached to open it and a smiling Cole motioned us inside.

"Hey, baby," he murmured as he brushed a kiss on my lips when I went to walk past him into his office.

"Hey."

"I see you've officially met Sam."

"Yup. She won't mistake one of your crazy ex-bitches for me again and she informed me that *she* isn't one of your crazy ex-bitches, either. We've decided to be new besties, so it's all good." Sam giggled as she proceeded to unload all the bags and placed numerous cartons on the table that was sitting in front of the couch. Cole's eyebrows shot up in question and I shot him a grin. He let it go.

"You think you got enough food?" He asked as he surveyed the scene, smirking.

"What? I'm hungry. You know I like my food." Cole chuckled and I heard Sam giggle again.

We all turned to the door when we heard someone enter. It was Max and Derrick. Max raised his eyebrows when he discovered the plethora of food spread out on the table, then shook his head on a half-smile, shrugged his shoulders and dug right in. Derrick introduced himself then followed Max's example and loaded up a plate with food. I shot Cole an I-told-you-so look, seeing as I had been right and Derrick looked exactly like the computer geek you would imagine. Cole chuckled and kissed my temple where he whispered, "All right, baby, you win."

"What did I win exactly?"

"You'll see," he told me in a low voice, making my insides quiver.

He led me to the table where we both loaded our plates before we sat down on the couch and waited for Max to give us the news.

Max looked at me for a minute, his face serious, then

started. "Liz, what do you know about your father?" I froze then lowered my eyebrows in confusion. My father? What did he have to do with any of this?

"My father? Why?" I asked. I wasn't all fired up to share that he had left us because he didn't want me.

"Just tell me."

I stared at him for a second then sighed. Judging by the look on his face he needed to know. So I shared, "Next to nothing. He left us before I was born. I saw a picture once but when I asked my mom about it, she got so upset that she locked herself in her bedroom with a bottle of vodka and didn't come out until the next morning. It was the only time I ever saw her cry. I must have been five or six. After that, I never asked about him again." Cole squeezed my knee in support. I covered his hand with mine and squeezed back to let him know I was okay.

"That's it?" Max asked.

"Yes, that's all I know. Well, and the reason why he left us. He didn't want me." Three sets of eyes turned to a mix of anger and sadness, Cole's being the angriest and Max's being the saddest, much to my surprise. Derrick's were somewhere in the middle.

"You don't know his name?" Max went back to interrogating me.

"No. Why is that important?"

"That's what I'd like to know. What does Liz's father have to do with what Courtney's been doing?"

Max's jaw clenched. Then he looked at Derrick and gave him a chin lift before his now concerned eyes came back to me. Derrick nodded and started talking.

"The first thing I did after Max called me last night was pull up everyone's record just to see if I could find anything that was important, that could tell us anything or get us any leads. Not just the criminal records, the public records. All three of you are from the same town. Call it a hunch, but I thought there could be more to that connection. I was right." His eyes came to me and stayed there. "Liz, your father's name is Walter Matthews." He paused.

Walter Matthews.

It felt strange to finally know my faceless absentee father's name. I nodded for him to go on, too anxious and nervous to form any words.

Derrick looked at me with compassion before he continued.

I braced myself.

"That same name is also listed on Courtney Miller's birth certificate as her biological father." My body locked in shock. What? Courtney and I had the same father? She was my sister?

What the fuck?

"Are you saying that Liz's father is also Courtney's father? That they are sisters?" Cole asked in bewilderment, echoing my thoughts.

"Yes," Derrick said.

"That's not possible. The records must be wrong. I've met Courtney's father numerous times. Our parents are members of the same social circle, so we would run into them during functions and such."

"According to your records, you moved to Ashford, Massachusetts, when you were ten years old."

"That's correct," Cole confirmed.

"Then you wouldn't know that Ann Matthews married George Miller when Courtney was three years old after her husband had died in a car accident the year before. George

Miller adopted Courtney and she took his last name."

Cole muttered under his breath.

I still sat quietly, shocked, my brain trying to take in and process the information.

And failing.

I didn't know what to feel. So many emotions and thoughts were swirling inside me I couldn't hold on to any one thing. I tried to do the math in my head. Courtney was three when her mother remarried, her biological father—our father — died a year before that in a car accident. Courtney was two years older than me. Which meant my father died when I was a baby. Or maybe even before I was born. He never left me willingly.

He died.

"So my father died? He didn't leave because of me?" I whispered.

Cole's head whipped around at my words. He turned his hand that was still holding my knee and grabbed mine tightly.

"Baby—" he started, but Max interrupted him.

"There is more."

I closed my eyes, not sure I could take any more revelations that would turn my life as I'd known it upside down. Derrick kept speaking.

"I found divorce papers that were filed by Walter Matthews three months before the car accident. He was leaving his wife. I can only speculate as to the reason why, but I think we all have a pretty good idea."

"When?" I still had my eyes closed, needing the privacy that gave me to control my emotions.

"When what?" Derrick asked.

"When did he file for divorce? And when was the car accident? What month?" Cole tightened his hand in mine. He knew where I was going with this.

"He filed for divorce in April. The car accident was on July 16th."

"I was born on July 17th." I whispered as I hung my head.

This changed everything.

Everything my mother had made me believe all my life. My father died the day before I was born. I had been a preemie, born six weeks early. My mother had told me many times that I should have died in that hospital, that she would be better off without having to care for me, that it was my fault she was worth nothing, it was my fault that people looked down on her. I never understood what she meant by that.

But it was crystal clear now.

She had had an affair with Courtney's father and got pregnant. My father was leaving his wife maybe because of that, because of me. It could have been for other reasons, but the timing would have been too coincidental if he weren't leaving his wife for my mom and me.

Because he loved us and wanted to be with us.

He didn't leave us because he didn't want me.

He wanted me.

He wanted to be my dad.

But he died tragically before he could.

And my mom went into labor six weeks early and had me the day after he died.

I can only imagine what sorrow she must have suffered that would make her go into labor early. Tears started to form in my eyes at feeling compassion for my mother. I understood now. Understood why she was overwhelmed, why she turned to alcohol and drugs, why she couldn't love me, why she needed to sedate herself to escape reality.

Not that that excused anything she had done to me, had

said to me. But understanding the reasoning behind it helped somewhat.

Fingers were brushing at the tears that were rolling down my cheeks. I opened my eyes.

"Liz?" Cole asked, concerned.

"I get it now. It all makes sense," I said through my silent tears. He looked back at me with sad eyes and nodded. "Yeah, baby. It does." I closed my eyes again and rested my forehead against his chest. His arms moved to rub my back soothingly.

"Liz," I heard Max call gently after a few moments. I turned my head on Cole's chest so I could look at him. "I know this is a lot and I can see what it's doing to you, but there is more to tell you." He paused and waited for me to collect myself. I took a deep breath and straightened out of Cole's embrace, but held on to one of his hands and nodded at Max to go on.

"It's about your father's accident. Foul play was suspected. Your father hit a tree at 50 miles an hour, without activating the brakes. He wasn't drunk or high. Drove a new SUV. There was an investigation, but nothing came of it. It was determined that he must have fallen asleep behind the wheel. Thing is, it wasn't late at night. Or after a long day at work. It happened on a Sunday afternoon. There is more evidence that could potentially lead to proving that his car was tempered with, but I have nothing certain yet. I promise you I will get to the bottom of this. Derrick and I will keep digging."

Holy shit! Was he serious?

"You're telling me that there is a chance that someone wanted my father dead? That something was done to his car to kill him?"

I couldn't believe this!

"Yes. Now, Liz, I'm not sure you've made that connection yet, but there's a good possibility that Courtney knows that you two are sisters and that her father was going to leave her and her mother for you. She was only two years old when everything went down, but the hate she has for you must come from somewhere. I suspect her mother has been feeding her with her own venom. That could be why she wants to hurt you, why she's been trying to make your life hell since you can remember. I'm sure I don't know all that happened between you two, since I only know what Cole knows." He stopped there and gave me a searching look. I nodded, slowly, confirming his suspicion that there was more than Cole—and inadvertently he—knew about how Courtney had tortured me all my life, to what lengths she had gone. Max returned my nod. "It makes sense then. First, her father chose you and was going to leave her behind, and now the man she has been in love with for years also chose you over her. That's the two most important men in her life tossing her aside for you. A woman like her would seek revenge."

I had felt Cole's body tense at the confirmation of there being more to the story between Courtney and I, but he didn't push me for details. We could talk about that later.

"Fucking hell," Cole growled under his breath. "This is a fucking nightmare."

Max's eyes moved to Cole.

"It is. At least we now know her motive and can act accordingly. We know her focus is on Liz, not on you, and we know why. That helps a lot. We've put the pressure on. She'll soon feel it and hopefully retreat, but a woman scorned like that? I'm not holding my breath. We need to prepare for the eventuality that she'll keep coming after Liz, and to protect her from it."

"Okay. That sounds like a plan," Cole agreed.

"We also found out who Courtney's partner in crime is."

"Who?" Cole asked when Max paused for long moments.

"It's your mother." Cole jumped up from the couch and started pacing, his hands grabbing his hair.

"You are fucking shitting me! My mother? Why?"

"I don't know why. That's something you're going to have to ask her. My guess? She wants you married to someone from your own social class, not someone from the wrong side of the tracks. No offence," he added, sliding his eyes to me.

"None taken," I replied. He tipped up his chin and swung his head back to Cole who was still pacing by the window.

"There's nothing that leads us to believe she is in any deeper than that. She might even believe that you are really in love with Courtney. I don't know. Courtney probably told her about the baby being yours, but that's just me guessing at this point. You need to confront your mother if you want to know the whys. Derrick and I are gonna focus on cutting Courtney off from messing with Liz."

Cole had stopped pacing and stood next to where I was sitting, a hand on my shoulder.

"You're right. Priority number one right now is keeping her away from Liz. She is not hurting her ever again."

"Hurting you means hurting Liz. You gotta keep that in mind. I figure the only thing she can really do to Liz after failing to drive her away from you is make her lose her job. We'll check if she has any connections that could help her with that. Liz is clean so she doesn't have much to go on. Her big plan hasn't worked. I have a feeling she won't back off, though. If she hasn't already, she is gonna find out soon that you two are engaged. That will fuel the fire and she'll be more determined than ever to get her revenge. Women can be crazy bitches, and something tells me this one is crazier than most. Derrick couldn't find anything that could compromise you professionally, Liz, but that bitch has got money, and we all know money can buy you pretty much anything."

"Well, I've got more money and I don't care how much of it I have to use to make her disappear from our lives." Cole's face was hard. So was his voice when he continued. "I want you to go on the offensive. Discredit her, take her job, her money. I want you to make it hurt."

"Cole—" I tried to interrupt. He was going a bit far and probably only making it worse by poking the angry lion.

"No, Liz. We talked about this and you agreed. She's gotta pay. Nobody tries to take you away from me. Nobody tries to hurt you and not suffer the consequences. And she's your sister for God's sakes! Who does that shit?" He was shouting now, working himself up.

"Maybe she doesn't know—" I tried again.

"Oh, she knows. That vindictive little bitch knows exactly who you are. Like Max says, it makes perfect sense. Fucking hell! I'm such a fucking idiot! I brought this on us. If I hadn't tried to protect you from me all these years, I would have never hooked up with her and none of this would have happened! Fuck!"

"Cole!" I shouted, pissed at him for blaming himself. I shot up from the couch since I couldn't very well put my hands on my hips when I was sitting.

"What?" He shouted back as he took in my stance and his eyebrows narrowed.

"Don't be an idiot! You had your reasons for not being with me! Yes, they were stupid, but you gotta let that go! Stop dragging us back there! You realized it was stupid and you did something about it! We're together now and that's all that matters! We're getting married for Heaven's sakes!" That last past I shrieked at him, too far gone to keep myself in check.

Cole realized this and started toward me, but I took a step back.

"No! You gotta hear this and get it through your head! I never told you about all the awful things she did to me, because I didn't want to be your charity case! You rescued me often enough as it was! If I had told you, you can't deny that you would have dropped her like a hot potato years ago. So according to your logic that makes it my fault just as much as yours, if not more so! *She* is making the choice to treat people the way she does! Nobody is holding a gun to her head, forcing her to ruin people's lives, Cole! It's not your fault and it's not mine! It's on her!"

"Okay, baby. You're right. Calm down," he said, his lips twitching.

"What's funny?" I was still shouting.

"You are, baby. You're hell on wheels when you're riled. I should piss you off more often." His amusement turned into something else as he stared at me. I narrowed my eyes at him. He burst out laughing and reached for me, grabbing me by the hips and pulling me into his arms. I wasn't ready to let it go.

"I'm serious, Cole. Don't take the blame for the things she does. It pisses me off."

"I think I got that, honey," he murmured, his eyes still dancing.

"The whole building got that. We done?" Max was ready to go.

"Yeah, we're done. Give me regular updates." Cole answered him and gave him a chin lift. Max looked at me. "Keep your eyes open, doll," to which I nodded. I thought they were a little overly dramatic. As far as I could tell, Courtney had played her major card and there wasn't anything else she could hurt us with. Other than physically hurting us, but I didn't think she would go that far. We were not in *Fatal Attraction*. No need to hide my bunnies. Not that I had any, but you catch my drift. Things like that didn't happen in real life. Trying to break us up out of jealousy? Sure. Risking getting arrested? No.

Chapter 20

Lizzy

Cole was taking me to dinner tonight.

On a date.

The last week had been super busy for both of us, trying to catch up on time we had lost at work due to all the drama. Then there was the wedding that needed to be planned in a hurry. I was so very grateful for Sam and all her connections. She had become my own personal wedding planner and I had realized quickly that she was a go-getter who didn't take no for an answer. A girl after my own taste. We were now on each other's speed dial and talked often and extensively, not just about the wedding. I really liked her no-nonsense yet chipper and upbeat personality. She was hilarious. Her constant, dry one-liners cracked me up. We were well on our way to becoming new besties, just like I'd warned Cole. It was kinda weird for me. I had never had a lot of friends, especially not female ones. It was always easier for me to get along with men. They were less complicated, there was no drama, what you saw was what you got. Most of the time. Now my female circle of friends was expanding and my initial bewilderment at that was turning into acceptance and delight at being able to talk to women I could actually trust.

A completely new experience.

As if that weren't enough to keep us busy, Cole and I had two more meetings with 'the guys' as he now called them.

The first meeting didn't result in any new information. It was the day after I had found out all there was to know about my father. The night before, Cole and I had snuggled in bed while we talked. Or while he talked, I should say. I was still too stunned to formulate a clear thought. Too many things were swirling in my head, options, possibilities, right next to confusion and the feeling of not knowing what to do with all that information.

One thing was clear. I had to go and see my mother. Talk to her, ask questions, get confirmation that Walter Matthews was indeed my father. Yes, he was listed as my father on my birth certificate, but I wanted my mother to admit it. I needed her to admit that she had lied to me all these years—that my father hadn't left us because of me.

That he had died.

I just wasn't looking forward to actually going to see her. I hadn't been back there in over six years. As soon as I could, I had left for college, right after high school, before the summer had even really started. I had sworn I would never set foot in that house again. Not for anything.

But this was something I had to do.

And it scared me.

"Liz? Have you heard anything I just said?"

I lifted my head from his chest and looked up at him. "Sorry. No."

His hand moved up and he brushed a strand of hair out of my face while he studied me. "Talk to me," he said, his voice calm and quiet, his eyes loving and worried.

I rested my head back onto his chest and sighed, then I said in a voice that was little more than a whisper, "I have to go back."

"Go back?" Cole repeated, confused.

"Back there. To my mother's house. I have to go and talk to her." Cole said nothing, just held me tightly and brushed his lips across the top of my head. He knew, of course, that I hadn't been back and had never intended to see her again. He also knew how hard it would be for me and that no words existed to make it any easier.

"I'll go with you."

Unless they were those words.

"We'll go this weekend. Get it over with. I'll need to have words with my mother as well and I'd rather not do it over the phone."

I closed my eyes and took a deep breath.

Great.

Now I was even less looking forward to that day.

Cole gave me a squeeze. "She won't hurt you. I won't let her."

"I know you'll try and I'll do my best to not let her get to me, but you know what she thinks about me. It's not like she's ever made a secret of it."

Now it was Cole who sighed. "I know.

We lay silent for a few minutes. Then I remembered something from years ago. "Do you remember that day we ran into yours and Courtney's mom in town?" Cole's body stiffened under mine. He remembered. "It makes sense now, doesn't it? Why she called me a home wrecker."

"No, baby, it doesn't. I get what you mean, but you never did anything to wreck anyone's home. If you need to blame someone, blame your mother and father. They shouldn't have had an affair. He should have left his wife instead of getting his girlfriend pregnant."

"It's not that easy when a child is involved. Courtney was still a toddler."

"I get that, but it was still wrong. He should have manned up and either gotten a divorce or tried to work it out with his wife. Not pull another woman into that mess and make the situation even more complicated."

"That's true. Still, I get where she was coming from."

Cole used his hand under my chin to make me look at him. "That right there is something we need to work on, babe. You always try to understand why people do what they do, why they act the way they act. And then you sympathize with them. There is nothing about the way the Millers have treated you to sympathize with—or anyone in that town who has ever looked down on you, for that matter. There is absolutely no excuse for what they have done. None of what happened was your fault. You never treat anyone with hate or animosity or resentment, and you're not rude or mean or evil, even though people have given you more than enough reasons to. You're the most compassionate, caring, honest, loyal, and fun person I know."

"Some people would argue with you about the not being rude part. A lot of people, actually."

"Then they're stupid." Cole was losing his patience now. "You aren't rude, you're honest and straight forward. You don't beat around the bush and people—especially women—take that the wrong way because they can't deal with it. That's their problem. Not yours. Let me ask you this, if the roles were reversed, would you have treated Courtney the way she treated you? Would you ever talk to anyone the way Mrs.

Miller or my mother talked to you?"

I shook my head no.

"That's right, you wouldn't. If you had known you had a little sister, you would have taken her under your wing, would have been her family, no matter what. You would have protected her from the shit people were dealing out instead of making it worse. And that makes you a better person than any of them combined. Don't try and find excuses for their actions, baby. There aren't any. None."

I thought about that for a second. It sounded so simple and logical if you looked at it like that. Cole was right. There was no excuse to treat someone like shit or a second-class citizen, no matter what, especially an innocent child. I had no patience with people who treated my kids with anything but compassion and respect. I wouldn't stand for it. I needed to learn to apply the same to myself.

"You're right," I said.

"Damn right, I am." My lips twitched. Cole smiled back at me. "I hate to spoil my victory, but since we're on the topic of the Millers, have you given any thought to what you're gonna do?"

No, I hadn't. It had only been half a day since I found out and I hadn't been able to wrap my head around all that Walter Matthews being my deceased father entailed. There were so many options, so many possibilities. And I wasn't sure I wanted anything to do with any of them.

Cole kept talking when I stayed silent. "You're entitled to your inheritance. More actually. You can sue them for keeping that information and your part of his estate from you. I don't know all the technicalities, but Max said you could probably bury them if you wanted to."

"I don't want that."

"I know you don't. But you should at least fight for the part that is rightfully yours, that has been yours for twenty-five years. At least think about it." Silence. I wasn't ready to talk about that yet, and thankfully, Cole didn't push any further.

We lay like that for a while, both of us lost in thought, before I whispered. "There is one thing I want."

"What is it?" Cole asked.

"I want to visit his grave. And..." Cole's arm around me tightened.

"And what, baby?"

"I would like to know what he looked like. If I look like him. I know I'm almost the spitting image of my mother, but...do you think we can figure out how to get a picture somehow?"

"I'm sure that can be arranged." Cole's lips were brushing the hair on the top of my head. "We'll get through this. You know there isn't anything I wouldn't do for you, right?"

"I know. You know I feel the same way?"

The smile he gave me was bright and happy. "I do."

"Good."

Not long after, we fell asleep holding each other, just like we did every night.

The next morning, I had told Taryn about the possibility of someone trying to discredit me. I dreaded bringing my personal problems to work, but things could potentially end badly if I didn't give my boss a heads-up.

"I don't want to bother you with this, and she might not even try anything, but I'd rather you knew what is going on, just in case." Taryn's eyes had gone wide when I had explained to her about my father, about how he had died before I was born, and how I had just found out. I told her a little bit about my past, just enough so that things made sense to her, before I explained the drama of the past few days.

"Jeez. I thought stuff like that only happened in books or movies."

I laughed. "Believe me, I thought the same thing. I still can't believe that all this is happening to me."

"No kidding." She smiled at me. "Don't worry about a thing, Liz. I know the type of person you are: one of the most compassionate and hard-working and loyal people I have ever worked with. The kids love you and respect you, you are always on top of everything and go by the book even though you loathe it. Yes, you are young and still have a lot to learn, but you live to help those children and everyone can see that. Don't worry. Let her try to slander your professional reputation. She's got nothing to go on."

As much as I hadn't wanted to share, it was a good thing I did.

Apparently, Courtney did have connections. The very next day, she had started her campaign to discredit me. Thankfully, she didn't get very far. I had made a name for myself as a compassionate, caring, and understanding social worker who took her job seriously, just like Taryn had assured me I had. Yes, I was known for sometimes being a little too direct and impatient, but I was nevertheless efficient. There had been a few fake complaint phone calls, but those had been disregarded almost immediately. So Courtney had nothing more to go on when it came to me.

For the next meeting, Max and Derrick had come to our house. Cole and I were going to visit our mothers in less than two days, so Cole wanted to make sure we had all the info we could get. But there was nothing new. Max had told him so over the phone, but Cole had insisted on a meeting. According to the guys, Courtney had gone to ground and everything was quiet.

"See? You guys are overreacting. She's got nothing to go on. I don't think she'll be stupid enough to come after you, Cole. She's used up her trump card with that fake pregnancy. She tried to come after me but failed. She's run out of ideas." I told them.

"The pregnancy wasn't fake. She just lied about Cole being the father," Max informed me.

Huh. I thought it had all been a ruse.

"I talked to my lawyer, just in case, but nothing has happened, which would prove Lizzy is right. She isn't coming after me." That was Cole.

"It's been too quiet. I don't like it," Max grumbled.

"She knows she's beat. You went on the offensive, found out that she was sleeping with her boss, used it, and she got fired. Your mother hasn't talked to Courtney from what Derrick could gather. Courtney is jobless, all her credit cards are maxed, and she's a pregnant single woman. If she's smart, she has reassessed her situation and come to the realization that she has other things to worry about."

"Yeah, a smart woman would do that, but she isn't smart. I say we stay alert, just in case," Cole said. Max nodded his agreement.

"All right. You guys stay alert all you want. I'm too busy to keep looking over my shoulder. I've got a life to live, kids to worry about, and a wedding to plan. And according to my fiancée's assistant, he is taking me some place special tomorrow tonight and I don't own fancy clothes. He has seen the only little black dress I own. I'm not that fond of shopping, but my new posse tells me that I have to look the part, so they're taking me shopping on our lunch break tomorrow. So you do what you gotta do and I'll do what I deem as more important."

"You don't like shopping?" Max asked me, seemingly shocked that there was a woman out there who didn't enjoy spending most of her time in a busy shopping mall.

"It's not one of my favorites, no."

He looked at Cole. "You're a lucky guy."

"Don't I know it. It's also very frustrating, though. The only woman I want to give anything she wants, and she doesn't want one single thing. It's a pain in the ass to buy her a gift. Always has been. Even when she was a little girl. Sweet as pie and hard as nails."

"Like I said. Lucky guy."

"Yeah," Cole agreed, then his eyes came to me and he grinned.

I rolled my eyes at both of them, making them both chuckle. I changed the subject. "You staying for dinner?"

"Wouldn't mind if I did," Max mumbled.

Derrick shrugged his shoulders. "Sure," he said.

"Good. Cole makes a mean lasagna."

Cole chuckled again and shook his head at me. Then he proceeded into the kitchen to start cooking, giving me a quick but deep kiss as he passed by me.

Now was now. I had gone shopping with my besties and had only received a few groans and stink-eyes when I had complained about trying on all the dresses they had picked. Even Rainey had joined us and had found the experience more than amusing. She was so much like me it wasn't even funny. At least that's what Marie and Sam had said. Rainey had shrugged and grinned at me.

But I had to give it to them. Sam and Marie knew what they were doing. I was ready to go, dressed to the nines, hair and make-up done. I turned in front of the mirror for one last check.

Wow.

I couldn't believe that was me. Sam had not been wrong. She knew her way around clothes, so I had trusted her judgment without question. Still, I had no clue that *I* could look like that. After finding the absolute perfect dress for me—her words—she took me to MAC to let them show me how to do my make-up and hair. I'd had some difficulties pinning my locks partly back the way they had shown me, but I got it on the seventh try. My make-up was light, but smoky, the grey bringing out the green in my eyes. Pale red lip-gloss. Silver waterfall earrings with little black stones at the end, matching the necklace adorning my ample cleavage. And what cleavage it was. Yeah, I had tits and ass, but holy hell! The dress was out of this world. It was green, which I usually didn't wear, not a fan of the myth that anything green looked stunning on redheads. But this shade of green went perfectly with my coloring. It hugged my hips and other important parts of my body, coming just to the top of my knees. Sexy, black, not too high heels completed the ensemble. No purse. I told Sam I wouldn't need it. Cole could put my lip-gloss in his pocket and that was all I needed. She had been a little disgruntled at not getting the opportunity to shop for the perfect clutch, but had let it go.

I heard a pained groan coming from behind me. Looking over my shoulder in the mirror, I saw Cole standing in the doorway, completely frozen. Only his eyes were moving, taking me in from top to bottom to top, then came to meet mine. At seeing the look in them, I caught my breath and shivered. It was almost animalistic. Pure desire and need stared back at me. Sam had been right. Cole didn't know what hit him. We were standing frozen like that, staring at each other's eyes through the mirror for several minutes until Cole broke the silence.

"I don't know if I should be happy Sam is your new best friend or if I wished I had never introduced you." He advanced on me. His hands went around my waist, gliding on the smooth fabric of my dress, resulting in another full body shiver. "You are the most beautiful creature I have ever laid eyes on," he whispered as he nibbled my ear. "I'm gonna have a hard time keeping my hands off of you tonight."

"Who said you had to keep your hands off of me?' I was starting to pant as his lips caressed the skin behind my ear.

"If I don't, the other patrons at the restaurant will get a show with their dinner," he mumbled. One last kiss before he stepped back, turned me, grabbed my hand in his, and walked us towards the door, down the stairs into the front hall where he helped me into my coat, and then took me out for our celebration dinner.

I smiled back at the waiter, who had just taken our orders, closed my menu, and returned it to him. Cole did the same without the smile, his eyes on me.

"I've made a decision," he stated after a few seconds of perusing the parts of my body that weren't hidden by the table.

"And what is that?" I asked.

"It'll take up all my precious free time if I follow my instincts and rip off every guy's head that dares stare at your glorious body. That won't do since I intend to spend every minute of that time with you for the rest of my life, however that comes about. So instead, I've decided to show you off and enjoy the envious looks *I* get, since no other man will ever come close enough to touch you. All they can do is look. You're mine, so I can kiss you and touch you whenever and wherever I want."

"That's a good plan. Though, I'm not so sure about the wherever part. I'm no exhibitionist."

"Neither am I." I gave him an 'Oh really?' look. He knew that I knew he had had sex in public places before. "At least not with you," he amended. "What we share when we're together is private and intimate. I wouldn't risk anyone seeing you like that. But don't get me wrong. If I see an opportunity to be adventurous but discreet at the same time, I'll take it. Like at my office. I'm dying to take you on that couch and have the memory of that with me at work." Thinking about christening his couch made me want to be adventurous. He could tell by the glaze that had covered my eyes.

"Behave," he growled.

"You started it. What do you expect me to do when you talk like that? It's not just you who has to control himself to not jump me every time I walk into a room. I feel the same way about you."

"That's good to know," he shot me a wide grin. Our drinks arrived then and we toasted to us and our future. Kind of corny, but I loved it.

Sam hadn't exaggerated. This place was *fancy.* I had thought I might be a tad overdressed, but I wasn't. Every woman in this room was wearing a dress just as lavish as mine. Where they dripped with diamonds though, I wore simple silver jewelry. I looked around. The restaurant was completely booked to capacity. It was close to Christmas, so there were a few bigger groups, not just couples. I noticed a few people looking my way. No, not looking at me. Glaring at me. They were all women. What? I looked at Cole, confused and a little uncomfortable. It wasn't the first time in my life women wanted to kill me with just a look, though I suspected this time it was for a completely different reason. He shook his head at me, quietly laughing.

"You see it, don't you?" I leaned in closer over the table so he could hear me when I asked in a quiet voice, "Why are those women glaring at me? You know them?" Cole's shoulders kept shaking.

"No, I don't know them. Baby, they're glaring at you, because you're a hundred times more beautiful than they are and they know it. They envy you."

"That's stupid."

"Maybe so, but it's true. They're also probably pissed because the men they are with couldn't tear their eyes away from you when we walked in."

"It's just the dress. Sam knows her way around clothes."

"It's more than just the dress. It just makes an already unbelievably gorgeous woman even more so. It's your eyes, your hair, your laugh, everything about you that men want and women are jealous of."

"They haven't heard me laugh."

"Not yet. Wanna bet how many heads are gonna turn when you do?" I crossed my arms over my chest, not liking his teasing or the situation at all. It brought up too many unpleasant memories.

"Maybe we shouldn't go out to places like this anymore. It makes me uncomfortable when people stare at me," I looked down at the empty table in front of me and fidgeted with the napkin on my lap.

"Oh, no. I told you I've decided to show you off. This is fun." My self-consciousness turned into attitude. "You know, crossing your arms like that really accentuates your generous breasts." I uncrossed my arms quickly and sat up straight, my eyes going wide, not wanting or needing any more attention on my body. Cole burst out laughing. Great. Now it felt like everyone was staring, though at least all the women were now looking at him instead of me.

"Maybe they were glaring at me because they're jealous I'm with you," I snapped. That made way more sense.

"It doesn't matter. None of them matter. Baby, as much as I like you riled up we are not going to argue tonight. Come here," he leaned over the table, stopping about mid-way toward me, waiting for me to do the same. He was right. It didn't matter if or why other people were jealous. What mattered was that we had each other. Again, corny. But it had always been our truth. And I didn't want to argue either. So I complied and leaned in, going in for a quick kiss on the lips. Cole had a different idea, though. When I started pulling back he held me by the side of my neck, keeping me in place, kissing the hell out of me. I was breathless by the time he was done.

"Now, tell me about your day. And how are Jesse and Chloe? They still happy in their new home?" My heart melted. That was only one reason why I loved this man so much. He genuinely cared.

"They're as comfortable and happy as they can be right now," I said in a quiet but proud voice. "Chloe is coming more and more out of her shell, and Jesse is starting to let his guard down not just with me but with the other workers and kids more and more as well. He's very funny actually, and quite the charmer. All the girls at the shelter are head over heels in love with him. They follow him around and hang on every word he says whenever the both of them stop by. They stopped by after school yesterday and I'm really happy at how settled they seem."

Cole was grinning at me proudly. "That's good to hear. I'm glad."

"Me too." I grinned back at him, but then scrunched up my eyebrows in worry. "It's just that I'm a little concerned about their father. He hasn't confessed to anything, says he doesn't know why his children hate him so much that they would make up stories about him, says they must be doing it out of grief for their mother, whom he couldn't save."

"That's bullshit. He's just trying to save his own ass. Everyone knows what happens to child molesters in prison. There's no way anyone believes him, right? No way they could send them back to him?"

The vehemence in his voice made me smile again. I really did love this man with everything in me. "No, honey, there's no way they could be sent back. He assaulted and beat his son unconscious in public. Both their x-rays show old fractures, Jesse more so than Chloe, but he's beaten them both. And he's touched his own son, threatened to do the same to his daughter if Jesse ever so much as hinted at what was going on at their house to anyone. That's why Jesse took his sister and ran, because he knew that sooner or later his father wouldn't be able to keep his hands off of her. Yes, it might be a case of their word against his, but the judges aren't stupid. And I've put Bobby on the case. We had lunch together today and discussed everything. Bobby will make sure Jesse and Chloe will stay safe, has ensured me that there's nothing to worry about, that there is no chance that their filth of a father will breathe free air any time soon."

"Who's Bobby?" Cole asked.

"Oh, only the most feared lawyer and child advocate in the field, graduated from Yale a few years ago and works pro bono most of the time; has no mercy when it comes to kids who have been abused or sexually assaulted. You should see it, the vengeance that lights in Bobby's eyes at a case like this.

Unstoppable. We don't work together often, but I reach out when I have a case like this where the children have no family left to be united with, no one to stand up for them and defend them. I want the best for them and Bobby is the best. You could say we have developed somewhat of a friendship over the years."

"I'm glad you could find them the help they needed. It sounds like this Bobby guy really knows what he's doing. How come you've never talked to me about him before?" My lips twitched. He was trying really hard to hide it, but I could see the jealousy in his eyes, jealousy at the idea that I had struck up a friendship with a man he didn't know, had never ever heard about before now.

I shrugged, trying to be nonchalant. "You know, I didn't think you'd be interested in hearing about everyone I work with. It's not like I see or talk to Bobby every day, not even every week or month. But we've got a lot in common. We always have fun when we go out for lunch. Turns heads like no one else I've ever met. Apart from you that is. Definitely hot, and you can tell with just one look that there is a lot of passion underneath that hard and shark-like exterior that everyone in our circles knows about. Probably breaking hearts left, right, and center."

Cole didn't say anything, just looked at me with his mouth in a straight line. I could tell it cost him a lot to not give in to his jealousy and do something stupid like forbid me to ever have lunch with Bobby again. My shoulders started shaking with mirth. His eyes narrowed. I burst out laughing.

"What exactly is it that you think is so funny?" he asked through clenched teeth.

"You! You're hilarious," I said through my laughter.

"Is that so?" More teeth clenching.

"Oh, yeah." I took a deep breath to calm myself down then let him off the hook. "Bobby is short for Roberta."

His eyes widened in shock and relief right before they narrowed on me once more. "You're gonna pay for that," he promised in a low and very sexy voice.

I leaned over the table and answered in a voice just as low, "I'm counting on it," then leaned back at his answering growl with a big and satisfied smile on my face.

For the rest of dinner we only had eyes for each other. We didn't talk much at first, just enjoyed the highly sexual tension between is. When we did after several long minutes, we talked about our dreams and wishes for our future. We had had conversations like this numerous times over the years, but this time it was different. This time, we talked about *our* future. Things we wished and hoped for as a couple. Where we wanted to travel, how many children we wanted, what our hopes were for our children. It was fun and perfect.

When we got home, Cole made true on his promise of retaliation, and I couldn't have been happier as he showed me how much he loved and adored me, how much I was his and he was mine. Exactly what I needed before I had to face our mothers on the weekend.

Chapter 21

Cole

We were on our way to my parents' house, about fifteen minutes out. Lizzy had insisted that we deal with my mother first before we went to see hers the next morning.

"I don't think I'll be able to handle anything else after I've talked to my mother. It's not gonna be pretty. I'd rather face your parents' wrath when I still have my wits about me."

I had agreed wholeheartedly. I knew she was nervous and anxious about coming face-to-face with her mother after such a long time and after what she'd learned from Max and Derrick. She hadn't seen or talked to her in years, had never intended to do so again once she left for college. I could only imagine what she must be feeling.

I had booked us a room in a nice bed and breakfast, a place we could go to— after I knew what would certainly be drama with my parents—to recharge for the next day and more drama. I wanted Lizzy to be able to relax, to not worry. But I knew that was a little too much to hope for. She was tense as she was sitting beside me, staring out the window and wringing her hands in her lap.

I had called my mother yesterday to let her know we were coming. She had ignored the fact that I'd said 'we', that it wasn't just me who was visiting. I hadn't expected any less. I knew she would never accept Lizzy the way she deserved, no matter what I did, no matter whose daughter she was. Hell, she probably thought being the bastard child of a cheater made Lizzy an even lesser person. My hands gripped the steering wheel tighter at that thought.

My father wasn't as vindictive as my mother. He just didn't care enough about anything I did to comment. Their marriage was loveless, had been for as long as I could remember. He put up with her whenever he was home—which wasn't very often—and as an extension, me. The very little consideration he had for me died when I hadn't gotten a business degree and joined him at the company he had worked at for over twenty years. I had gone for architecture instead, following in my grandfather's, his father's, footsteps.

I took one of my hands off the steering wheel and placed it on top of her fidgeting ones, giving them a light squeeze. "It'll be okay. Stop worrying."

She let out a long breath. "We both know that's not true, Cole. Your mother hates me. She will never accept me as part of your family, you know that just as well as I do."

I sighed. "I know, baby. She isn't too fond of me, either. But she doesn't get to decide anything about us. She has no say in what we do. All I want to do tonight is put her in her place, tell her that it has always been and always will be you, whether she likes it or not. None of her antics will ever change that fact. And she needs to know that if she ever tries to break us up again, if she ever so much as says another word against you, that that's it. I will no longer be part of a family that does nothing but spread malice and bitterness. I'm not like her, never was. And she has to understand that she has no power over me."

"I know this is important to you, and I understand, but why do I have to come?"

I gave her hands another squeeze, firmer this time. "What happened to my feisty little firecracker?"

"She's feeling more and more worthless the closer we get to Ashford." Her small and defeated voice ripped my heart in two. I wish I could just turn around and drive back home, but this was just as important for her as it was for me. Lizzy needed this, even if she didn't know it. She needed to stand up for herself, needed to face the hatred that had been thrown in her face and rise above it. My Lizzy didn't realize how strong she was, and until she did, I would be that strength for her, even if it meant pushing her to do something she was scared of doing. I would love for her to face Courtney's mother at some point, would love for her to see that she was stronger than her, better than her, so she could be confident in herself, could believe in her own goodness. It would happen eventually, but first they had to deal with their mothers.

"It won't be as bad as you make it out to be. I won't let her treat you like the outcast daughter of the town whore's mother." Her whole body flinched at my words, breaking my heart yet again. "Because that is not who you are. It never has been, Lizzy. Keep that in mind when she throws shit at you. You are not who she says you are. You are my Lizzy, the love of my life, my fiancée. The sweet girl whom I fell in love with the second I laid eyes on her when I was twelve years old, the only girl I have ever loved, the one person I would do anything for. Think about that when it gets too much." Those words awarded me a return squeeze.

"I'm not sweet," she said still in that quiet voice, but I could hear a hint of steel in it now, too.

Thank God.

"You can be when you want to. It usually happens when we're both naked," I teased.

"Cole," she snapped, "don't you dare make me horny right before I'm about to face your witch of a mother."

"There she is, my feisty little firecracker. Don't let go of her again. And baby, you know I love making you horny. I will enjoy doing it for the rest of our lives, I don't care where we are or whom we are about to meet." That earned me a slap onto my thigh. I chuckled and grabbed that hand and held it where it was until I pulled into my parents' driveway.

Lizzy

I knew what Cole was doing. He was right, of course. That didn't change the fact that my stomach plummeted with dread when we pulled into the driveway and I looked up at one of the most impressive houses in my hometown of Ashford. It screamed sophistication and money.

It also scared the ever-living hell out of me.

I felt like I was fifteen years old again, worthless, trash, unwanted, like I had been told so many times. How stupid of me to think I had overcome all of this when I moved away and made a life for myself in Boston, a life I was damn well proud of. I closed my eyes and took a deep breath, trying to gather my wits and steel myself for what was about to happen.

"What the fuck?" I heard Cole's voice beside me. I looked over to him and saw that his eyes were pointed toward the two cars parked beside us.

"What is it?" I asked, confused.

"That's Courtney's car. And my guess, the other one is her

parents'."

"You're kidding." My whole body froze. Not in fear, though, in anger. I had a debt to settle with that bitch. Before Cole could say anything else, I opened my door, got out of my car, and stalked to the front door. Cole caught up with me right before I was about to reach it, and turned me to face him, then wrapped his arms around my tightly strung body.

"Easy there, baby. I know you're hell bent on settling your score, and believe me, I would love nothing more right now than to watch you do it, but we gotta go into this with a clear head. There's a reason why she is here with her parents and we gotta be prepared. My guess, she told her parents that she's pregnant with my child, and they're all here to try and set me straight."

"That fucking bitch," I growled. I would relish scratching her eyes out, couldn't wait actually.

"Baby, look at me." Cole lightly shook my body and my eyes went away from the front door to his. Besides amusement and pride, I saw worry and dread in them, and a whole lot of anger. He was seething, but was trying to keep himself in check for me. Because he was worried about me having to face not only his parents, but Courtney's parents as well. "You'll get your chance to go head-to-head with her, I promise. But promise me you'll try and keep a clear head. We don't know what that bitch is capable of or what twisted story she has told everyone. She might say things about me, about us, to try and hurt you, to try and make you run." The apprehension was obvious in his eyes as well as his voice. He wasn't just worried about me. He was worried I would leave him if I heard something I didn't like.

"Is there something you haven't told me about you and Courtney?"

He shook his head. "No."

"Is there a sex tape I don't know about?"

Another "No."

"Have you had threesomes with her?" His lips twitched slightly as he shook his head.

"Have you ever told her that you loved her? Promised her anything besides a good time in bed?"

"No, Lizzy. You know this already."

"Then what are you so worried about?"

His eyes roamed my face as his fingers brushed a strand of my hair aside before he cupped my cheek. "Nothing, I guess. Just ignore me."

I leaned into him and touched my lips to his. "I love you, Cole. And I know that you love me. I trust you. Now, let's go kick some bitch ass."

"Sounds good to me." He pressed his lips against mine and slipped his tongue into my mouth for a quick touch, making me moan and gasp at the same time. Before we could get into it, though, the door opened.

"Cole! How dare you bring your whore to this house!" his mother hissed. Cole's body locked, and so did mine. He pulled his lips from mine and turned to his mother.

"Don't you dare speak about my fiancée that way, mother." His voice was low. And threatening, as was his body language. He towered over his mother, his body taut, his hand firmly grasping mine. His mother gulped, but recovered and narrowed his eyes on him. "I have taught you better than this, Cole. You have no idea how disappointed your father and I are with what you have done, how much of disgrace you have brought to this family."

"Oh, believe me. I know only too well. What you never understood is that I don't give a fuck what you or anyone else think. And I'm putting an end to this fucking charade right fucking now."

He moved his mother out of the way with the hand that wasn't holding mine and pulled me behind him into the foyer, through the hall, and into the dining room. Everyone was there, sitting at the table, all prim and proper, dressed up in their Sunday finest while they were waiting to be served. There was one open spot next to Courtney, which I assumed was where Cole was supposed to sit. That was so not going to happen. I tightened my hand around his and got a reassuring squeeze in return. My eyes never left Courtney.

I could smell her game from a mile away. She sat there, pretending to be almost demure, playing the confused and hurt pregnant girlfriend who had to put up with her boyfriend's escapades. But her eyes betrayed her. That glint that told me she thought she would always get what she wanted no matter the collateral damage showed the person she truly was: a vindictive, manipulative, and spoiled little brat. My body heated with my rising anger. It took everything in me to not stride toward her and rip her fucking head off.

Out of the corner of my eyes I could see Cole taking them all in before his eyes settled on Courtney as well. "What the fuck do you think you're doing?" he growled at her, his anger unyielding, his voice uncompromising.

Courtney's eyes flicked to her mother then settled back on Cole. "Cole, baby, I've been patient, but—"

"Do not call me 'baby'. Only one woman has that right, the woman whose hand I'm holding right now. And cut the shit. Why don't we tell everyone what's really going on here. How you tried to trap me with a baby that's not mine, how you stalked me, threw yourself at me, how my own mother helped you try to drive Lizzy away from me. Let's talk about that."

"I have no idea what you're talking about, Cole. That baby is yours. All I was trying to do was stake my claim on you, to make her see that you're taken—"

"Oh, I am taken, all right. But not by you. I would never commit to a hateful and cruel bitch like you. All I ever did was use you to get off. And you were only too happy to offer."

That's when the unthinkable happened. Courtney started crying, shedding desperate and distressed tears, her body shaking with uncontrollable sobs. Oh, she was good. It was almost believable. I had the crazy urge to clap.

"Daddy," she whispered for help, her eyes going to her father in desperation.

"Fucking unbelievable," Cole muttered under his breath as he shook his head. I could see Courtney's mother gear up to say something. Her face was full of hatred, her eyes swinging from me to Cole then back to me. But before she could say anything, a loud boom startled all of us.

"For fucks sake, enough with this farce already!"

My eyes went to the person who belonged to the unfamiliar voice. It was Courtney's father. "We all know what is really going on here. I thought we were invited for dinner with friends, but now I see what the real reason is behind the invitation. And let me tell you, I will not be a part of it. I told you to get your life together, Courtney. You're neck-deep in debt. On top of that you just lost your job. I will not bail you out any longer. I gave you an ultimatum and what do you do? You get pregnant and lose your job. We all know that baby you're carrying isn't Cole's. Do you even know who the real father is? You're twenty-seven years old and still behave like the spoiled little brat your mother created." Another reason to jump up and down with applause. Looked like Courtney was finally getting the years-overdue whip-lashing from her father that she deserved.

"I have had my life ruined by my loyalty and commitment to my family. I will not stand by and watch while you try and do the same to someone else. I know both of you think I'm stupid enough to fall for the games you're playing because I've always turned a blind eye. But believe me, Courtney, I've always known you are nowhere near the sweet little daddy's girl you pretend to be to get your way. I've always known you were just like your mother. I tried, I tried so hard to do right by my cousin and raise his daughter to become a kind young woman. But I didn't stand a chance against your mother's bitterness, her games and manipulations. But this is the last straw. I'm done."

I gasped as his words registered. His cousin's daughter? What the hell was going on here? Cole pulled me close and wrapped his arm around my shoulders, tucking me into his side tight.

"George, what the fuck are you saying?" He had caught it, too. Courtney's father's, George's, eyes turned to Cole at hearing him speak, then to me and softened.

"You must be Elizabeth. Lizzy. It's nice to finally officially meet you." His voice had softened considerably as well as he was addressing me now. I couldn't say anything, so all I did was stare at him as my mind went into overdrive, trying to make sense of what this man had just said.

Cole answered for me. "Yeah, this is Lizzy. My fiancée. Now, tell us what the fuck you meant." Cole was getting impatient, and I had to say, I was right there with him.

"George," Courtney's mother hissed under her breath, at the same time Courtney whined, "But daddy—," but George cut both of them off with one look and a "Not one more word from either of you." Courtney's mother was seething, it was easy to see, while Courtney dropped the act and narrowed her hateful eyes on me right before she spat, "You fucking bitch! You worthless, meaningless little slut! Not only did you take my real father from me, now you've turned my other father against me too. But I will not let you take Cole! Mark my words—"

"I said, enough!" George's voice boomed once more. "Sit down and be quiet, Courtney. I don't want to hear one more word come out of your mouth." She glared at her father, but sat down. As did her mother, whose eyes hadn't moved from me through any of this.

George turned back to me. Then he started to explain, and his words once more tipped my world upside down and over its own axis. "Shortly before your father, my cousin, died, he told the family that he was filing for divorce. He couldn't stand his wife, didn't want to be with her for one more second. Their marriage had been arranged, it was never a love match. He also claimed that he had found the love of his life. Your mother."

I made a whimpering sound in the back of my throat. Cole pulled me in closer, wrapping his second arm around me, cocooning me with his body. I had known about the intended divorce, of course, but hearing it first-hand from his cousin, my—what exactly was he to me anyway? My head was spinning too much to figure that relationship out at the moment—and hearing the truth and sadness in his voice, was something different altogether. It made it real.

"He said that they were pregnant, and that he wanted to marry your mother. He loved you. Both of you." My body started shaking and tears were forming in my eyes. My father had loved me. The love of a parent was something I had no idea how to grasp. I was struggling. George went on, not giving me a chance to get myself together. "He wanted to marry your mother. And he wasn't just going to file for divorce, he was going to file for sole custody for Courtney as well. Your mother was delighted to raise your half-sister as her own, he said." My eyes went to Courtney, whose eyes were shuttered and resentful. Then they went to her mother. Bitterness, loathing, and hostility rolled off of her in waves. George continued. "My family is old-fashioned. Divorce is not acceptable, no matter if you're miserable or not. You have a duty to your family, and nothing or no one is ever to interfere with that duty. But my cousin didn't care. He was getting divorced, no matter what that meant. My parents were furious with him and threatened to disown him. Then he died unexpectedly." His voice grew grave at his last words. He really seemed to have loved his cousin, my father. He missed him. "When he died, everyone pretended that your mother and you didn't exist. I had heard about your mother going into labor the same night of the accident and giving birth to a girl, but I was too devastated by the loss of my cousin to think straight, to do the right thing." His apologetic and sorrowful eyes shifted from me to over my shoulder as he got lost in his memories. "I was four years younger than your father. I adored him, looked up to him, was proud of him. He was my idol. But then my parents started talking about how he had gone against the family's wishes, and how that had resulted in his death. I was stupid and grieving. I know that is no excuse, but it's the only thing I can offer. They talked me into marrying my cousin's widow, for the sake of the family, said that I needed to honor his memory and take care of his wife and child. I thought I was doing a good thing, convinced myself that I was. So I married her and adopted Courtney."

My mouth hung wide open at this point. Who were these

people? What kind of world did they live in that they thought they could make decisions like that about other people's lives? They were immoral and selfish, and I hated every single one of them. My anger was coming back, making the shock and sadness recede.

Good!

"Now I wish I had been braver," George continued. "That I had been smarter. I've been living a lie, covering up many a lie and deceit for my family's sake, while you and your mother had to endure the life you were doomed to live. I wish things had been different, that I had helped you, had supported my cousin's true love. It's what he would have wanted. I know that now. If I'm honest, I've known for a while. But I didn't. I was a coward. I have not only failed my cousin, I have spat on his memory, and I have to spend the rest of my life with that knowledge." He swallowed hard, then his eyes came back to me and he finished with, "But there is one thing you need to know, and again, I know this is poor as excuses go, but when I learned that Cole had taken you under his wing, I knew you had him to rely on. I have always known he was a good kid, so I knew he would take care of you, protect you, make sure that you were okay as much as it was in his power. I knew you were in good hands."

This was all too much. I didn't know what to think, what to do with this information. My father had loved me. Had loved my mother. Had wanted me. And Courtney's stepfather was my first cousin once removed, which in return made her not only my half-sister but also my what? My second cousin? How fucking messed up was all this? And all these people had been in on it. I just knew it. Even Courtney, by the looks of it.

"Did you know?" That was Cole's voice. I looked up at him to see that his eyes were going back and forth between his parents several times before they finally stopped on his mother's face.

"Of course we knew. Everyone in our circle does. Why do you think I wanted you away from that whore's daughter? Her mother brought enough disgrace to this town. I didn't want you to fall into her clutches. Don't you see? She is just like her mother, trying to take a man away from the woman and their child." Her voice was filled with venom. This woman could not be believed. Did she not hear what George had just said?

"You knew. You knew this whole time that Lizzy was Courtney's sister, that their dad wanted them to grow up as sisters with the woman he truly loved as their mother. You knew all this and yet you did nothing but look down on Lizzy and her mother, did nothing but make life miserable for them, spread rumors, fabricate lies, lock me up in the basement so I couldn't go see her. Lizzy was a child, mother! How could you do that to an innocent child?"

"Ha! Your *Lizzy* was never innocent. She probably doesn't even know what that word means or how to spell it. Those low-life white trash women are all the same. It's in their blood. Thank God that filth left town and took her foulness with her. Ashford has been a much better place since."

And there they go again, throwing me for yet another loop. Was she referring to my mother? Was she gone? "My mother left?" I asked in astonishment at the same time Cole asked, "You made her leave, didn't you? Both of you, or all three of you. You did something to make her leave." The glee in his mother's eyes was unmistakable. She had done something to my mother. She had made her disappear.

"I bought her a bus ticket myself," she said triumphantly.

A red haze settled over my eyes at that knowledge. My mother wasn't my favorite person in the world, not even close.

She had made my life a living hell, but now that I had all this information, now that I knew what exactly had happened, I could somehow understand how and why she had changed into that god awful person she had been all my life. It didn't excuse her treatment of me, didn't excuse the blame and guilt she put on my shoulders, but it did explain why and how she had sunk so deep. She had been lost in her grief. And all those bitches in town with their noses up their asses had done everything in their power to make her sink even further into the abyss of hell. All because she had fallen in love with a married man. They shouldn't have had an affair. My father should have gotten divorced before he started anything with my mom, but the extent these women went to for revenge was unfathomable. I saw now why my mother took delight in the fact that she was sleeping with their husbands. It was her own type of revenge. The only revenge she had been capable of meting out.

Absolute fury controlled my body as I tore away from Cole, the complete disregard for another human being these people lived and breathed on a daily basis boggling my mind and making me livid. "How dare you? How dare you people treat another human being that way? What the fuck is wrong with you? Where is she? Where did you send her?" Without realizing it, I had taken a few steps towards Cole's mother and was now only a couple of feet away from the chair she was sitting in with no intention to stop. I was going to kick her ass and not regret one single second of it. Strong arms wrapped around me from behind, holding me back. I knew they were Cole's so I didn't struggle.

His voice was low in my ear, soothing. "Calm down, baby. She's not worth it."

Cole's mother hadn't moved an inch, had stayed in her

chair while calmly and malevolently scrutinizing me. "That's right, son. Keep your whore in check. She wouldn't want to be charged with assault."

At the word "whore" being directed at me, I struggled to get free of Cole's hold, but he only tightened his arms around me and pulled me back a few feet. Then he kissed the top of my head and murmured, "Calm, baby. She's just looking for a reason to get you in trouble. She won't hesitate to have you arrested if you so much as touch her. Don't let her get to you. Think about what I said in the car." His calm and soothing tone did wonders in helping me breathe through my fury. When I opened my eyes again, I saw that Cole's father was standing now, though he hadn't moved closer to his wife, which was surprising since I had almost attacked her. George was also still standing, but he had moved closer to me. Almost protectively. Courtney and her mother were missing from the room. I didn't give a rat's ass where they had disappeared to, I was just glad that there was now only one hateful woman to deal with.

"Richard, I think it's time you control your wife before something happens." Richard, Cole's dad, was standing a few feet away from the table, a little off to the side, as he took in the scene. His head started to shake when his eyes landed on his wife. "Jesus Christ, Claire. I knew you always had it out for that woman and her daughter, but don't you think this is a little ridiculous?"

"Ridiculous? Did you just call me ridiculous?" Cole's mother hissed at her husband at the same time Cole asked him, "So you didn't know?"

Cole's father looked at his son. "Yes, I knew. Everyone in our social circle knows the connection between George and Walter and what preceded George's and Ann's marriage.

Everyone knew about the woman Walter cheated on her with and the daughter who resulted from that affair. But I stayed out of it. You know me, I try to not be around your mother too much if I can help it."

God, these people were unbelievable!

"Yeah, dad, how could I forget? Staying out and staying away has always been your solution to everything that had to do with mother and me," Cole replied disdainfully. Cole's father just stared at him and shrugged his shoulders, seemingly not giving a shit about what his son thought about him, not caring about anything really. I felt pity for him. He had lost out on getting to know his son, his amazing and wonderful son. I looked back at Cole's mother, thinking the same. She had no idea who her son was, never tried to get to know him, never supported him and his dreams, never encouraged him to be a good person, never showed him any love. It clicked for me then. These people really didn't matter. What they thought about me didn't matter. They were pitiful and sad. Miserable. They were rich in money and possessions, but poor in love and meaning relationships. I pitied them, all of them: Cole's parents, Courtney, her mother. The jury was still out on George, since he at least regretted his mistakes and was trying to redeem himself in some way.

I turned in Cole's arms and rested my hands on both his cheeks, cupping his face. "You know how much I love you?" I whispered. This man, this caring and loving and protective and kind man, had grown up exposed to nothing but viciousness, bitterness, and indifference, and had come out the other end the man he is today. No, he had always been that man, even when he was a little boy. Yes, he could be brutally honest and should not be proud of how he had treated women before he claimed me as his, but he was not evil, or hateful, or bitter. And I loved him all the more now that I realized the enormity of that fact.

"I do. You know I love you just as much? Probably more?" he asked, his confused but happy eyes studying me. I nodded, then placed my lips on his and kissed him softly and lovingly. When I ended the kiss I could see George standing close, his eyes sad.

"I know this is a lot to ask, but once you've wrapped your mind around everything you learned today, I would like to meet with you, get to know you, tell you about your dad, show you some pictures maybe."

I gave him a small smile. "I would love that." He returned my smile, relieved if hesitant.

"Over my dead body! I didn't let her have Walter, and I won't let her have you!" we heard screeched from the other side of the room.

It was Ann.

I turned my head just in time to see her holding a revolver. In the next moment, a deafening noise exploded in the room, like a bang, and seconds later, I landed on the floor.

Then everything went black.

Chapter 22

Cole

"Lizzy? Lizzy!"

No! No, no, no, no, no!

She wasn't moving.

Fuck! She isn't moving!

This isn't happening! No! No, Lizzy!

Her eyes were closed and her body was limp in my arms. Frantically, I started searching for blood, for a wound, my heart beating in my throat at a rapid pace, my breath coming out in labored pants, the panic over losing her threatening to overwhelm me as I ran my hands over her body, her neck, her chest, along her sides, over her abdomen, her legs, the back of her head. Finding nothing, I carefully turned her to look at her back to repeat my frantic search.

Nothing.

I couldn't find anything.

No wound.

No blood.

No nothing.

She was okay.

She was just knocked out.

She was okay.

I lifted her limp upper body and pulled her into me, cradling her, tucking her face into my neck and mine in hers, breathing her in. Now that I knew she wasn't shot, I could feel her strong pulse beating against my lips, her breath against the skin on my neck. I closed my eyes and kissed her smooth skin as relief washed over me.

She was okay. Lizzy was okay.

God! I can't ever lose her.

I placed another kiss over her pulse point and softly ran my fingers over the back of her head.

There.

A bump was forming where she must have hit the floor.

I kissed her forehead, murmuring, "You're okay. We're okay. Everything will be fine. I love you so much, baby." Then the commotion going on around me started to penetrate. There was shouting and screaming.

And groaning.

Someone was groaning in pain.

Someone close to me.

I turned my head to see George lying not three feet from me, blood seeping out from somewhere in his torso. Ever so carefully, I placed Lizzy's body back onto the hardwood, onto her side, so as not to put any weight on that bump. I crawled over to George and grabbed his hand. His eyes opened as he groaned once more, then his breaths started coming in pants.

"Fuck, that hurts," he said on another moan. "How is Lizzy? Is she okay? She didn't get her, did she?" He rolled his eyes to the side, trying to find Lizzy. I squeezed his hand.

"She's fine. Just bumped her head." My eyes went to her as well. She still wasn't moving. If she didn't wake up soon, I would lose my mind again. I needed to see her gorgeous green eyes, needed proof that she was truly fine.

Another pained groan snapped my eyes back to George. He was in bad shape. There was a lot of blood. It needed to be stopped. I ripped open his shirt to find the wound. "Shit," I swore under my breath. His whole torso was covered, but I could see the wound as it steadily seeped blood onto the floor.

He had been shot in the gut.

I took off the sweater I was wearing and whipped my t-shirt over my head, then scrunched it up and pressed it to George's wound, trying to stop the flow. "Hold on, George. Don't die on me."

"It's okay. Fine. As long as she's safe. As long as I saved her." He was in a lot of pain. His eyes were closed once again and his face was scrunched up in what could only be agony. His breathing was labored. But at least he was still conscious. I took that as a good omen.

"You did. And she is." He nodded his head weakly in acknowledgement.

High-pitched shrieks made me look to the other side of the room, finding Ann on the floor, on her stomach, her hands behind her back. She was struggling, kicking, fighting whoever was restraining her.

Max.

Max was here. Thank God.

"Max!" I called across the room. His head whipped around and his eyes landed on me, roaming first over my body then over George before they came back and stayed on me.

"You good?"

"Yeah, it's not my blood. But George needs an ambulance."

"It's on its way. Our girl?" Despite the circumstances, my

lips twitched at his reference to Lizzy as 'our girl'.

"She's fine."

Relief washed over his face before he turned back to Ann, who was still screeching at the top her lungs, spouting some nonsense about filing assault charges. That woman was unbelievable. I scanned the room and saw my parents off to the side as they surveyed the scene in utter shock. My mother had her arms wrapped around her middle, her eyes wide with bewilderment and disbelief. Good. Maybe this shook her shit up. My father's eyes were on me, shocked just like my mother's, but I could also see remorse there. And sadness. I would deal with that later. Now, I needed his help.

"Dad, come over here and keep the pressure on George's wound. I need to see to Lizzy." He flinched as if woken from a daze, then strode over without hesitation, his face now alert and focused. He took over pressing the shirt against the wound and grabbed hold of George's other hand.

"I've got him, son. Go and look after your girl." He hadn't referred to me as 'son' in years, but I had bigger things to worry about, so I ignored it for now. I hurried back to Lizzy and took her hand gently in mine, stroking my thumb over her knuckles. My other hand went to her cheek, cupping it softly and lovingly.

"Lizzy, baby? I need you to wake up now. Can you open your gorgeous green eyes for me? Please, I need to see them."

Her eyelids fluttered and she moaned. I squeezed her hand. Then it happened.

She opened her eyes.

Lizzy

I felt a hand squeezing mine.

A voice calling to me.

Cole's voice, asking me to open my eyes.

I tried, but it was hard. My head was pounding, and there was so much noise. Someone was screaming. Someone else was shouting. Then there was another someone talking in a low murmur. So many voices, I couldn't make them all out.

What is going on?

The last thing I remembered was kissing Cole.

I tried again to open my eyes and this time, I was successful, even though it hurt like a bitch. The first things I saw were Cole's eyes. They were filled with concern and relief as they held mine.

"Hey," he whispered through a small smile.

"Hey," I whispered back.

"How are you feeling?" His hand gave mine another squeeze.

"Groggy. Confused. My head..." I turned my head to better see him. "Ow," I moaned.

"Easy, baby. You hit your head when we went down. You've got quite the goose egg."

"What happened?"

"Do you think you can sit up?" Cole asked.

I nodded then flinched. He reached for me and held me by my shoulders, supporting me as I sat up, then sat next to me, holding me to his side. I could see the room now. It was filling with even more noises, more people. First with cops, then with a group of EMTs. And Max was here. What was he doing in Cole's parents' house? Then I saw George. He was lying on the floor close to me, with Cole's dad talking to him quietly as he pressed something against his abdomen.

My confused and now panicked eyes found Cole's when

he started to explain. "It's okay. He'll be fine. Ann had a gun and was about to shoot you, but she hit George instead. He got shot in the gut, but he's conscious and the EMTs are here now to help him. It seems like I owe your cousin. He saved your life when he threw himself in front of that bullet."

"He threw himself in front of a bullet?" I asked in astonishment.

"Yeah. He saved you. She would have shot you in the back, could have possibly killed you and me. He saved both our lives."

"Are you okay? You're not hurt?" My eyes started roaming his body. He was shirtless. And there was blood all over his hands and arms. "Cole," I whispered, another completely new wave of panic hitting me.

"Shh, I'm fine. It's not my blood. I'm not hurt." Relief washed over me as I leaned my head against his shoulder, forgetting once more that it was not a good idea to move said head.

"Ouch," I groaned once again.

"Easy, sweetheart. We need to have you looked at."

"I'm fine."

"Lizzy." Cole's voice was stern as he lowered his head to give me a reproachful look. "You are letting the EMTs look at you. You bumped your head hard and were unconscious for several minutes. I want you checked out. No arguing." Yes, his voice was stern, but it was that way because he was worried about me, worried that I was more hurt than I seemed. It was written all over his face. I lifted my hand and cupped his cheek. "Okay, honey. I'll let them look at me," I gave in instantly.

"Thank you." He turned his face into my hand and kissed my palm, murmuring, "You scared the shit out of me. Don't ever do that again." I moved my hand to hold the back of his neck and pulled him toward me, placed my lips against his, and whispered, "I won't." Then he kissed me, oh so gently and carefully.

"Ma'am? I was told you needed looked at?"

We broke the kiss and looked up to see an EMT standing next to Max. Both of them were looking at us, smiling. Well, smirking in Max's case, though I could see the worry etched in his face nonetheless.

"Yes. She bumped her head when she fell and passed out. There's a big goose egg on the back of her head and she's in pain," Cole explained as he shifted me away from him slightly so the EMT had enough room to check me out.

"All right, then. Let's take a look. My name is John, by the way."

"Hi, John. I'm Lizzy. This is Cole and the big, burly guy standing next to you is Max."

"Nice to meet you, Lizzy," John murmured through a smile as he prodded my head gently until he found the bump. Yeah, it hurt. My head was throbbing, though it wasn't nearly as bad as after that punch in the nose by Jesse's and Chloe's father a few weeks ago. Out of the corner of my eye I could see Cole shaking his head.

"What?" I asked.

"Nothing, baby."

I rolled my eyes at him, making him and the two other men surrounding me chuckle.

"All right, roll those pretty eyes back down so I can look at them." Cole's body tensed next to mine.

"Less flirting, more working. She's taken," Cole told John. Now it was my turn to shake my head, which uh...was a bad idea.

John's smile faded when he saw me flinch. "That hurt?"

"Yeah. I need to remember to not move my head so much. It's not that bad, though. It's gone already."

"Any blurriness? Dizziness? Feeling nauseous?"

"No. None."

"Good. As your friend here said—"

"Fiancée," Cole interrupted him. I shoved my elbow into his side and he tightened his hold on me.

John started over. "As your *fiancée* said, you have a nasty goose egg on your head. But your eyes look fine and you're not dizzy or feeling nauseous, so I'd say you're probably okay. But just in case, I would like to take you in for some x-rays."

"Thank you, John. I don't think that will be nece—Hey!" One minute I was sitting on the floor, the next I was up in Cole's arms and he was striding toward the front door. "What the hell are you doing?"

"I'm taking you to the hospital and you won't say a single thing about it. Now, do you want to ride in the ambulance or my car?" There were a lot of things I would have said to him under normal circumstances for hauling me around the room and making decisions for me, but I bit my tongue. Cole wasn't acting out of his usual bossiness. He was genuinely concerned, and I needed to keep my pigheadedness in check. This time at least. He needed this, needed me checked out thoroughly for his own peace of mind. So I would give it to him.

I sighed in defeat. "Fine. Let's take your car, though. I don't want to have to come back here."

"Fair enough," he said and walked us to his car, opened the passenger door while still carrying me, then deposited me gently in the passenger seat.

Low voices woke me. My left cheek was resting on Cole's

thigh while I was curled up in a chair in the hospital waiting room.

After the doctors had re-examined me and the x-rays and CT scan—yes, I had agreed to undergo one for Cole's sake even though I knew I was fine—had been performed, and luckily showed that nothing was fractured or swollen or at all concerning inside my head, I had refused to go back to the hotel to rest. I wanted to wait and hear about George's surgery. That man, no matter how deeply he had been involved in the deceit that had controlled my and my mother's life for so long, had saved my life. I could be dead if it weren't for him. So I had insisted on waiting, had marched right to the waiting room and planted my butt in a chair. Cole argued, telling me I needed my rest and promising me we would come back first thing in the morning to check on George. I had dug my heels in. Seeing that there was no way he would win that argument, he had begrudgingly given in under the condition that I would try to get some sleep here. Which at first didn't happen since the police had come to the hospital to get our statements. So we did that. It took longer than you might think, since we had to explain the relations in our oh so happy little family, which was difficult to do since I had a hard time figuring that part out for myself, let alone come to terms with it.

I have to admit that after we were done and the cops had left, I had been more than a little tired. I didn't even have enough energy left to give Cole the evil eye when he got me a pillow and a blanket and ordered me to lie down. I forewent the pillow, though, and used his thigh instead. It didn't even take me two minutes to fall asleep when his fingers started running soothing circles on my shoulder and upper arm.

Which brought us to now.

I opened my eyes to see Cole's father sitting in the chair across from us. He was alone. Cole's mother wasn't there. They weren't really talking. Richard was wringing his hands as it seemed like he tried to find the right words. He wasn't very successful in that endeavour.

"Cole, I...Son...I..." was all he seemed to be able to get out.

"Not now, dad." Cole's voice was stern and dismissive.

"We need to talk. I wasn't aware that your mother—"

"Don't start with that shit. You knew exactly what was going on this whole time. You might not have known all the details, but you knew about Lizzy's dad, you knew about her mom, you knew who Lizzy was this whole time. Don't pretend you didn't." Cole's voice was getting more and more agitated towards the end of his little tirade. His thigh was tense under my cheek.

"You're right. I knew. But I didn't imagine it would—"

"Oh no, dad. Don't you dare start spewing any of your pathetic excuses. I'm not interested, and neither is Lizzy. Unless you came here to apologize in earnest and try and make amends, you can leave."

"I..."

"Apologize and mean it or go."

"She's sleeping—"

"She's awake." Damn. Of course he knew I had woken up.

Richard's eyes came to me, and I lifted my cheek off of Cole's thigh and sat up, flinching slightly when the movement caused my head to throb.

"You okay, baby?" Cole asked quietly, his voice so much softer now that he was addressing me.

"I'm fine. Any news?" I asked him when he pulled me into his side.

"Not yet." I looked at the big clock on the wall. George had been in surgery for over four hours now. Worry gnawed at my stomach and I bit my lip.

"No news is good news in this case, Lizzy. He'll be fine. He's made it this far. That's a good sign."

"Where's Max?" Max had come to the hospital with us. He had also given his statement when the police were here and had stayed after.

"He's trying to find some decent coffee and something for breakfast. It's almost dawn.

"I could do with some coffee," I murmured.

"I thought you might." He smiled. "And you need some food in you." I wasn't going to argue about that. I was starving. We missed dinner last night and had been up most of the night, so my stomach was craving food like nobody's business.

"You think he could find me some pancakes?"

"You want pancakes?" Cole asked as he leaned back so he could pull his phone out of his pants' pocket. He didn't need my answer. He knew how much I liked my food, especially pancakes.

"Max? Lizzy's awake. She wants pancakes. You mind getting her some?" Silence for a second before he said, "Thanks, man." Then he hung up and put his phone back in his pocket. "He's at a diner down the street. Already ordered a bunch of food for all of us. He'll be back soon."

"Good," I said.

He smiled at me and I returned that smile, then both our eyes went to his father, who hadn't said a word during that whole exchange. He looked uncomfortable as his eyes moved back and forth between the two of us. I had to give it to him, he really did look contrite to some extent, but I wasn't sure if that was good enough. Yes, he seemed to be sorry, what exactly about I wasn't sure since there was so much for him to be sorry about; the list seemed endless. And no, he had never actively done anything to hurt me, but his passiveness and indifference as well as his elitist attitude had contributed to this whole dilemma. And then there was the fact that he has never been a good father to Cole. That was something I wasn't going to forgive easily. And neither should Cole. It might make me a cold-hearted bitch, but I didn't care. His parents had caused him a lot of pain and self-doubt throughout his childhood and teen years, and even if he didn't admit it to himself, Cole wanted his dad to be proud of him.

Richard cleared his throat when neither Cole nor I said anything, but instead just looked at him, waiting for him to speak.

"Dad," Cole prompted him with a growl after another minute passed.

He sighed and trained his eyes on me. "Elizabeth. Lizzy. I came here to apologize. I'm aware this probably isn't the right time or place, but I didn't think it could wait. I didn't want the two of you to leave and miss my chance." He stopped and gave his son an apologetic look before he continued. "I am truly sorry for what has transpired, for not caring enough to do something, for not caring at all. What has been done to you and your family is truly tragic and I am sorry that I played a part in that." Another pause. This one lasted a little longer, as Richard seemed to be troubled. "When Ann tried to kill you tonight...when she pointed the gun at you...she would have done it. She would have killed you. I could see it in her eyes. And she didn't care if she hurt anyone else. She could have hurt Cole, could have killed him, too, and she didn't care. You can say that that was a real eye-opener. When the two of you went down, my heart stopped. I..." He took another deep breath and then finished with, "I confronted your mother, Cole. She admitted to trying to break you up, told me the lengths she went to, to accomplish that goal, told me that she had been conspiring with Ann for years to get you to marry Courtney. That viper. I'm glad you never got serious with her. You're much smarter than your father. Anyway, I told your mother I was leaving her, that I was going to file for divorce. I packed a bag and moved into a hotel a couple of hours ago."

Wow.

I had expected nothing more than a forced apology, an apology out of duty so that Cole wouldn't cut him off completely maybe, but this...this...I didn't even know what to do with this. For the second—or was it the third? —time tonight, my head was spinning with the information given to me. Not only had his apology sounded genuine, he had left his wife and was getting a divorce?

"You left her?" Cole asked, sounding just as shocked as I felt.

Richard nodded. "Yes. I should have done it a long time ago."

"Why didn't you?"

He sighed and ran his hand through his hair, exactly like his son does when he is frustrated or stressed. "We grew up in a different time, son. I was never going to tell you this, but I married your mother because I got her pregnant. Back then you didn't really have a choice. If you were stupid enough to get a girl pregnant, you took responsibility for your actions and married her. It's the way it was done. I...I didn't particularly like your mother even back then, but..."

"Let me guess. She put out. Or rather trapped you."

Richard nodded. "Yes, your mother trapped me into

marrying her. She got pregnant on purpose. That's probably where she got the idea and helped Courtney try to do the same to you. Your own mother tried to trap you into marrying a girl you despise. There is a reason we were never happy. Believe it or not, I wasn't always this hard and indifferent man I am now. In fact, you remind me a lot of myself before I married your mother."

"You're kidding." Yes, that's what came out of my mouth. I slapped my hand over it, covering it. I didn't need to be embarrassed, though. Both Cole and Richard chuckled at my faux-pas.

"I know it's hard to believe, but it's true. I see a lot of myself in my son. And I never told him this, but I am proud of him." Cole's chuckle died as his body tensed. His father saw the change. "It's true, son. I *am* proud of you. You are stronger than I ever was, you fight for what you believe in and never back down. For that fact alone I couldn't be prouder. Then add to that what you have made of yourself. You're a successful young man who is already making a name for himself in his field of expertise. And you went after the woman you've been in love with all your life. An independent, strong, and kind, young woman from what I hear. Not to mention beautiful."

My eyes went wide at the unexpected compliment. He liked me? And he was proud of Cole for being with me? If my world hadn't been turned upside down a few times already in the past few months, or rather weeks, hell, hours, I'd be looking around for the cameras, thinking I was getting punked or getting set up in some way. Cole was just as surprised, though his eyes weren't bugging out of his head quite as much as my eyes were out of mine.

"And you realized all this tonight? Because I could have

gotten killed?"

"No, son. I didn't just realize it tonight. I've known for a long time. But you and I...We never had the kind of relationship where we talked about any of that, or rather talked much in general—"

"And whose fault is that?" Now Cole was getting angry again. I understood. If Richard had reached out to his son sooner, if he had been more approachable, his life could have been a lot different.

"It's mine and mine alone. I take full responsibility for my failure to get to know my own son, to be there for him when I knew he needed me. I know I left you to your mother's devices. I was selfish and ignorant, disappointed in myself and angry for destroying my life, for being stuck with a woman I knew I would never love. I should never have taken any of that out on you. And if that wasn't enough, I resented you for being close to my father, a father who all but disowned me when I got your mother pregnant. And when he supported you in your choice of profession, and then left you all his money, I'm ashamed to say that I was jealous. You will never know how sorry I am. I just hope I haven't lost my last chance at making things right between us." Richard's eyes were pleading with Cole. He was asking for another chance. His last chance. Wow. This was big. And I could tell that Cole had no idea how to react. It was a lot to swallow, a lot to think about, a lot more to talk about. But for now, all I could do was show him that I would back him up no matter what he decided. I grabbed his free hand that was resting on his knee and squeezed it in reassurance and support. His eyes never left his father's, his jaw stayed tightly clenched, but he returned my squeeze, letting me know that he understood.

"I appreciate you saying all that, dad. I really do. But I can't give you an answer right now. I can tell that you mean every word you said, but I don't trust you. If I decide, no, if *we* decide that we want you to be part of our lives, we'll have to take it slow, take one day at a time. But let me assure you one thing, my mother will never be a part of this. I do not want or accept that poison in our lives any longer. If you ever decide to not go through with the divorce, that's your call, but she will not enter my and Lizzy's lives ever again. That includes the children we will have."

Richard nodded. "I understand. And I wholeheartedly agree."

Father and son stared at each other for a long minute until Cole lifted his chin in male understanding, making Richard exhale and close his eyes in relief. The moment was interrupted when Max strode into the room, carrying two bags of what I was hoping was delicious diner breakfast. He took one look around the room, assessing the situation, and greeted me with, "Hey, doll," then to my surprise fixed his gaze on Richard and said, "I'm surprised he hasn't kicked you out yet."

Richard held his eyes and said, "Believe me. So am I. My son is a better man than I ever was."

"Can't argue with you there."

"What? You guys know each other or something?" Cole asked.

"Not personally, no," Max said. "Know his type. Can't say I like it."

"Neither do I. I'm trying to turn a leaf." That was Richard.

"That so?" Max didn't sound convinced. But then, he hadn't been here when Richard apologized. "What about Lizzy? You trying to turn a leaf with her too?" My heart melted at hearing the protective undertone in Max's voice.

Richard's eyes came to me and softened. "Absolutely. I already apologized for my behaviour towards her and I'll do my best to make up for it."

Max grunted but didn't say anything else as he busied himself with the boxes of food, looking through them until he found one filled with pancakes, then grabbing a cup of coffee and handing me both.

"Have I told you that I love you?"

There was silence for a few moments as Max froze in his tracks. Then his face spread into a wide grin and he winked at me before he sat down and dug into his breakfast. Cole chuckled and squeezed my knee. I beamed at him, happy that I had found a new close friend in Max, then I dug into my own breakfast.

"Damn, these pancakes are good." Cole shook his head at me, laughing, while Max gave me another huge grin.

We were all eating silently for a few minutes until Cole asked, "Max, why were you in Ashford last night? I'm grateful you were, don't get me wrong, but what made you follow us here?"

"I didn't follow you. I was already there. Keeping an eye on little Miss Courtney. Making sure that she wasn't planning some new scheme or worse. Never considered keeping my eye on her mother, though I should have. It makes perfect sense. That's on me. I was about to follow Courtney when she came running out of the house, but then I heard a shot fired and ran inside instead."

Something he said piqued my curiosity. "Where *is* Courtney? Her dad is in surgery with a gunshot wound and her mother is in jail. Has anyone seen her?"

"Shit. I completely forgot about that bitch," Cole said, which I have to admit made me really happy.

Max shook his head. "Nope. Far as I know, the police tried to track her down for a statement but couldn't find her."

"So she's gone? Just like that?" I wondered.

"She'll resurface at some point. I wouldn't be surprised if she went to her baby daddy, whoever that might be. But for now, yeah, I'd assume so. She has no more cards to play. Their house of lies has crumbled and she's alone. Her father cut her off financially a while ago, her mother is in jail and will stay there for a long time, and she lost her job. Last night was her last-ditch effort to get what she wanted and she failed miserably."

"Do you think she knew about her mother having a gun?" I was curious to know.

Max shrugged his shoulders. "I wouldn't be surprised if she did, but you never know."

I stewed on that, a little upset that it seemed like I wouldn't get the chance to give her the smack down she deserved,

"There is something I would like to know," Richard spoke up. "Do you remember what Ann said right before she tried to shoot Lizzy?" I froze. I hadn't remembered her words until now.

"Fuck," Cole swore.

"What? What did she say?" That was Max. He had hurried into the house after the shot had been fired, so he hadn't heard.

"She said something along the lines of not letting Lizzy get Walter, and she wouldn't let her get George either."

"I knew it," Max growled. "I knew she had something to do with Walter Matthews' death." His eyes landed on me. I could feel all eyes in the room trained on my face. Cole put his plate aside and pulled me into his side, trying to soothe me. Me? I didn't know what to think or feel. The magnitude of what

Ann's words and actions entailed astounded me. I felt like I was trapped in some cheap soap opera.

I shook my head in disbelief and sadness. But before I could say or do anything, the doors to the waiting room opened and a doctor strode in.

"George Miller?"

I got up, and so did Cole since he refused to let me go, and braced for the news.

Chapter 23

Lizzy

Eight months later.

I giggled as I felt small, soft kisses being traced all over my face. My eyelids fluttered and when they opened, landed on the man I was going to spend the rest of my life with. The man I had been in love with for sixteen years.

"Good morning, beautiful," Cole murmured as he continued down the side of my neck.

"Good morning, handsome." I tilted my head to give him better access, feeling his answering grin against my sensitive skin.

"How did my gorgeous wife sleep last night?"

I giggled again. "Your *soon-to-be* wife slept very well for the two or three hours her soon-to-be *husband* let her." That earned me a chuckle and a quick lip touch, raising goosebumps all over my body. His mouth was close to my collarbone now, one of my most sensitive spots.

"My *very*-soon-to-be wife is too addictive for her own good. That's why her *very*-soon-to-be husband can't keep his hands off of her." His teeth grazed my skin right before he started sucking it lightly into his mouth. My body quivered in anticipation.

"Cole," I moaned as I arched my body against his, seeking more skin-to-skin contact, my nipples brushing against his hard chest as he kept himself just high enough above to keep our bodies from touching more. He was in a teasing mood, which meant I was in for a treat. Or a torture session, depending on how you looked at it. I smiled to myself, only too ready to play. I wrapped my arms around his back and lightly ran my fingernails from his shoulder blades down to the top of his ass. Cole loved it when I scratched his back. It was one of his triggers.

"You're a little minx, aren't you, very-soon-to-be Mrs. Brooks? My minx."

"That's right, Mr. Brooks. I am that."

"A minx?"

"Yes."

"Mine?"

"Always," my whisper turned into a long moan when he pulled my nipple deeply into his mouth and circled it with his tongue before he gave the same attention to my other breast. His hands were roaming my sides, the soft touch driving me absolutely insane. God! He made me feel so good. Every time he touched me, my body was craving more. And more and more. His mouth kept working my nipples, going from one to the other, then back again, until I couldn't take it any longer. I knew what he wanted. He wanted me to beg for it. It turned him on immensely when I begged him for more, begged him to take me.

"Please, Cole. I need more." I was delirious with want and need and wasn't too proud to ask for it. At least not with Cole.

He had shown me what it felt like to let go, to not be embarrassed of my reactions, to trust that he would give me what I wanted, what I needed, what I craved. He made me feel beautiful and desired and perfect for him. I knew I was absolutely, one hundred percent safe.

Always.

"What do you need, baby? Tell me." His lips and tongue left my nipple and moved over my ribs down to my belly button, stopped for a quick but sensual nip and dip, then kept moving until they found my clit. "You need this?" The vibrations caused by his voice and the heat from his breath against my clit made my whole body twitch.

"Yes," I breathed. "No...I need you inside me." I was panting, my hands gripping his hair tightly.

"Like this?" he asked right before he pushed his tongue inside me. I arched my neck, my body bowing off the bed. "Or like this?" Two fingers entered me, circling, scissoring, pumping, while his mouth went back to my nub. It felt so good I knew I wouldn't be able to hold on for much longer. Cole was really good with his mouth and fingers. "Tell me, Liz."

"I want you," I whispered. "Please, Cole."

"You've got me. Tell me how you want me." His lips closed around my clit once more, his tongue flicking, while his fingers kept playing with me. God, I was getting close now. "God, baby, you're so wet. And you taste so fucking good." He gave his tongue another turn while his hand spread me wide, opening me to him. My breath hitched. I could feel my muscles tighten, the heat pooling. I was ready to explode.

"Cole," I screamed.

Then he was gone, and less than a second later we were face-to-face and his cock was pushing inside, stretching me oh so perfectly. "You're not coming without me, baby, not today," he whispered as he held my eyes. "Wrap me up tight." I did as asked, wrapping both my arms and legs around him, holding him as closely and tightly as possible, while his arms went around my back, pulling me up and into him. "Keep your eyes on mine. I need to see those gorgeous greens when you come for me."

"Okay," I whispered.

Then he started moving, slowly at first, and shallow, then faster and deeper. Our eyes stayed connected, both of us completely open and vulnerable as we looked deep into each other's souls.

It was building again. Quickly. "Cole—"

"I feel it, baby. Your pussy is starting to clamp down on me. God, baby. You have no idea how good you feel. Let go!"

"Come with me." I held on, needing him to join me.

"I am. Let go, sweetheart," he ground out through clenched teeth. He increased his thrusts, going deeper, then grinding, then pulling out to the tip and thrusting in again, once, twice, three times. I let go. His eyes grew wide, just like I knew mine did, and he came on a shout of my name while I came gasping his, our eyes staying locked while we joined each other in pure bliss, making this the most perfect pre-wedding sex ever.

Cole

I was standing by the cottage windows, looking out over the water, sipping a cup of coffee. Lizzy was finishing up in the bathroom.

Only a few more hours until she was my wife.

Four to be exact.

It was busy out on the beach where our ceremony would

be performed. People were milling about, setting up chairs and arranging flowers. It had been a long time coming and I couldn't wait to finally give the love of my life my last name.

A lot of things have happened after that night at my parents' house.

When the doctor told us that George had made it through the surgery and was optimistic towards his recovery, Lizzy and I had gone to the hotel after a quick visit with a still half-unconscious George. We had stayed in town for a few days until Lizzy was reassured enough to go back to Boston and back to work. She had bonded with George. For her, he was just another victim of the games and deceit our families had started, and she had forgiven him. I hadn't been as forgiving. For me, George had played a big role in that whole scheme, but after seeing the love and adoration in his eyes whenever they were on Liz, and after he had proven that he regretted everything he had done or not done, that he wanted nothing but to get to know her and be a part of her family, I had relented. But not without giving him one last talking-to.

"You hurt her once, you lie to her once, you deceive her once in any way, you're gone. She's had enough of that shit in her life and I won't let her big heart lead her to more pain. You treat her like the diamond she is every time you see her, every time you even think of her. If you don't, if I get even the slightest inkling that you're not being true and honest with her, I will make sure that you are gone from her life forever. You understand?"

"I understand. I absolutely do. I have learned my lesson, Cole. You can count on me. I love her like my own daughter, like I should have all those years. There is nothing and no one in this world that could make me hurt her ever again," George had replied without hesitation.

I still kept my eye on him, but during the past few months I had relaxed somewhat. He was genuinely interested in being Lizzy's family and I wanted that for her. I knew she needed it, to know she had at least one blood related family member who wasn't embarrassed by her existence.

George is now back on his feet, his slow recovery being the reason why we had postponed the wedding. Lizzy had wanted him here and I had understood. I'm not gonna lie and say I wasn't disappointed when she told me, but I had understood. Better yet, I had come up with an idea that would have earned me her eternal love if I hadn't already owned it.

"I'm sorry, Cole. I want to marry you; everything in me wants to be your wife. But can we wait a few months until George is feeling better so he can come?"

I sighed and hung my head. I wasn't a patient man, especially when it came to officially making the woman I had loved all my life mine. But I understood her need to wait for George to be able to attend. "How long?" I asked her.

"I don't know. The doctors say anywhere from six to nine months for him to be back to normal." Six to nine months would make it anywhere between May and August. My face had split into a wide grin as an idea formed in my mind. "What? Why are you grinning like a crazy loon all of a sudden?"

"I have an idea," I said through my smirk. "A great idea, actually."

"Uh oh. Do I want to hear it?"

"Yeah. You do. Come here."

"I am here. I'm sitting right next to you."

"Closer." I pulled her onto my lap and cupped her face. "Let me ask you something." She nodded. "If we wait six to nine months, that would make it the middle of summer. Would you still want a destination wedding or would you like to get married here instead?"

She shrugged. "I don't really care where we get married, as long as we get married."

"Thank you for that, baby." I softly brushed my lips against hers. Then I asked her a question that had her eyes go wide with understanding. "Do you remember the day we first met?" She nodded as tears filled her eyes. I am not embarrassed to say that I had to fight back my own. "It was in the beginning of July, two weeks before your tenth birthday."

"I know," she whispered as the first tear started falling. I kissed it away.

"How about we make that date our wedding day?"

"I would love that." Her tears were now running freely.

"And how about we get married at that beach where we spent our first weekend together?" She had thrown her arms around me at that point, full on crying.

I smiled to myself at that memory and how grateful she had been that night.

George had been delighted, to say the least, that we had postponed the wedding so he could attend. Lizzy and he had spent a lot of time together in the past eight months. Every Sunday, he came to our house for dinner, and they talked many times on the phone during the week or met up for lunch. Through George, Lizzy got to know her father. He showed her photos and shared tons of memories and stories with her from when they grew up together. Something that Lizzy cherished. And George had helped me find the perfect picture of her parents I had framed as her wedding gift. In the picture, her mom was pregnant and her father was holding her from behind, his chin on her shoulder as he nuzzled her neck; her mother's eyes were closed and she had a small, happy smile on her face. The same smile I see on Lizzy's face when she is content and happy. The smile I live to see every day. I hoped seeing the picture, seeing her parents this happy, would give her some peace and help her overcome the pain I knew still lingered.

It didn't take long for Ann to be convicted for attempted murder. It was a clear-cut case and she was serving a life sentence at the Massachusetts Department of Correction in Framingham. She had the possibility of parole, but that wasn't for another few years. Walter Matthews' case had also been re-opened. A lot of time had passed and it was doubtful that they would find anything after all these years, but it was worth a shot.

Getting a divorce had been easy and quick for George, especially now that Ann had been convicted. He had sold their house in Ashford and was now working and living in Boston. He was starting over, which couldn't be easy at his age, but he didn't seem to care. Just like Lizzy's father Walter had when he'd decided to go his own way, George had split from his family, and as a result, their business. He was good at his job as an attorney and I had no doubt that he was doing fine. He had even started dating again and was seeing a woman he had met at his new company, a widow with two teenage children. They were attending our wedding together.

Another important development had been the relationship my father and I were starting to build. He was still getting divorced from my mother, though she was putting up a good fight. My father didn't talk to me about it; in fact, he never even mentioned my mother, but I knew through Max. I also knew that the only contact they had was through their lawyers. I was glad that my father would be rid of her soon. Over the months, I have come to see him in a different light.

When he had told me at the hospital that I reminded him a lot of himself when he was in his twenties, I hadn't quite believed him. How could I? All I had known was this reserved, removed, and indifferent man who never had time for his son. Now though, he made it a point to call me frequently. At first, those phone calls had been somewhat awkward, filled with many uncomfortable silences, but we had gotten over that and were finding our way to an easier and more relaxed father-son relationship. He was here today as well. My mother wasn't. She hadn't been invited. After that night, she had phoned me once, which hadn't gone as she'd undoubtedly planned, a last-ditch effort to pull me to her side. Though she should have expected nothing less. Her shock over Ann trying to kill Liz and shooting George hadn't lasted long and she had reverted to the cold-hearted bitch I knew her to be. Just like I had expected. That phone call was the last contact I had with my mother, and I didn't intend to ever speak to her again.

The last major change, and something we were still dealing with right now, was Lizzy working with a lawyer to look into her father's will. At first, it seemed like all she would get was the compulsory portion that she had been denied when Walter died. And she had been more than content with that. But when George went through one of Walter's old boxes before he sold the house to find some pictures of her father he could give to Lizzy, he had come across a very interesting document: a copy of his changed will and testament. Before he died, Walter had changed his will in Lizzy's, her mother's, and Courtney's favor. Ann was taken out and both Lizzy and her mother were added, splitting all his money between the three girls he undoubtedly loved. Lizzy and her lawyer were now using that copy to sue Ann. It was still in the works, but soon enough, Lizzy would come into a lot of money. She didn't care about the money itself, but she told me that it felt good her father had wanted to take care of her and that being the reason why she was fighting for it. They had all been wronged. Not just Lizzy and her mom, but Walter too. And Courtney, though neither of us had any compassion left for her.

From what Max has told me, Courtney was fighting her own battle in court, over the custody of her two-month-old daughter. She had used the father to get pregnant so she could trap me, but she had tried to play the wrong person. When Max had found out who the father was, he had made sure that he got the information he needed to get custody of his child. And even though the courts usually favored the mother, it didn't look good for her. Not that I cared, though I wouldn't want a child left in that woman's hands.

Lizzy's mother hadn't been found. There was no trace of her. We know that my mother paid for her bus ticket and we know that it was a ticket to California, as far away from Massachusetts as she could send her. But it had been two years and there were too many possibilities for her to disappear between here and California to find any leads. Nobody cared or paid attention to a woman in her late forties who was addicted to drugs and whored herself out to get her next fix.

Lizzy was struggling with it. Things in her life—in our lives—had never been better, and somewhere deep inside her I think she had hoped that she could somehow fix their relationship and help her. God bless her, but she was way too forgiving. Though I understood. Now that she had a fatherly relationship with George, she craved a relationship with her mother. But Sarah Watson was too far gone, had been for many, many years. I just hoped that Lizzy would eventually get over that sadness. Maybe George's new girlfriend was a keeper and Lizzy would build a connection with her. I hoped she would.

My thoughts came back to the here and now when I felt Lizzy's arms wrapping around me from behind. I lifted my arm and moved her under it, tucking her to my side and kissing her temple.

"I have to go. Sam is probably waiting already." I could hear equal parts reluctance and excitement in her voice. She still wasn't comfortable with people fretting over her and getting dressed up. Even for her own wedding. I chuckled.

"Want to make a run for it?" I asked conspiratorially, making her smile.

"No, but thanks for asking. I guess there's no way around getting prettied up today. Though I would much rather stay here with you until it's time to go."

"Me too, baby. But I'm sure once you're there, you'll have fun. I want you to enjoy it, let yourself get spoiled, just this once. Do all that girly pre-wedding stuff." I laughed as she scrunched up her nose, then couldn't resist but kiss that nose.

"I'll try," she said, forced. "I don't have a problem with getting my make-up and hair done, but at a spa? For three hours? Really? I didn't even think this town had a spa." She wouldn't. She didn't pay attention to things like that.

"Less than four hours and you'll be mine for real," I changed the subject.

"Yeah," she whispered.

I kissed her one last time before I turned her and gently pushed her out the door. She had been right. Sam was waiting outside the cottage, waving from her car. I returned the wave then went back inside when they had disappeared around the corner and got ready to marry my woman.

Three and a half hours later, I stood in front of our friends and family, waiting for my bride to appear. Any second now she would come out of those doors and walk down the beach to meet me.

And then there she was.

She looked like a dream.

Jesus Christ. My woman was perfect.

From head to toe, she was pure perfection. I couldn't contain the smile that spread across my face or the tears that sprang to my eyes. She was absolutely gorgeous in her vintage sleeveless lace dress as she walked barefoot toward me, her face equally alive with happiness. A light rose band around her waist made her legs seem like they went on forever. I knew she was carrying a bouquet, but I didn't see it. All I could see was her in that dress, and her beautiful face, her green eyes that, just like mine, were wet with tears. I couldn't stand here and wait. I had to hold her and tell her how much I loved her, how beautiful she was, and that I was the luckiest son of a bitch in the world to call her mine.

Right now.

So that's what I did.

George chuckled as he saw me come up the aisle towards them and handed her over without argument. Not that he would have stood a chance. As soon as I was within touching distance, I gently grabbed her face and pulled her in for a long and deep kiss. Hollers and catcalls were erupting all around us, but I didn't give a damn. I had to feel her, taste her, brand her as mine. When I ended the kiss, I kept my lips on hers and whispered all the things I had said to her a million times, all the things I couldn't say often enough. By the time I was done, the tears in both our eyes had spilled over.

"Let's get married," I murmured lastly.

"Please," she answered.

Ten minutes later, to loud cheers of our closest friends and family, I kissed her again, for the first time as my wife, Mrs. Elizabeth Brooks.

Lizzy

Cole and I were on the dance floor of the small tent that had been erected on the beach. Twinkle lights shone from all around the tent, illuminating the place with a soft glow. I had wanted a simple wedding, so the decorations had been matched with the vintage theme. We used small, colored glass jars filled with wild flowers as centerpieces and simple vintage china as dinnerware. Some of the kids from the shelter had helped put them together. I had been touched that they had wanted to be involved and had been more than happy to include them. Some of them had even come to the ceremony, as had all my co-workers. We'd asked our colleagues from another shelter to fill in for us, since everyone wanted to celebrate with Cole and I. Of course, Jesse and Chloe were here as well. A live band was playing an old and romantic song while we danced. It was absolutely beautiful, more beautiful than I could have ever imagined.

And I was now Mrs. Brooks, dancing with my husband.

Was there anything more perfect?

My face split into yet another wide grin when I realized that yes, things could be more perfect.

"I have a surprise for you. Well, two actually," I told Cole as we were slowly swaying to the music.

"Do you now?" His nose was stroking mine. All afternoon, he hadn't been able to take his hands off of me, not since he had stalked toward me in the aisle.

"Yup. I do. And I have to give them to you now."

"I'm not gonna stop you."

"You'll have to let me go."

"Not a chance, Mrs. Brooks." He kissed me. I smiled.

"Give me thirty seconds."

He sighed. "All right. Thirty seconds. Not one second more."

"Stay right here," I gave him a quick peck then hurried out of the tent and up the small, short walkway to the cabin I had been getting dressed in, retrieved the surprise, and hurried back down to the tent. People were laughing and smiling and oohing and aahing when they saw what I was carrying in my arms. My eyes stayed glued to Cole's when I re-entered the tent and his mouth dropped open.

"Cole, meet Cash. Cash, this is your daddy, Cole." The cute Australian Shepherd puppy wiggled in my arms as he licked Cole's chin.

"You got me a puppy?" he asked in amazement.

"I did. Sixteen years ago today you told me about how you wished you had an Australian Shepherd and how you would name him Cash. You knew I was sad and you tried to cheer me up."

"I remember. I can't believe you did this."

"You're gonna have to share him, though."

"I don't mind. I'll share anything and everything with you, baby, you know that," he said through a grin as he scratched Cash behind his ear.

I did know that, but that wasn't what I meant. "I'm not talking about me."

"Whom are you talking about then?" His eyebrows were raised in confusion and mild amusement.

My heart was beating so fast I thought it would jump out

of my chest any second. "You'll have to share him with our son or daughter." I took his hand and placed it on my stomach. Cole was standing in front of me, his body frozen, his mouth hanging open, his eyes filled with shock. I watched as shock turned to comprehension, and comprehension turned to happiness.

Pure and simple happiness.

"You're pregnant?" he whispered.

I nodded.

He whooped, then grabbed me—and Cash by extension—and whirled me through the air, his face alight with nothing but joy. Cash was yapping at his daddy, happy that he was happy.

And I was laughing so hard I could hardly breathe.

This was it.

This was us.

We were as happy as we could be.

With nothing but a bright and joy-filled future spread out in front of us.

The End

Acknowledgements

First and foremost, I would like to thank my incredible husband without whom none of my books would have ever been written. You gave me the opportunity and the proverbial kick in the behind to make my dreams come true. I love you. Always and Forever.

A special Thank You goes to Teeny, my sista from another mista, the sister I never had and always wished for. Thank you for all your tips, for letting me vent, for making me laugh, for being there whenever I need an open ear, for motivating me when I'm ready to give up, for your all around support. And of course, for your fabulous job on the formatting and cover. This book is for women like you and me, the flowers that grew through the crack in the sidewalk.

Another special Thank You goes to Mayra, one of the sweetest women I have ever had the pleasure of meeting. Thank you for all your kind words of motivation and encouragement, for your ideas, for being my beta reader and my amazing teaser designer.

Thank you, Neva Carter, my new editor. I loved your suggestions and am glad we found each other.

Thank you to all my friends (you know who you are), to my beta readers, and to the bloggers and reviewers who took a chance on a new author and give their continued support.

And last but definitely not least, a big thank you to you.

The readers.

Enjoy other works by Julia Goda

The Cedar Creek Series

Bent Not Broken

Be Here Now

Bent Not Broken (Cedar Creek #1)

Life has taught Ivey Jones early on that with trust come pain and betrayal. Out of survival she has created walls around her to keep anyone from getting too close. Though she lives in her dream house in the Rocky Mountains and loves being the owner of the town's quirky little bookstore Serendipity, her life is narrow and governed by strict rules that she never deviates from...until Cal Bennett enters her life.

For the past nine years Calvin "Cal" Bennett has stayed away from Ivey, thinking she deserved better than to be saddled with a single dad who has never been good at relationships. Until a few chance encounters show him what he's been missing and he can't stay away any longer.

Little does he know he's got a fight on his hands that he might not be equipped to win. Shadows from Ivey's past lurk in the dark, ready to strike and bring her low once and for all. But Cal swears he will do whatever it takes to break through that wall of steel to win Ivey's heart and keep her safe.

Now available on Amazon and Kindle Unlimited

Be Here Now (Cedar Creek #2)

Six years ago, Loreley Cooper thought she had it all. Head over heels in love with her boyfriend Jason and ready to take on the future after college, she landed the internship of her dreams. But things came crashing down during a fight when she believed she found out he'd done something she knew she could never forgive. Completely heartbroken, she walked away and hasn't talked to him since.

Now, six years later, Loreley is recovering from a painful tragedy that almost killed her. She is finally finding her way back to herself when now famous rock star Jason Sanders returns and seems determined to win her back. Why he would seek her out after all this time, Loreley has no idea. She has sworn to never talk to him again after what he did to her.

Jason Sanders has regretted not chasing after Loreley to fight for what he knows would have been a life filled with happiness. Now he is back and he is determined to remedy his mistakes and not let the love of his life walk away from him again. He is willing to do anything and everything to make her give them another chance.

But misunderstandings are uncovered and secrets are revealed that lead to pain and heartbreak yet again. Will they have what it takes to forgive each other and themselves and fight for their happily-ever-after or is it too late?

About the Author

Julia Goda has been writing stories in her head since she can remember. Much to her teachers' dismay, given the task of writing a short essay she would always come back with way too long and detailed stories. Many discussions (she has always been somewhat of a smart-aleck) and bad grades were the result, so that for most of her life she thought she couldn't write worth a damn and pursued other careers. But the dream of being an author wouldn't be ignored and kept lingering. With a little help from her fantastic husband, who gave her the necessary kick in the behind, she was finally brave enough to start writing her first novel. Since then she has enjoyed giving herself over to her stories and making them come to live.

Her novels jump genres and touch on all kinds of different topics, but the things she tries to focus on no matter what are romance, strong women, and a good sense of humor.

When she is not in her writing cave, she enjoys reading, drinking coffee, eating good food, and listening to rock music.

Julia Goda has lived in Germany, Virginia, and Colorado (where she fell in love with Boulder and the Rocky Mountains). Her current home is Southern Alberta, Canada, where she lives close enough to the Rockies with her husband and chocolate lab to enjoy the beauty and excitement that is mountain living.

Connect with Julia Goda:

www.juliagoda.net
www.facebook.com/juliagodaauthor
Amazon: https://www.amazon.com/author/juliagoda
Google: www.google.com/+JuliaGoda
Goodreads: https://www.goodreads.com/author/Julia_Goda
Twitter: julia_goda

68322983R00160

Manufactured by Amazon.com
Columbia, SC
30 March 2017